CLOUD 9

A VACATION REVERSE
HAREM ROMANCE

STEPHANIE BROTHER

ISBN: 9798377548065

1

DAWN

"Can I get you another mojito?"

I eye the barman, with his faded white logo shirt and strange mullet hairstyle with disappointment. When I fantasized about coming on this trip, this wasn't what I expected at all.

"No thanks," I say, twizzling the straw in my existing drink. There's only the essence of alcohol left and it's mostly melted ice water flavored with mint and lime. My head is swimming, and my bladder is urgently warning me to make a trip to the restroom. Worst of all, my heart feels lonely.

I miss home.

I miss my friends.

I miss going to familiar places and seeing familiar faces.

I'm even starting to miss my stupid boss. He was an ass, but predictable at least.

Cringing, I suck the last of my diluted drink and give

myself an internal pep talk. What the hell was the point of me getting the YOLO tattoo if I'm desperate to live for yesterday? Today is where I need to be, focusing on the present, enjoying whatever life throws in my direction.

I need fun and laughter. I'm in Australia for goodness' sake. It's the trip of a lifetime and all I can think about is home.

Kyla, my bestie, pops into my head. She's living her best life, shacked up with eight gorgeous tattoo artists. She's living YOLO every day. I may have been the one to encourage her in their direction, and I'm so happy for her it hurts, but I'm also the color of Shrek jealous.

There's not a single man in this whole bar who could hold a candle to one of Kyla's harem. Or maybe I just haven't looked properly. I started this trip bubbling with enthusiasm, but it's slowly ebbed into something darker and sadder.

Ugh.

I am not this girl.

Sliding off the wooden bar stool, I swipe my hand over my tight dress, smoothing out the wrinkles and tugging at the hem so it's a little closer to decent and a little further from panty-revealing. Although maybe a little panty revealing would go some way to improving my night.

The sign for the restrooms is in the corner and I stagger slightly on my heels through the throng of bodies. I'm almost there when a drunk man with blond braids and a pink shirt comes flying towards me, nearly knocking me off my feet. I'm sent hurtling directly into a tray of drinks that overturn all over the poor person carrying them, splashing my legs and feet in the process.

"Oh my god," I shout, stumbling to right myself. The man is soaked from his feet, to his jeans, to his shirt. My eyes trail upwards inch by terrible inch, taking in the catastrophe I've caused. It seems to take an eternity to reach what can only be described as a very surprised face.

It must match mine because not only is this dude tall enough to play for the NBA, but he's also built enough to get into my pants. Seriously. I've suffered through a week of drought and the first man I come across with any kind of potential is the one I've showered with so much alcohol that his cock must taste like beer!

"I'm so sorry," I say, patting his shirt, finding it cold and wet and clinging to a ripped muscular chest and abs that roll in waves. Damn, he's sexy. "You're so wet, and so am I."

"That's quick," he says, his mouth quirking into a gorgeously mischievous grin. "It usually takes a little more than a grope of my chest to get a girl ready."

My eyes bug out for a second as I absorb the fact that he's flirting rather than mad, and then I burst into nervous laughter. "Yeah, this chest is something close to spectacular." I add a wink for extra flirtatious effect which he seems to appreciate.

He folds in his full lips like he's imagining tasting the wetness he's referring to, and my mind is already there. I bet he'd be amazing at oral. Men with sharp wit usually have very capable tongues. Combined with his flop of messy auburn hair and a nose that could give Julius Caesar a run for his money, this guy is the full package.

"Only close?" he grabs the hem as though he's going to give me a flash of the good stuff, but it's only a tease.

At that moment, before I can ask Mr. Hilarious-Sex-God for his number, the mullet sporting barman appears with a mop and bucket to deal with the lake of beer congealing around our feet.

"I'm sorry," I say again.

"It's okay."

I stare at his lips as he replies and wonder if this is the first Australian dude with a hope of making my trip worthwhile.

"Mitchell, you bringing those drinks or what?" a man yells.

Mitchell shrugs, and I take the hint that he's under pressure to go back to the bar. My bladder is about to call time too, so I tiptoe to dry land in the direction of the restroom, glancing over my shoulder as he disappears back into the crowd.

Wow. Maybe this trip isn't going to be the washout I was dreading.

When I find a free stall, I do what needs to be done. A sniffling sound from next door interrupts my flow, but I don't say anything.

I stand at the mirror and wash my hands, using a piece of toilet paper to dab at my legs and feet. I'm almost done when the girl emerges with red-rimmed eyes and a face covered with blotches of distress. Our eyes meet in the mirror, and I give her my most sympathetic face.

"Are you okay? Tell me to mind my own business, but I like to think that girls in restrooms should be there for each other in times of need."

She sends me a watery smile and washes her hands. "I'm having a bad night," she explains.

"I'm not having the best one," I say. "My legs were just moisturized with Bud."

Raising her eyebrows, she scans my soaked shoes. "Probably not Bud," she says. "More likely to be Victoria or Tooheys. You're from America?"

"Is it that obvious?" I don't even know why I'm asking. Of course it is!

"Well, I could offer you my welcome to down-under speech, but it looks as though someone has christened you already."

I grin, watching as the girl scans me from head to toe. I

have plenty of female friends, but I'm very aware that other women are often wary of my confidence and my tattoo makes them jittery. Girls who like to live for today are more likely to be the ones who fuck boyfriends and husbands. That's not me at all, but it still hangs over me. "Is this an Australian custom I didn't read about in the Lonely Planet?" I toss the bundle of wet tissue in the bin and focus on my new bathroom buddy. She's dressed in a smart skirt and white blouse which seems more appropriate for work than bar-hopping. With dark hair twisted into a bun, and small glasses perched on the end of her nose, she's any man's librarian fantasy brought to life.

"Not really." She sniffs and blots her face, her expression changing from friendly and open to worried and closed.

"Wanna tell me what made you look like someone stole your Twinkie?" The girl blinks at me, confused, and then I realize my reference isn't something she'd understand. I guess they don't sell Twinkies in Australia. "What's causing the tears?"

"I got fired," she says with a shrug. "I'm good at my job, but my boss wanted extras and I'm not that kind of girl. I mean, I'm dedicated and hardworking and I go over and above to achieve but sucking cocks or bending over my desk for a fifty-year-old balding asshole is too far."

My mouth drops open. "He fired you because you wouldn't sleep with him?"

"Yep. He tried hard enough. I can still feel his gross hands on my skin and smell his sour breath." She shivers, her hand rustling her right cuff as though she's searching for something to distract her. "And he's made up some bullshit about me to cover his tracks, so I can't even get a decent reference or fight him in a work tribunal. He's too powerful and scary, anyway. I just feel like a bug he squashed under his shoe. I came out to drink myself into oblivion, but I can't even do that without crying."

"I'm sorry this is happening to you," I say. "And I'm totally on board with drinking myself into oblivion. My issues are small potatoes compared to yours but having one too many mojitos was the only thing on my to-do list tonight."

She blinks her bloodshot eyes and gives me another watery smile that seems less sad. "I like mojitos."

"Then, let's drink and forget our woes. Tomorrow is another day."

"Okay. Sure."

I grab my new friend's hand even though I don't know her name and march decisively to the bar. I may have been miserable three seconds ago, but now I'm a girl on a mission to uplift a sister. "Two mojitos, please."

We perch on vacant barstools, and I can't resist a scan of the bar, searching for the beer-soaked Adonis but not finding him anywhere. Shame.

"So, first things first. I'm Dawn." I hold my hand out for a formal handshake.

"Chantelle," she says. "And thanks for this."

"No problem." I smile, feeling all the warm fuzzies that come with being someone's knight in shining armor. In my case, it's more of an avenging angel in lycra.

"So, who's the mean guy and why can't you press charges?"

Chantelle shakes her head and hangs it mournfully. "He's too rich and powerful. You probably wouldn't have heard of him." I shrug and she continues. "I wouldn't stand a chance. To be honest, I'm scared of making it worse. You didn't see his face when I told him no. His eyes were black and dead, but his mouth pulled into a twisted smirk that chilled my soul. The way he touched me." Her shoulders bunch and she shivers. "When I got the job, I didn't realize how shady he was. The way he does business..." She shakes her head and grimaces.

"...let's just say it was all underhanded."

"Ugh. He sounds like a peach." I pay the bartender for the drinks, even though I could do with saving my money for more important things. "I think we should make a toast." I pass her the tall, cool glass and hold my drink close. "To finding new jobs and happier times. And wishing your asshole boss's cock withers up and drops off."

She clinks her glass against mine and snorts with amusement, both of us taking long sips of our very strong cocktails. "At least if it withers up and drops off, he wouldn't be able to bother anyone else with it," she giggles nervously. I catch her looking around as though she's worried he could be listening. The asshole has really gotten under her skin.

"Exactly. He's probably got a tiny pecker, anyway."

"Probably. So, you're not enjoying your trip?"

I shrug, not relishing the pathetic feeling of being homesick. "I'm enjoying the scenery, and everyone I've met has been perfectly friendly. It's just..." I trail off, not sure how to explain that unless I'm living life in the fast lane, my time is wasted.

Chantelle raises her eyebrows. "Are you here with anyone?"

"No. I came by myself."

"That's brave. I'm not sure I'd be that brave."

"My dad thinks I'm crazy. He spent days berating me for leaving a perfectly good job and a perfectly nice apartment to slum it on the other side of the world."

"Yeah, mine would probably do the same. So, what would make this trip more interesting?"

"That's a good question." I stir the straw in my drink, making the ice swirl amongst the mint leaves. "I guess meeting interesting people and finding adventures."

"Do you have an itinerary planned?"

Shaking my head, I recall Kyla asking me the very same thing. "Itineraries feel too organized. I like living from day to day, not knowing where the wind will blow me."

"Well, the wind blew you here." Chantelle looks around and so do I. The bar has emptied a little and not for the first time, my heart sinks. "I think it was fate."

"Yeah?"

"Yeah. I was going to go home and cry myself to sleep, but maybe I should just wake up tomorrow and plan myself an adventure."

"You absolutely should."

"Does trawling websites for a new job constitute adventure?" She rolls her eyes at the lameness of her question.

"I guess anything can be an adventure if it's taking you somewhere you haven't been before."

"So that's the definition. Newness?"

"Yep. I'm like a rolling stone. I like moving on."

"So, I guess I shouldn't bother giving you my number? You know, in case you get a craving for another mojito?"

I smile broadly. "I start craving another mojito as soon as I've finished the one in my hand."

Maybe I was too hasty at judging this trip after all.

2

DAWN

I'm old enough to know that adventures that start at the bottom of a glass only lead to hangovers, but not mature enough to care. I crawl out of my bed after noon, throwing on a pair of cut-off denim shorts and a white tank, and slide my feet into thongs (well, that's what they call them here!).

The hostel I'm staying at has a cool surfing vibe, and the café bar area serves all day brunch, which is about the best thing I've eaten since I arrived in Byron Bay. The owner, Craig, must be in his early-fifties and still loves to surf at the crack of dawn every day.

His eyes scan me, and without me having to ask, he pours a black coffee and brings it over with the menu.

"I have a hangover cure that will put the pink back into your cheeks," he says. "But it involves raw egg and hot sauce."

I mime gagging and shove my hand out, palm facing him, to protest any further mention of such grossness. "I think I'll stick with the pancakes."

"Good choice. Drink up that coffee and I'll squeeze you some OJ too."

Smiling gratefully, I hand back the unopened menu and, while he puts my order into the kitchen, I swipe through my phone, catching up on the news from back home.

It was Carl's birthday and Kyla has posted a cute photo of him surrounded by friends on her Insta. Allie tweeted about an article she wrote on the female orgasm, and I spend five minutes scanning through it so I can make a witty comment below. My dad's Facebook page hasn't been updated for a month. The anniversary of my mom's death is looming, and he always withdraws for a while. Each year he writes a lovely post about her. Each year I'm worse for reading it.

I scroll through other friends, and family updates, knowing it's probably a mistake. The more time I spend thinking about home, the more unsettled I am. To counter my homesick feelings, I scan through my camera roll, searching out some of the beautiful pictures I've taken since I arrived and uploading them onto Insta. I come up with captions like 'A slice of heaven' and 'So beautiful it doesn't seem real' and use filters to give the natural beauty a vibrant and hyper-enhanced gloss.

There's a picture I took of myself outside the hostel yesterday before I went to the bar. My smile is broad, my eyes are bright, and my arms outstretched. In the background there's a dramatic, flame-red tree, so it has an exotic feel about it. Anyone looking at the image would assume I was having the time of my life, but all I can see is the pretense of my forced smile.

It might be fake, but at least it will please everyone back home. Admitting the truth would only make it worse.

When Craig returns with my pancakes, he flops into the empty chair opposite which I'd usually take as an invasion of space, but things here just seem more laid back than at home. "So, tell me about your plans," he says.

"No plans," I tell him, cutting a bite-sized piece and popping it into my mouth.

"Is that why you've been walking about as though someone killed your cat?" He stretches out his legs, and drops his head to one side, assessing me as if I'm a slide under the microscope. "It's normal to feel like a fish out of water. The first time I went to a surf competition outside of Australia, I didn't know what I was doing."

"Yeah," I say. "Even though you guys speak the same language, kind of, everything is different."

"Even the pancakes?"

"Even the pancakes," I smile. "But good different."

That seems to reassure him. "What about getting a temporary job? That would help you settle and meet some people."

Settle. That's about the worst word he could have used to sell his idea.

"My buddy Jared has a bar and hostel called Cloud 9. They're looking for some help with bar work."

"Bar work?"

"Yeah. It's a cool place. Owned by nine guys who met here and decided this is the place they wanted to grow roots."

"Roots aren't my thing," I say, chewing thoughtfully.

"It's all beanbags and hammocks and drinks in fruits. It's chill, and the owners are great. I think you'd fit in and have some fun."

Now fun is more up my street.

"How old are the owners?" I ask.

"Mid-twenties to thirties," he says. "Younger than me, anyway."

The white-toothed grin he sends me is meant to be self-deprecating, though it's really laced with confidence. He knows he looks good for his age. Kind of a silver-blond surfing fox type.

"Anyway, if you decide to go, tell them Craig sent you. I'll message you the details."

Of course, he has my cellphone number from my booking. "Sure. Okay. I'll think about it."

I eat the rest of my pancakes as Craig serves a couple who've arrived and ordered lunch. With my day wide open, I wait for his message to come through and decide to take a stroll to scope out Cloud 9. If it's a dive, I won't bother going inside. But if I get a good feeling, maybe I will.

From the outside, Cloud 9 screams laid-back Australia. Craig is right, it does seem to have the right vibe. In fact, without even stepping over the threshold, I can tell I'll like it.

Tropical plants spill over pots that surround the perimeter, and a circular wooden bar fills the center. A mixture of hammocks, beanbags and rustic wood and woven chairs keep everything at a low level. And even though it's early, chill-out music spills from inside.

"Lachlan, do we need more sparkling water?" The voice is gruff with an Australian drawl.

"Yeah and get a wee box of lemons while you're back there."

Whoever Lachlan is, he isn't local. Nothing like a Scottish voice to warm parts other accents don't quite reach.

"Who's making lunch today?" someone else asks. "I could eat a bear."

"You drink too much," Lachlan says. "That's hangover munchies."

"You think what I had last night was too much? That's nothing."

"Anything's a lot to a man who doesn't drink." The accent is so Texan I have to stifle a laugh. Scottish, Australian, and American. Interesting.

I listen to their banter, still hesitating about going inside. People pass me on the sidewalk and their gazes linger with curiosity. It's hotter than Dante's Inferno out here, and I'm sure I'm developing third degree sunburn as I stand here waiting.

This isn't like me.

I'm the girl who sees opportunity and runs headlong into it. I seem to have an instinct for the natural direction that fate is pushing me in, and I love to go with the flow. If it means moving from place to place and person to person, I don't care. Living life to the fullest is my most important priority. I touch my hand to the tattoo at the base of my spine, the one dad was mortified with. He couldn't see how YOLO was something that anyone would want on their skin, but much like the yearly post he writes about my mom, the sentiment behind 'you only live once' is for mom, too.

I wonder what Mom would have thought about me working in a bar in Australia. She used to talk to me about all the different career options that might interest me, even when I was a kid. It's as though she wanted to inspire me to think about my future, even when things were going so wrong in the present.

Who would I be now if things turned out different? Maybe I'd be like Kyla, settled down in a relationship and making plans that don't involve giving up a job and a home to flee across the world. Maybe I would have hung onto Brett, who was a perfectly good guy and awesome in the sack, rather than sending him back onto Tinder to find a replacement for me.

I don't know. How can we ever know what we would be like if our past was different? Like a patchwork quilt, you can't just remove the center square without the whole thing falling apart.

"Hey, can I help you with anything?" A deep baritone voice asks from inside, and I almost jump out of my skin.

"Craig sent me about a job," I say, squinting into the lower light of the bar to take in the gorgeous face that's staring at me with interest. He's tall with sun lightened brown hair and warm brown eyes that make my skin feel too hot and too tight. The worn gray shirt that hugs his chest and arms like it's in love with the feel of his skin doesn't help reduce his appeal, either.

"A job?" He raises his chin as he sizes me up, too. Does he like what he sees? Who knows? I think I look cute in my outfit, but it's nothing like I would usually wear for an interview. Then again, this bar isn't anything like any of the places I've worked at before. "You'd better come on in then," he drawls, the Texan twang now out in full force.

So I do, because fate has played her card, and I never refuse a game.

3

MITCHELL

I look up from the box I'm currently unpacking to find Bradley crossing the bar with a girl who looks familiar. I squint as she gets closer, taking in her loose light brown hair, cute white shirt and sexy cut-off denim shorts that leave very little leg to the imagination. Damn, she has nice thighs. The kind of thighs I love wrapped around my hips or my face.

Her green eyes meet mine, and I get a flashback from last night.

That's who she is! The girl who drenched me with beer and cost me another round. The girl whose sassy mouth and mischievous smile left a lasting impression.

"It's you," I say, grinning. "The Tasmanian Devil who overturned my tray."

Bradley glances down at her with a surprised expression, raising his thick brows. "You're the one who wet him down to his underwear?"

The girl has the decency to look guilty but smiles

broadly with a mischievous twinkle in her eye. "That's me. Except I'm not a Tasmanian Devil, more an American kind of demon."

"You guys must know each other," I say, and both of them roll their eyes in response.

"What is it that you don't get, Mitchell? There are over three hundred million people in the US. The chances of me bumping into someone I know from home are so small it's not even a thing."

"We should have pretended to be cousins," the girl says, grabbing Bradley's arm. "We could have pranked them."

"That would have been fun." Bradley's eyes drift to where her hand is currently wrapped around his forearm.

"Do you have a resume? Experience?" I ask as she smiles up at Bradley and draws her hand away.

"I'm on vacation, and I haven't done any bar work before. The closest experience I have is when I worked retail when I was in college."

"So, you've worked in the service industry?"

"Yeah." She shrugs her shoulders and I get the distinct feeling that she doesn't care if we offer her the job or not. She's like a butterfly that's blown in on the breeze.

"And you like the idea of working here?"

She glances around, pivoting on her foot as she takes in the bar. "I think it looks awesome."

"But you're on vacation," Bradley says. "How long will you be around for?"

Shrugging again, she tucks her hair behind her ear. "I don't have a return ticket. I'm leaving my plans open."

"So you could work a couple of months, minimum?" I ask.

"Sure. If you're nice to me!" The grin that splits her face reminds me of last night.

"Nice is a very unsexy word. I could be good to you. Exceptionally good, in fact."

"I'm not sure this conversation is appropriate for an interview," Bradley warns.

"This girl spilled so much beer on me yesterday, my cock had a drink."

She points at me and laughs hard enough that she doubles over. "I knew it. That's exactly what I thought to myself, that your cock would have tasted like beer."

"You thought about what my cock tastes like?" It's not often that people surprise me enough to drop my jaw, but it just happened.

"Well," she says, wriggling her eyebrows. "I do like beer."

Shit. My cock stirs in my jeans, as an image of this girl on her knees, licking the beer off him, floods my mind. Food and drink and sex can be fun, but I've never imagined dipping my cock in beer for a blow job.

"Definitely inappropriate," Bradley says again. "Like employment tribunal worthy. Maybe you should get Lachlan."

Maybe he's right.

"Well, have a seat here." I point to a barstool. "I'll get the man who makes the decisions."

"Lachlan," she says. "He's the boss?"

"Self-appointed," I say without malice. Some people like taking charge, and I'm happy to let them if it means I have an easier life.

"Well, send the self-appointed boss my way, and if he doesn't like me, I guess I'll go look for something else to do."

Bradley follows me to the office at the back of the bar, sending me an amused look on the way. "You know she's got a tattoo on her ass that says YOLO."

"The fuck?"

"You guys have matching shit tattoos!"

"If you're referencing this…" I point at my right bicep, tugging up the soft fabric of my white shirt at the FOMO tattoo I have there, "then you are absolutely right."

"I am," he grins. "And I know."

"Well, matching shit tattoos must mean we should hire her. It feels like fate."

With his hand on the handle to the office, Bradley pauses. "If you want Lachlan to consider employing her, I suggest you don't mention the cock conversation or the tattoo. Neither makes her a poster-child for being a reliable bar waitress.

"But both say she's fun, and fun is what we need around here."

He nods, his brows drawing together, and I get a flash of the likeness between him and his twin. "Mention fun. Even Lachlan might see the benefit in that."

Minutes later, we return to the bar, and I half expect the girl to have left.

The girl.

I still don't know her name.

Lachlan wasn't impressed by my interview skills.

He approaches her, holding out his hand to shake hers. It's so formal and I can see her amusement in the sparkle of her moss green eyes and the way she presses her lips together as though she's stifling a laugh.

Her lips.

They look soft and the fact that they emit so much wit only makes them more appealing.

"Hi boss," she says. "I'm Dawn."

"Nice to meet you. I'm Lachlan, this is Mitchell, and this is Bradley. They tell me you're looking for employment."

"Sure."

Lachlan's jaw ticks but he continues. "I can offer you a day's trial. If you like it and we like you, we'll talk after. Is tonight, okay?"

"Absolutely," she says. "What time?"

"Get back here for five-pm."

"Bossy," she smiles. "It suits you."

I stare, open mouthed, as Lachlan's cheeks redden. I don't think I've ever seen my serious Scottish friend flush. Dawn really does have a special skill for getting under people's skin with her unbelievably relaxed attitude.

She slides from the bar stool and glances around again. As she strolls past me, I glance at her ass, catching sight of the tattoo Bradley mentioned. It really is bad. "Nice tat," I say, easing my shirt up my arm. "We match."

When she sees what I'm pointing to, she stops immediately and reaches out to run her finger over the words. "You have a fear of missing out?"

"I guess," I say. "I was drunk when I asked for it."

"What are you fearful of missing out on?"

Dropping my shirtsleeve, I push my hand into my pocket and relax my stance, gazing down at the fireball of a woman in front of me. "You."

The word slips out without my conscious brain taking in the gravity of it.

Dawn's eyes widen, and she folds her bottom lip into her mouth and bites down. I'm not sure whether she's trying to subdue her amusement or if my admission has surprised her enough to render her temporarily mute.

In the end, her mouth twitches, she releases her lip and sends me a megawatt smile. "Well, lucky for you, Lachlan has given me a reason to come back later."

"Lucky me," I grin. "And don't forget YOLO."

"How could I?" She twists, lifting the back of her shirt to reveal a narrow waist, curvy hips and the full spread of ink across her skin. "I've got a permanent reminder to make the most of absolutely every day."

"Before you go," Lachlan says, temporarily interrupting our connection. "Can you leave your details here?" He hands Dawn a form and a pen and she scribbles down her name, contact details, current address and next of kin.

"Mitchell?" I ask, seeing her surname on the paper.

"Yeah. Not only do we have matching tattoos, we also have matching names."

"It's fate," Bradley says sarcastically, but maybe he's right? Maybe it is? Stranger things have happened.

"The other important thing that Lachlan forgot to mention is that the job comes with a room and three meals a day."

Lachlan's head swivels and his eyes narrow. We hadn't discussed it, but there's no way I'm letting Dawn travel across town to that other hostel when she could sleep soundly under the same roof as all of us.

Chivalry isn't dead at Cloud 9. Neither is my optimism that Dawn is going to be something more to me than just a colleague.

4

COOPER

"You're coming back tomorrow?" Mitchell says as we leave the bar after my first shift.

It's dark, but the warmth of the day still clings to the night, and I inhale the scent of the ocean into lungs that are hungry for everything unfamiliar about this place.

"Sure," I say softly, deciding right then that I will. Working in a bar as big and busy as Cloud 9 proved to be harder work than I anticipated. I spent most of the evening running with drinks in my hands and telling myself that there are other, easier things I could be doing with my vacation.

But as the patrons began to leave and the nine men who own Cloud 9 gathered to clear up, I was drawn in by their easy smiles, teasing conversation and relaxed approach to life. Even as a stranger, in their company, I'm more comfortable than I've been in a long time.

Lachlan, with his dark brows and hair, and watchful eyes that seem to take everything in, has made me feel cautiously welcome. Jared and Joshua, the twins from London, are bubbly and fun with green eyes and messy light brown hair that begs to be tamed. They've given me guidance on how to move around the bar in an easy and methodical way. Thomas is dark and mysterious, playing haunting guitar and singing with the voice of an angel. I'd put money on him having Greek or Italian ancestry. Bradley and Bryce are laid back, as I'd expect from Texans, with straight brown hair and eyes flecked with gold. They've cooked up a storm and filled my belly with tastes of home. Cooper, the DJ, has blue eyes that remind me of the ocean nearby, and close-cropped blond hair that looks like velvet under the flashing lights. Logan is the one who's asked me the most about my trip. With sun-bleached blond hair and a serious mouth, he's the one who feels the most like a protective big brother.

And Mitchell has made me laugh nonstop, which certainly helped the time pass.

"You didn't have to do this," I tell Mitchell. "I'm a big girl. I managed to get all the way to Australia by myself. A short walk alone won't kill me."

Mitchell shrugs his broad shoulders and purses his lips. "I didn't have to, but I wanted to."

His deep voice resonates with a part of me that craves all the things that make men so different to women. His size and strength are attractive. His easygoing attitude is appealing. And when I like what I see, I usually don't waste any time trying to get it.

"Does your fear of missing out stretch to boring walks with almost strangers?"

"I don't think being in your company could ever be described as boring."

I grin, tugging the handle of my purse higher on my shoulder. My feet feel a little swollen in my sneakers and I'll be grateful to slump into my bed and get some sleep.

"Do you think Lachlan was happy with me? Or did you force him to hire me?"

Mitchell begins to cross the road, resting his hand on the small of my back to guide me. The man has manners. "No one can force Lachlan to do anything," he says. "I think he might be soft on you."

"Soft?" I mime sniffing skin. "Did I wear a different kind of perfume today?"

He grins as we approach the entrance to the hostel I'll be leaving in the morning. "It's not your perfume," he says, dipping his head and looking at me through his thick eyelashes. "It's your winning personality."

"Not my butt then?" I turn and smooth my hands over my fitted jeans, and he eyes my curves lustfully.

"Well, a good butt never hurts anyone's case."

"Good to know."

A few seconds of silence tick past, disturbed only by the rustle of insects in the bushes next to us. There is so much about Mitchell that makes me want to drag him into my room and appreciate him. It doesn't hurt that he's serious eye-candy, but aside from his handsome face and crazily sculpted body, he's also fun and seems like a good person, too.

Ideal boyfriend material if I was looking for one, which I'm not.

"So, I guess I'll see you tomorrow," he says, already turning to look back in the direction we just came from. He's cute, displaying that he has zero expectation of a reward for his escort. That only makes me want to drag him into my lair more.

"Tomorrow," I say softly. "Or you could come in to appreciate my winning personality some more."

His mouth pulls into a one-sided smile and those soft brown eyes of his crinkle at the sides. "How about your butt? Do I get to appreciate that, too?"

"Absolutely," I say, taking hold of his big, warm hand.

I know some people will think that having such an easy attitude to sex is problematic. There's so much judgment around how people choose to share their bodies, especially when it comes to women.

I like eating and sharing food with other people. I like dancing and finding a partner to vibe with which only makes it more exciting. And I love sex in the same way. When I find a man I'm attracted to, and he ticks the boxes like Mitchell does, I don't see the point in waiting around for love. Love is complicated and takes long-term focus. I'm happiest existing and enjoying the present, and that's where me and Mitchell are right now. The future is a distant ethereal thing that never solidifies in my vision.

Mitchell only lets me lead him for a few paces before he scoops me into his arms. My bag trails in my hand and I giggle like an idiot, swaying as he strides forward. "Number?"

"Twelve," I gasp as he almost passes the door to my room in his enthusiastic haste.

"Where's the key?"

I drag my bag onto my belly, searching frantically to find it. My hands shake with anticipation as I unlock the door and twist the handle. We're inside the dark room in a flash, and Mitchell tosses me onto the bed unceremoniously. I bounce and laugh some more, staring up at his smiling face. In the low light, with his hair flopping over his forehead, he suddenly seems much younger.

"You're kind of a caveman, Mr. Mitchell," I say, patting the bed next to me. "I think I like it."

Even though the room is an unfamiliar space, he doesn't take time to familiarize himself with his surroundings. In fact, as he removes his shoes, his eyes cling to my face and then my body, feasting in a way that sends a shiver over my scalp.

Now, this is me living my best life. Living in the moment. Living each day like it could be my last. My body feels alive with energy, thrumming with blood and vibrating with excitement. Only yesterday, I wondered if I'd made a mistake coming to Australia, and now, it's as though I'm stepping into a new era of excellent possibilities.

"When you spilled all those drinks over me, I never thought we'd end up here," he says. He folds in his lips to moisten them, and I can't wait anymore. I rise to hook my hand around his neck and draw him so that he's propped over me, resting on one very nicely toned arm.

"Maybe you should kiss me."

His grin is smoking hot. "Maybe you give Lachlan a run for his money when it comes to bossiness."

I guess my demanding attitude doesn't put him off because he does slant his lips over mine, and he does explore my mouth with the hot, sexy slide of his tongue. His hands roam my body in a perfect way, focused on discovering new territory. My mind goes to a hilarious place where Mitchell is an explorer and I'm a wild new country.

I like the idea of being untamed.

Drawing away from my mouth, his lips trail a soft path down my jaw and my neck, finding the dip at the bottom of my throat.

"Dawn Mitchell," he whispers against my skin. "You taste like heaven."

"You haven't got to the best part yet," I say with a grin.

"Oh, don't worry. I will, but I'm going to take my time."

He doesn't lie.

He explores me inch by inch, and I've never felt so

worshiped. He does things with his lips and tongue that I'm sure are illegal in half the countries of the world. And I lap it all up, because who doesn't want to feel like a queen? When we're both naked and I'm trembling, he groans that he didn't bring protection.

It's cute that he doesn't have a condom with him and even cuter that he assumes I also don't have one. When I reach into the nightstand and pull out a packet, he cocks an eyebrow. "A girl scout has to be prepared," I say, handing him the shiny square.

"You're a little old to be a girl scout, and I'm not sure condoms are on the official kit list."

We both laugh, but the atmosphere in the room changes when he tears the packet open with his teeth and begins to roll the latex down his very long, very thick, very hard cock. My mouth waters at the sight of him; gorgeous tan skin with a dusting of light brown hair across his chest and a happy trail leading to all the good stuff. He's got the physique of a man who lives his life and eats and drinks what he likes but also loves outdoor exercise and construction tasks. A man built on both hard work and enjoyment.

"What's your favorite position?" he asks, and I'm immediately intrigued. Not many men ask that. They're usually more interested in heading straight into their preference.

"Doggy," I say, even though it's not strictly true. There have been times when I've let a man fuck me in missionary and it's been awesome, but it also ends with me catching feels. The eye contact makes sex deeper and more meaningful, and what I'm looking for is fun and frivolity.

"Seriously?"

"I'm a freak. What can I say?"

I roll and push up on my hands and knees, lining my ass up with Mitchell's cock, desperate for the stretch that I know he will be able to provide. His hands stroke over my back and hips lazily, appreciatively, and I stifle the moan that fights to bubble to the surface. It's not that I don't want him to know how good he is. It's just that I always feel like I need to keep something back. A little fleck of control. An ounce of restraint.

But when his finger begins to trace the line of my YOLO tattoo, I tense.

"You get this when you were drunk?"

"Nope," I say, twisting to look at him.

It's on the tip of his tongue to say something along the lines of 'interesting' because I can tell he's trying to figure me out. It's funny, but in my experience, the less you give away to people, the more they want to discover.

When he bends to kiss the top of the Y, my heart does a weird little skittery thing in my chest. And when he braces himself on top of me, with one hand next to mine on the bed and the other wrapped around my waist, I almost swoon.

Be still my heart, I think.

Mitchell really is a man who understands what a woman needs.

Or is it just what I need?

Kyla always tells me that I don't think in the same way as most women do. She couldn't hack it when sex with her men was just about pleasure and enjoying each other's company, and that is the only kind of sex I enjoy. So, maybe Mitchell is more about fitting my needs and expectations rather than womankind in general.

The press of his cock at my entrance brings me welcome relief from my churning mind. As he nudges forward, stretching me open, I focus only on the physical feelings, the beauty of our bodies joining, the sweet relief of being filled. We move together like lovers do when they understand the other totally, and that's another surprise to me. I don't need to teach him how fast to move or how deep. I don't need to communicate the angle or the way he can use his hands to make everything between my legs feel so much more urgent and good.

This is a rare experience. A one-night stand which feels like amazing relationship sex but without the commitment.

If I didn't know better, I could get addicted to Mitchell; his smile and his laughter and his perfectly sized cock.

"Fuck, you feel good," he says, his voice so close to my ear that it's like the rumble of a storm.

"I'm close," I gasp, and he hums his approval, keeping the same rhythm and depth, understanding that my body is building towards release inch by slow inch.

There's no painful switch to mindless pounding or shift to focus on his epic finish. He simply fucks me until I break apart, then eases me down onto the bed so that I can enjoy the ride.

Limp and breathless, I twist to stare at him in the darkness. His expression is satisfied, and a little amused, but I can't fault him. He did good.

"You can finish too," I pant, as my pussy flutters through yet another happy wave.

"I'm enjoying everything your body is doing right now," he says, still buried deep. "And there's no rush, is there? I can go all night."

Shit. This man just went from almost perfect to fucking ideal.

"What would Lachlan say if I turn up tomorrow half-asleep?"

"Well done, probably."

"Well done for fucking his friend?"

Mitchell touches my face, tracing my cheekbone and the bridge of my nose, using the pad of his finger to pull out the center of my bottom lip.

28

"Life is for living," he says softly. "It's what brought us all together at Cloud 9. The desire for more. The need to push out of the confines of our lives."

"That's what I'm doing."

"I know."

He leans in to kiss me again, tugging me into his lap until his cock is back inside me and we're moving in a beautiful rhythm. I watch Mitchell as he takes pleasure in my body, relishing the flush across his cheeks and the sweat that dampens his chest. When I sense he's close, I clench around him, knowing the additional squeeze will trigger his orgasm. When he comes, he clutches me to him, pumping deep in that primal way that suggests an instinct to impregnate.

And fuck, if that isn't as sexy as hell, then I don't know what is.

Mitchell doesn't spend the night with me. He has things to do in the morning, and that's cool. I like my own space in bed, anyway. But he does stay long enough to make me feel good about everything we did together. And by the time he kisses me goodbye, I know we're going to be great friends. Great friends who fuck occasionally, hopefully.

Isn't that the best kind?

5

JARED

Dawn's moving in today and I still can't believe that Lachlan suggested it. A girl living among nine men. What's the saying? She's a rose between thorns, that's for sure.

When she arrives tugging her suitcase, I'm the first to see her and I jump to assist her with her bags. "Here, give them to me."

"I managed to get them across town. I'm sure a few more paces won't hurt." But she passes me the handle anyway and then the bag on her shoulder and the one on her back. By the time she's unloaded everything, I look like a donkey.

I lead her through the bar to the back, where the hostel accommodation and staff quarters are. We each have rooms off of a hallway. Lachlan has his own, as do Mitchell, Logan, Cooper, and Thomas. I share with my twin, Joshua, just like Bradley and Bryce bunk in together. The last room we've mostly kept free if there's a requirement for privacy or to house a visiting relative.

Now Dawn's going to take up residence in the eighth room.

When I throw open the door, I allow her to pass and inspect the accommodation. It's basic but clean, and I hope she's going to like it enough to stay.

"So, you're British?" she asks, in that American drawl that I find so damned sexy.

"What gave it away?"

"The cute accent," she says.

I rest her suitcase against the wall and place her carry bags on the bed. "Cute is not a masculine word," I say, raising my eyebrow in mock disgust.

"I could say sexy accent. Would that be better?"

"Infinitely," I add. "I miss being in America. People love our accent so much over there."

"And they don't here?" she asks, standing next to the window and looking out at the view. She's got a good room with a clear view out over the central communal area, complete with pergola, bean bags, and hammocks.

"Here they sometimes call us Poms, and it's not meant in a complimentary way."

"Really. I wonder what they call me?"

"Cute?"

Dawn places her hands on her hips and eyes me from across the room. "Sexy would be an improvement."

Oh, she is that, for sure. Before I heard that Mitchell spent half the night in her room, I'd already vowed to get to know Dawn with a view to something more. She has the look that I love. Pretty in a girl next door kind of way, but with enough confidence bubbling under the surface to wipe out a small country. Her eyes are green and sparkle with mischief, too.

Mitchell didn't disclose, but the smile on his face said it all. The girl's dynamite.

Dynamite, and not looking for a committed relationship.

"So, what brought you to this part of the world?" she asks. "You're a long way from home."

"The surf," I say. "Me and my brother Joshua, we love to surf. There are parts of England where you can catch some waves. Cornwall, mostly. But it's nothing like here."

"Really?" Dawn says. "I've never surfed."

"Really," I confirm. "We can teach you, if you like?"

I'm cut short by Joshua who knocks on the open door. "Is my brother doing a good job of being on the welcoming committee?"

"Well, he carried my bags and offered to teach me to surf. He's doing well so far."

"No offer to assist you with your unpacking?"

I shake my head at my brother's frankly ridiculous suggestion. "You think Dawn wants us rifling through her underwear?"

"I've never heard it called that before," she quips, and we all laugh. My eyes meet my brother's, and with twin communication, I can already see he's interested in her too. It's not unusual for us to like the same woman. It's not even unusual for us to sleep with the same woman. My brother is like my own flesh and blood, and we're so similar it can seem strange to others. Between the two of us, it just feels normal.

"So, surfing?" I ask, keen not to lose more of the day than I have to.

"I guess I don't have anything else to do," Dawn says.

"Other than rifling around in your own underwear," Joshua says, earning a startled laugh from our new housemate.

"Thankfully, I don't need to do that much. There's always a helpful hand around to take on the task."

"Like Mitchell?" Joshua asks, with a glint in his eyes and a crooked smile.

"Perfect example," Dawn says without a hint of discomfort.

In my experience, women can take issue with discussing their sex life, especially one-night stands. Not that Mitchell had labeled what happened last night as that. He was as relaxed as Dawn when he talked about what happened. Happy for it to happen again if the opportunity arose. Happy for it to lead to more. Happy if she decided it was a one-time thing. I swear, between the two of them, they could freeze the world with their chill attitudes.

There was one thing about Dawn that Mitchell did bring up. Her YOLO tattoo has him intrigued. He thought it was a drunken mistake like his, but it turns out, she chose it. Tattoos like that have a story, but apparently Dawn wasn't keen to share hers. It left us all intrigued.

"What do I need?" she asks.

"Just put on your swimwear and sunscreen, and we'll sort the rest."

Dawn beams happily, already unzipping her suitcase to find what she needs.

"See you out there?" Joshua asks.

"I'll be less than ten minutes."

"Perfect," he says.

When we've made our way out of the room and closed the door behind us, we immediately share glances. "She's cool," my twin says, rubbing the back of his neck.

"Very cool," I say.

"And hot." He blinks and opens his green eyes wide to emphasize.

"Very hot," I agree.

"Am I the only one wondering if this is going to end in disaster?".

Bradley appears in the corridor as we head back to our room to collect our gear. "See you guys later," he says, knowing our routine is going to take us to the beach.

It's only when we're in our room and I've closed the door that I answer my brother's question.

"It's not only you," I say.

6

DAWN

The British twins, Jared, and Joshua, leave me to decide on which sexy two-piece to wear to our first trip to the beach. They sound pretty serious about surfing, so I hope they won't be annoyed at how clueless I am. Slathering myself with sunscreen is a necessity. The sun in Australia is strong and I've already burned a little since arriving. Pink blistering skin is not an attractive look, and with mostly tanks and shorts in my bag, it's not like I have clothes available to cover it up.

When I've pulled on my trusty denim shorts and electric blue tank, I make my way outside.

The design of this place is unreal. The rooms are good sizes, but they don't dominate the setting. So much effort has been put into the layout and landscaping, it's almost as if the bar and hostel are part of the natural environment.

I should probably worry more about what I've agreed to do this morning than I am. Surfing looks easy when you watch the enthusiasts and pros, but something tells me it's a lot harder when trying to navigate the tempestuous ocean for the first time.

I drop my beach bag onto the ground and flop onto a green and orange striped bean bag. Not for the first time since the start of my trip, I get an urge to call home, but I can't. There are no normal conversations that I can have with my dad. There's only one question on his lips and I don't have an answer for him. At least, not one he'll be satisfied with. I must be staring into the distance because I don't notice Jared approaching.

"Ready to go?" he asks, making me jump.

I bring my hand to my heart quickly, letting out a whoosh of breath with shock. "As long as you promise not to scare the bejesus out of me again, especially when we're surfing."

He laughs, shaking his head slightly, and those sparkly green eyes just come to life with amusement.

Those eyes make my heart flutter. "Where's your brother?"

"Loading the boards into the truck."

I try to scramble off the beanbag with dignity but end up almost falling on my ass. Jared grabs my hand and helps me to my feet. "These babies take some practice."

"You're telling me!" he laughs.

We walk to the back of the hostel, where there is a small parking lot. Joshua is leaning against the side of the truck, all ready to go and looking like the sexiest surfer-dude I've ever seen. The sun spreads streaks of light through his blond hair and his tan skin glows with health and vitality. Glancing at Jared, I marvel at the luck of such a hot man multiplied by two.

And then I marvel at my luck at getting to spend the day with such delicious eye candy.

"You promise I'm not going to get hurt?" I say as I climb into the back of their truck. "I'm supposed to be working tonight and I've heard my bosses are real assholes."

Both twins laugh and turn to grin at me through the gap between the seats like sexy bookends. "No promises," Joshua says. "But isn't it the risk that makes life exciting?"

"It is," I agree. "But I don't think Lachlan will be that impressed with a bar waitress with a black eye or a broken leg."

"We'll do our best to take care of you," Jared says.

"Perfect," I say.

We're at the beach in less than five minutes. In fact, it probably would have been quicker to walk, but they have a lot of gear, so driving serves a practical purpose. Joshua passes me a board that is slightly smaller than theirs, but still weighs a lot. "Are you okay to carry?" he asks.

"Of course," I say. "Let's go."

The beaches in Byron Bay are some of the best in the world. The sand is so clean and white that it's almost blinding, and squeaks as I walk on it. The ocean is turquoise tipped with white frothy clouds that top the waves as they make their way to the shore.

We dump all our stuff near the shoreline, and Jared and Joshua begin to tug on their wetsuits. All I can say is, wow. They leave almost nothing to the imagination. When he's ready, Jared hands me a wetsuit, too. "Zip at the back," he instructs, using a long string to tug his own zipper closed.

"You say zip, I say zipper," I sing as I'm shoving my feet into the rubber outfit. It's a snug fit and, as I wriggle, it is as though I'm having to wrestle myself into something at least two sizes too small.

"Crazy Americans, changing a perfectly good language!" Joshua says, running his hand through his mess of dirty blond curls and already staring longingly at the surf.

"You have no idea."

Jared is kind enough to pull my zipper into place, and he grabs two handfuls of the fabric at my waist and yanks it up, lifting me off my feet in the process. I squeal, as he drops me. "Better?" he asks, and it really is.

"Right. Let's get you out there."

We each grab a surfboard, and stride into the ocean. The water is colder than I expect, and the waves hit my legs with a force that's a little intimidating. Jared and Joshua walk in front of me, their amazing physiques making light work of the push back from the surging waves. Beneath my feet, the sand churns sideways with a strong current that wants to drive me to the right.

"The ocean is fierce, isn't it?" I say.

"She's a force to be reckoned with," Joshua says. "But you should feel right at home with her." The smile he sends my way is so open and genuine that it sends my heart into a weird fluttering rhythm, and Jared joins him, as though they both agree on Joshua's sentiment. I love being thought of as a force to be reckoned with, especially by men who haven't known me for long. It means my vibe is coming through loud and clear!

Before we get too deep, they begin to instruct me on how to get on the board and how to paddle out further. I manage to get on for a few seconds but slide off the other side, much to their collective amusement. I resist the urge to feel disappointed with myself because this is something totally new and I have absolutely no idea what I'm doing.

When I'm finally on with both Jared and Joshua's amused assistance, I start to paddle out deeper. The waves push at the board, splashing me in the face and nudging me backward. I push harder, scooping water with my arms, trying to keep up with Jared and Joshua who seem to cut through the water with the grace of sea creatures.

They don't go too far, before they turn. "Okay, Dawn. Get ready to paddle." They focus behind them, waiting for a wave that will take us all back in the direction of the shore. "Now," Jared yells.

Paddling furiously, the wave takes the board, propelling it along faster than my hands can keep up. Jared and Joshua stay on their bellies too, flying through the water on either side of me. The rush of traveling just a few meters, driven by the power of the water, is immense, and I can see instantly why these boys have moved from England to Australia for their passion.

"Woohoo," I shout as I almost careen into the sand.

"Fun, isn't it?" Joshua's grin says it all.

"Can we do it again?"

"Of course," Jared says, helping me turn the board around and get back on. "Time to paddle again."

"Yeah, the paddling isn't fun," I groan, as my arms begin to feel the strain. No wonder the twins have such amazing biceps. Surfing isn't just about fun. It's physically grueling and takes a whole lot of mental concentration.

We go deeper this time, and I'm panting and bleary-eyed from the ocean spray. Jared and Joshua move to sit on the board with their legs hanging on either side, so I try to do the same. The balance it takes to achieve what they make look so simple is extraordinary. My core strength is letting me down.

"Have we converted you, yet?" Joshua asks.

"I think I need to join a gym before I come back out. It's hard work."

"But so worth it." Jared gestures to the horizon and back to the shore and I take in the bright blue kiss of the sky against the ocean, and the glittering white strip of sand in the distance. It's so beautiful my throat burns.

I share a love of the beach with my mama. I have a few photos of me as a toddler with my pants rolled up and my feet in the water, clutching her hand and smiling with glee as the water tickles my toes.

If she could see me now, she'd be cheering with excitement.

"You'll be surfing in no time," Joshua says. "You're already doing better than a lot of new starters."

"Yeah. We tried to teach some of our friends who visited last year, and they couldn't hack the salt in their eyes."

"It's not my favorite thing." Using the back of my hand, I smooth over my eyes as the sting begins to dissipate.

"All good things come hard." Joshua nods seriously as though he just delivered a nugget of wisdom that we should all reflect on.

His twin almost falls off his board laughing. "That is a line I've never heard you use before," he splutters.

Shaking his head, Joshua flares his nostrils in disgust. "Your mind is constantly in the gutter."

"My mind too," I say, twisting my mouth into a mock-bashful sideways smile.

Joshua waves his hand to dismiss us both.

"Hey," I say. "I think mine and Jared's interpretation is a lot more interesting."

"It definitely is," Jared agrees. "We have a favorite saying," he says with a filthy grin.

Joshua shakes his head, but a smile plays across his full lips.

"Oh yeah. And what's that?"

"If it swells, ride it!" they both shout, punching their right arms in the air.

"Yeah," I agree, following their gesture. "Maybe I'll get

that tattooed below YOLO."

Joshua stares at me as though he's trying to work out whether I'm serious or not. "I told Jared we should get it tattooed on our shoulders, but he doesn't want to, and I don't want to do something that will make us different."

"Seriously?" These guys are in their twenties, and they still relish the idea of being identical.

"We're mirror twins," Jared says, as though that explains everything.

"I have no idea what that is."

"When we look at each other, it's like looking in the mirror. My nose is slightly crooked to the left and Joshua's is to the right, so it's like we're a mirror image rather than just simply identical."

"And the tattoo wouldn't work because it couldn't be mirrored?"

"Exactly."

"Twins are weird," I laugh. "I'm so happy there isn't another one of me. The world wouldn't cope."

"We'd like it if there were two of you," Joshua says.

"More to go around," Jared smiles.

"Oh, there's plenty of me to go around." I widen my eyes suggestively, knowing that I'm flirting and feeling good about it. Mitchell is a lovely guy, and we had fun last night, but I'm not looking for anything exclusive and neither is he. If the twins wanted to make me the filling in their delicious looking sandwich, I'd be more than happy to oblige.

When Jared and Joshua glance at each other, I notice a question passing between them. The slight raise of Jared's head tells me everything I need to know.

If I suggested we hook up, they'd be down for some fun.

"Shall we go again?" I ask, feeling like it's the right

moment to break the ice.

"We're always ready to go," Joshua says with a wink.

I lie on the board, feeling the waves and trying to sense when they're going to tell me to paddle. It takes a few seconds before the water swells behind me with enough force.

"Now," Joshua yells.

This time, as I'm propelled forward to my belly, the boys fly past, somehow standing and riding their boards like it's the easiest thing in the world. With the wind rushing through their sun-streaked blond hair, they're like Greek gods. Was it Hermes who had wings on his sandals? That's what they're like, flying with boards as wings.

And even though I'm nowhere near standing, the rush of flying across the surface of the ocean with just a thin board beneath me is exhilarating.

I go a few more times before my arms begin to hurt, then I make my excuses and head inland, resting the board on the sand by our bags and sitting to watch Joshua and Jared do the thing they love enough to leave their lives behind and travel halfway around the globe.

Will I ever love something that much?

The prospect feels remote.

It hits me that I've never found a thing that I love as much as the twins love surfing. I've never found something that truly sets me on fire, despite trying every opportunity that presents itself.

Even though I'm faced with one of the most beautiful vistas, there's an itch beneath my skin that I can't quite reach. As a distraction, I reach for my cell phone, snapping pictures of Jared and Joshua in their element.

I take a few selfies, even though my hair is matted from the salt water, and my skin pink from the spray and sun. There's a part of me that is desperate to create memories, and this day feels strangely important.

The sun moves across the sky, time passing too slow and too fast all at the same time, and my heart skitters with panic at the thought of another day behind me.

There are never enough hours, minutes, or seconds. Every beat of my heart feels like a step too far.

I scoop up handfuls of sand and watch it slip between my fingers, hating the reminder of the egg timer that stands next to the stove at home. Hating the knowledge that with every grain that leaves my palm, I'm a little bit older and not at all wiser.

By the time the twins have had enough, I'm more than ready to go back to Cloud 9 for some alone time.

I get to my feet as Jared nears and shakes his hair, spraying me like a dog. "Where's your smile, pretty girl?" he asks.

"Did you miss us?" Joshua throws his dripping arm around my shoulder and the shock of the cold makes me jump.

"Of course," I say. "Who else is going to take the time to cover me with seawater?"

"Exactly," Joshua says. "When you find two men who can make you wet, you should hang onto them."

"That's a phrase that should be printed on a shirt." I smile, the melancholy that had been hanging over me, washing away with their smiles and humor.

"Stick with us," Jared says, pulling a box from his bag and flipping it open. Inside is a strange brown cake covered in white flecks and divided into squares.

"What is that?" I ask.

"It's a lamington. The best cake you'll ever eat."

"Lamington? Never heard of it," I say, but I reach into the box and snatch one up gratefully. All the paddling has left me hungrier than a horse. My first bite is tentative, but once my taste buds detect all the yummy sweetness, I don't hold back. "Mmmm," I groan. "That is frickin' delicious."

"Isn't it?" Jared agrees, demolishing a whole cake in just a few seconds.

"I thought athletes are supposed to be obsessed with eating protein, not cake."

Joshua snorts. "We never said we were athletes. Just enthusiastic surfers who love lamingtons."

"…and know how to make a girl wet. Don't forget that part."

"That's the best part." Joshua puts his arm around my shoulder again and tugs me into his chest, planting an affectionate kiss to my forehead. It feels so natural and easy, like we've been dating for weeks and are in that comfortable zone where two bodies become one.

And I decide, at that moment, that when we get back to Cloud 9, I'm going to find out exactly how good they are at riding the wave and taking me to the crest of pleasure.

7

JOSHUA

When we get home, there isn't much time before our shift starts. But Dawn is looking at us with hungry eyes and zero reservations.

She's the first girl we've ever hung out with who's shown an interest in surfing, and I didn't realize how much I would enjoy sharing my passion with someone of the opposite sex. She's also the first girl in a long time who's made me and Jared laugh. Maybe it's her easy American humor, or maybe it's just the fact that she doesn't seem to have any inhibitions. That easy way of approaching life is refreshingly unlike the girls back home.

"Let me carry your bag," I say, easing it from Dawn's shoulder as we make our way from the truck to our living quarters.

"Why, thank you," she smiles, surrendering it. Now back in her own clothes, the skin of her shoulders is dusted with salt that sparkles like glitter in the sun. Her sun-kissed hair is twisted into a messy bun that's begging to be unraveled.

At her door, her pretty green eyes drift over me and my brother, crinkling at the corners with whatever she's thinking in that fascinating mind of hers.

"So," I say, leaving it hanging as a potential opening to more, or a way of closing out an awesome outing.

"So," she says, with a cheeky smile. Then she opens the door to her room and reaches for both our hands. "All that surfing has made me horny. Is that something you can help me with?"

"That's something we can definitely help you with," my brother says.

For a fraction of a second, Mitchell runs through my mind. I know he won't care what we're doing with Dawn. He's not territorial like that. It's more that his perspective on what happened between him and Dawn lingers. He's convinced there's something behind the YOLO tattoo, but Dawn wouldn't tell him.

She's like a puzzle just waiting to be solved.

A beautiful, fascinating puzzle who is looking at me and Jared with hungry sex-eyes.

The next few seconds pass like a dream where time seems to move slower than reality. The door slams behind us and Dawn doesn't waste any time. Before I have a chance to even kiss her, she has a hand in my swim shorts and my cock in her hand. Jared gasps and I realize she's done the same to my twin, too. "If it swells, ride it," she whispers with a grin, and we all laugh. I bite on my bottom lip, loving the tight pressure she's giving my dick, wanting to taste her mouth and where she's salty-sweet between her legs. With two hands busy, I take the opportunity to push down the straps of her top and untie the strings of her bikini. When Dawn's full breasts are exposed to the room, there's no more laughter. Just the sound of her quickening breath as both me and Jared squeeze and tease her perfect light brown nipples into stiff points. The skin of her breasts is so much lighter than her arms and chest, exaggerating the reveal of previously concealed flesh. I bend to take a tight nipple between my lips and teeth, making Dawn shiver with pleasure.

Her hand tightens around my cock, and Jared gasps. "Fuck."

"Yes," Dawn says, breathily. "Let's do that."

"I thought you'd never ask." Before any of us have a chance to think, Jared has grabbed Dawn's wrists, pulled her hands away and backed her onto the bed.

Dawn shoves off the rest of her clothes, so impatient to get naked that my mouth falls open. My twin is keeping up, standing in nothing but a pool of his clothes and shoes, gazing down at Dawn's very pretty, very spread pussy.

"You know, my friend has eight lovers," she announces, her eyes drifting over our revealed bodies as I finally catch up with Jared. Her words throw me off guard.

"Seriously?"

"Yeah. Eight tattoo artists."

"Wow. And here I was worrying that two would be too many for you," I joke. It had crossed my mind, back at the beach, when Dawn's flirting became more obvious, that she might like more than just one of us. Now, I'm wondering whether we should just recruit the rest of the Cloud 9 boys and get this done properly.

"Two's good," she says, sliding a finger into her mouth and then slicking it over her clit. Fuck. My cock kicks with arousal. "But apparently eight is good, too."

"I'm surprised your friend can walk," Jared says, bending to kiss Dawn's inner thigh. She sighs loudly, and relaxes back against the bed, entirely at ease with the situation.

"Women have an amazing capacity for orgasms,"

Dawn says. "With the right men, of course."

"We're definitely the right men," Jared says, finally getting to the good stuff. I can't tear my eyes away as he flicks the point of his tongue against Dawn's clit, making her jump.

Her hand slides in his hair, gripping as he repeats the action over and over. My cock is like an iron bar, hard and straight in my palm. "While your brother's busy, give me a taste," Dawn says.

Oh god. She doesn't need to ask twice. As I kneel on the bed, she props herself on her elbows, and opens her pretty pink lips to the tip of my cock, moving to take me deeper than I had anticipated. The swallow of her throat against the sensitive head is intense and I have to grip her hair, desperate to find some control. It's too much to feel so much sensation and watch my brother do filthy things to this girl at the same time. He has two fingers inside her now, pumping, twisting and scissoring until her hips are bucking against his mouth and hand, and her lips grow tighter and more desperate around my cock.

Jared watches what she's doing to me through heavy-lidded eyes, and I know in a way it's like watching himself get head. Fucked up and a little twisted, but insanely hot at the same time.

"Fuck, you look good," I say, stroking Dawn's cheek as she works me to the precipice of pleasure.

She hums her appreciation and I have to pull back before I come down her throat and miss the chance to feel what it's like to be buried deep inside her.

I turn all my attention to helping Jared make Dawn come, using my hands to stroke and squeeze her breasts and my fingers to work her nipples into sharp points. It's only when I use my mouth to suck, matching the rhythm of Jared's licks, that she gasps, coming so violently that she almost tears off my twin's head with her clamping thighs.

The noise she makes is so low and desperate, I want to take her in my arms and hold her through the experience of such intense pleasure.

You only live once, is Dawn's mantra and I guess we're helping her make the most of today because what is life about if it isn't doing what you love and experiencing connections with other people?

Jared stands and our eyes meet. Wordlessly, he asks me what happens next. We don't have to go any further. We've done the important bit and sent Dawn into the stratosphere. If she's done, we are both man enough to deal with it. The issue of protection hangs in the air between us, too. When we left for the beach, sex wasn't exactly at the forefront of our minds.

"I have condoms," Dawn says. She still has her eyes closed and her legs clamped tightly together, but there's a small smile on her face that confirms she's ready for more.

I couldn't be fucking happier.

"Where, baby?" Jared asks.

"Front pocket of the suitcase, for easy access," she says, cracking her eyes open to look at us. "Damn, you both look sexy naked."

"You should see you." I run my hand up the outside of her thigh, loving the soft sighing sound she makes and the way her body relaxes under my touch.

Jared returns with a silver foil packet for us both, and we're sheathed and ready with identical efficiency. I glance at my brother again, wanting to share my thoughts about what happens next. One at a time, or together? The raise of his eyebrows suggests together.

Dawn isn't the kind of girl who would balk at the idea of two men at once. Her friend has eight lovers! She tugged us into her room without even a hint of shame. She embraces new experiences. At least, that's what her tattoo would suggest. We should try to make this as new and mind blowing as possible.

I lie on the bed next to Dawn, using my hands to explore all her warm curves. I lean in to kiss her pretty lips, finding her mouth soft and welcoming. When she's pliant and hungry, I scoop her on top of me in one clean movement, making her gasp in the process. When she stares down at me, it's with eyes crinkled with happiness and the cheekiest grin on her face.

"Joshua, are you manhandling me?"

"Yes, I am," I say, grabbing her hips and pressing my fingers into the roundness of her ass, drawing her sweet, wet pussy in a slick line over my waiting cock. Her eyes roll as I do it again, controlling her body until we're both gasping. When her pussy squeezes against me, I know she's ready, but I ask anyway.

"You ready for my cock?"

"Hell yeah," she says, with an accent that sounds thicker and more southern.

And she is. In one easy thrust, I'm buried deep, and Dawn's back is arched, her rounded tits pointing to the sky.

Jared curses behind us, watching it all.

As I encourage Dawn to lie against my chest, he moves closer.

"Ready for Jared's cock, too?" I ask.

"You boys really do like to share," she says, turning to hold her hand out to Jared. "If you think he can fit inside me too, then I say we should try."

"Oh, I can," Jared says. "All you have to do is relax."

"Relaxation and anticipation are not easy to combine," she says, but I sense her exhaling and softening against me.

I stroke my hand down her spine and over her ass, letting my fingers dance across forbidden places that make her shiver. "When Jared's buried deep in this tight, sweet pussy, he'll move. You just let us know if it's too much."

"Too much can sometimes be just right," she whispers against the corner of my lips. "Too much can sometimes be exactly what I need."

"It can be." I smile, thinking about all the times we've looked at the waves and judged them too rough, but thrown caution to the wind, anyway. They've been some of our best days.

The first press of Jared's cock has Dawn's fingers gripping my shoulders. "You're wetter than a river," he tells her, and she shrugs in response. "You're both sexy as fuck. What do you expect? I mean, look at you."

Her hand trails over the ripple of my six-pack and over my rounded pecs like she's showing off a supercar in a game show. There isn't a man alive who doesn't relish this kind of appreciation from a woman. It makes me want to rut into her from beneath, but I can't. Jared's the one in the driver's seat.

He makes slow work of easing into Dawn's pussy alongside me. Inch by slow inch, her body gives way until we're both buried deep.

"Fuck," she gasps, her fingernails almost drawing blood through the skin of my pec. "I've never felt so full."

"Just wait until I fuck." Jared presses a soft kiss between her shoulder blades to give Dawn time to accommodate him and get used to the idea that she's going to have to take even more.

"Fuck me," she orders, in control even though she's effectively powerless and pinned between us. But when Jared moves, Dawn's eyes are wide, and her mouth drops open. "Oh fuck," she gasps, and I know how she feels. The sensation is pure, white-hot pleasure. She is so tight around us that Jared almost struggles to pull out and push back in.

I grip Dawn's hips as though my life depends on ensuring she doesn't float away, and Jared rolls his hips with a finesse that comes from having done this a few times before. Well, what can I say? Sharing comes naturally when you've shared a womb.

Dawn's hips are mashed against mine, her clit grinding against my pelvic bone with every thrust, and she begins to twitch, seeking just the right kind of contact to send her over the edge into sweet oblivion all over again.

"That's it," Jared says. "Come on our cocks."

Dawn groans, flopping until her face is resting against my breastbone and her breath is gusting hot and out of control.

"That's it," Jared croons, and out of nowhere, he plants a slap that ripples Dawn's ass and pulls a gasp from her lips. Her pussy tightens like a vise, which is enough to reveal how much she likes a little light punishment.

"She liked that," I say, and Jared responds with another spank. This time, the tightening grip around my cock is like rippling waves, and Dawn's face scrunches as she orgasms almost painfully. My thighs feel wet from her arousal, and between us we are slick with sweat. I tug her close, wanting her to feel safe and secure between us, even as Jared takes us closer to our own release.

"Fuck," Jared grunts as his thrusts become less controlled. I know my brother's close, and I am too. Maybe we'll come together as a weird kind of grand finale. I close my eyes and lose myself in the sensation, feeling like I do when I hit a wave that's going to go and go and go.

And then it hits.

A swell of pulsing pleasure that spins me out of the moment. Jared is only two seconds behind me, jerking his release until it's almost painful to still be inside Dawn.

For a long moment, we all dwell within our own

bodies, relishing the sensations, knowing that our time together is almost done.

Duty calls, and we all need to be showered and ready within twenty minutes, or Lachlan will hand us our arses on a plate.

"You guys rocked my world," Dawn says, half dreamy and half amused.

"I think it was you who rocked ours," Jared says, easing out slowly. He takes time to kiss her shoulders and her neck and tell her she's the hottest thing he's ever had the pleasure of sharing a bed with.

I kiss her lips, soft and slow, until she's squirming on my half-hard cock. "You could go again, couldn't you?" I laugh, surprised.

"Hell yeah," she says.

"Forget your friend Kyla. I think it's you who needs the big harem of boyfriends."

"Yeah," she laughs. "Do you know anyone who might want to join us?"

I do, actually. There are nine men in this place who I'm sure would sacrifice a nut to feel what I felt just now. Well, maybe not a nut, but something else almost as important as a vital body part. I don't tell Dawn that because I wouldn't ever want to pressure her to do anything with anyone.

She's not a girl who's shy about taking what she needs.

She doesn't need me to hold her hand.

She lives each day as if it's her last and it's refreshing as fuck, but as we dress, kiss, and say easy, smiley, affectionate goodbyes, I can't help but wonder, like Mitchell, why she got that tattoo in the first place.

8

THOMAS

It's early evening and Cloud 9 is just starting to get busy with the after-work crowd and the before-dinner people. This is my favorite time of day because there's still a mellow vibe about the place, and I get to spend some time adding to the atmosphere with my music.

Lachlan's more than happy to have my easy guitar and my gravelly voice to entertain the masses. He doesn't enjoy Cooper's DJing but understands it's what our customers want when it's late and everyone is drunk.

I have a simple wooden chair in a raised area in the corner where I strum out the music I like and hope that the crowd enjoys it, too.

Dawn is flitting from table to table, helping Jared and Joshua deliver the drink orders. With a permanent smile on her face, she seems to be loving the work. The customers enjoy her easy, friendly attitude too, and I don't miss the appreciative looks some of the men are sending her tonight. Her yellow sundress sets off her sun lightened hair drawn into a messy bun, and her catlike green eyes.

Every time she passes, Dawn shoots me a smile, and I respond because her happiness is infectious.

I think I know why she's happy. We all heard the noises coming from her room this afternoon, and Lachlan caught Jared and Joshua leaving the room. Good sex obviously has a positive effect on our newest employee. It'd have a positive effect on me, too. It's been a while, not because there haven't been opportunities, but because those opportunities just haven't been that appealing. Pretty girls don't always hit the spot if they don't have a special spark. I'm not sure I could identify exactly what it is that I look for in a woman, but I know when I know.

I finish singing an upbeat tune, and the crowd ripples with low applause. Jared brings me a beer, and I take a grateful swig.

"Good tune," he says. "That one new?"

"Yeah. Thought I should freshen up the playlist."

He grins, his eyes drifting from me to follow Dawn, who's carefully crossing the bar with a tray of beers resting on one hand.

"You look smitten," I say.

He shrugs in his laid-back way, like everything washes off him like water off a duck's back. "Dawn's cool. Like, really cool."

"Cool. That's an interesting word."

"You'll see what I mean when you get to know her." His eyes continue to trail her as she returns to the bar and starts a conversation with his twin.

I clear my throat. "You guys really fuck her too?"

He nods, focusing his attention on me. "Fuck's a harsh-sounding word."

"You made love?" I ask.

"Nah...it was more like we enjoyed each other's

bodies."

"Funny…that's what Mitchell said."

"Dawn's just really relaxed about life. She doesn't seem to have any hang-ups. She just wants to enjoy herself, and sex is part of that."

"Sounds like the perfect girl."

"Yeah," he says, without any hint of doubt in his voice.

"You really like her?"

"What's not to like?"

Joshua shouts his brother's name and Jared leaves to help with a big order.

As Dawn passes me, I wave her over, deciding it's time for me to see what all the fuss is about.

"How are you getting on?" I ask, taking another long drink.

"Good," she says. "Everyone is just so friendly. You guys are all making me feel so welcome."

"Welcome is our middle name," I say, hearing the cheesy line and cringing. This isn't me. I'm usually not flustered by women, but Dawn has an energy pulsing from her that's both vibrant and sexual, and I completely understand why three of my best friends have already fallen for her charm.

"Thomas Welcome. Your mom had a sense of humor."

I snort, and tip my head to the side, letting my eyes trail over Dawn's high cheekbones and soft mouth, the curve of her breast and the firmness of her thighs. Before I think about what I'm doing, I ask her if she'd like to learn how to make two of the bar's signature cocktails.

"Sure," she says. "Are you allowed to stop playing?"

I shrug, and lumber off the stage, finding myself looming over Dawn, who's smaller than her big personality allowed me to perceive. "We're all equal partners here. We don't tell each other what to do. We just work in the best interests of everyone."

"That sounds very democratic," she says, following me to the bar.

Lachlan is mixing drinks with Cooper and Logan. It's Mitchell's night off and he's taken the opportunity to sleep.

I pick up a fresh coconut and begin to show Dawn how to make a Cloud 9, feeling the interested eyes of my friends.

With coconut cream, pineapple, vodka, and rum, it's a lot like a pina colada, except there's a special ingredient. A swirl of dark chocolate sauce.

Dawn's eyebrows shoot up as I add the sauce. "Chocolate?"

She sounds as skeptical as I was when Lachlan came up with the idea. I finish dressing the coconut with two straws and two cherries on a stick and then hand it over to Dawn. "Here. Try it. You're going to love it."

She holds the large coconut in two hands and wraps her soft pink lips around both straws. Her cheeks hollow as she sucks, and she keeps her eyes on mine the whole time. I don't think she intends for me to start imagining filthy things. This is all about her trying a drink concoction that she suspects is going to taste gross, but all I can imagine is her lips wrapped around my cock and her eyes staring into mine as she takes it deep.

In my jeans, my dick stirs, ready. And I feel like a dick for not being able to look at a pretty woman without thinking about sex. Should have grown out of that in school. "So, what do you think?"

Dawn lowers the cocktail and I notice the coconut is nearly empty. "That is goooooood," she drawls.

Grinning broadly, I grab another shaker and fill it with ice. "See, I told you you were going to love it. Now we'll see if you like Seventh Heaven."

"There's a theme going on here," she says, grabbing the cocktail list and glancing down. "Where did the Cloud 9 thing come from?"

"There are nine of us," Cooper says from behind. "It was the only phrase we could think of with nine in."

"What about nine lives?"

Cooper nods his head, pursing his lips. "That's a good one, too. Wouldn't have made such a good name for a bar, though."

"True. Dressed to the nines? Or even A stitch in time…"

"…saves nine," Lachlan finishes.

"What are you? Some kind of phrases dictionary?" Logan asks, passing Jared eight bottles of beer for a large rowdy table in the corner.

Dawn shrugs. "Must have picked them up from somewhere." A dark look fleetingly shadows her expression before she pastes her smile back on.

I continue mixing the drink, letting Dawn see each of the ingredients before I shake it. I pour it into a glass and pass it to her to try. This time, her sip through the straw is quick and less suggestive.

"What do you think of that one?"

She shrugs, handing it back. "Seven isn't as good as nine."

"Really?" Lachlan interjects. "I had you pinned as a girl who'd like the sour cocktail more than the sweet."

"I don't know how to take that." Dawn rests a hand on her hip and raises her eyebrow. Lachlan, realizing his comment could be misconstrued, has the decency to blush.

"I just meant you're not a typical woman."

"Again, I'm not sure how I should take that."

"As a compliment," I say, rushing in to save my friend before he tumbles headfirst into an abyss of his own

58

making.

"Well, alrighty then," Dawn says happily.

"Do you want to try to make them now?"

"Sure," she says, already reaching for a coconut. I stand by, expecting her to query the measures or the method at some point, but after five minutes of concentrated work, Dawn has two perfectly prepared cocktails in front of her. Lachlan has stopped what he's doing to watch and nods his head with approval.

"She's got it," I say, sipping Dawn's Seventh Heaven.

"She could work behind the bar," Logan says, peering into the Cloud 9 coconut.

"I'm a woman of many talents." She grins, obviously pleased with herself and our approval.

Jared smiles. "I can confirm that statement."

Most girls would blush at his very obvious sexual reference, but Dawn doesn't. Instead, she reaches across the bar and presses her palm to his face. "You're very talented too, baby," she says.

Lachlan, watching everything, nods in my direction. "Time to play some more guitar, Thomas."

"I guess it is."

Dawn follows me as I make my way back to my makeshift stage. "Thanks for teaching me. That was fun."

"Anytime," I say. She smiles when I pick up my guitar and rest it in my lap, fingering the strings. I mentally flick through my playlist, considering what to sing next.

Dawn steps back, folding her arms across her chest as she waits for me to begin. There's a connection between us already, a thread of mutual attraction that tugs at my mind, my body, and my heart.

Is it the musician thing that appeals to her?

Usually, when I start singing, people stare appreciatively, or smile. I'm used to warm responses to my voice and my guitar. I may not be fame-hungry enough to go pro, but I like to think my voice is good enough.

But when I begin to sing Iris by the Goo Goo Dolls, Dawn's smile drops. Her shoulders brace and head lowers, and instead of smiling, she backs away and rushes in the direction of the women's toilets.

Shit.

I keep singing because that's what I have to do. It's a popular song with an awesome guitar part, and customers around the bar sway and look over to where I'm sitting, happy to hear an old favorite. But not Dawn.

Something about this song set her off.

At the end, I rest my guitar against the wall, and head to the bar, keeping my eyes focused on the door where Dawn disappeared and hasn't yet emerged. "Did you see that?" I ask Jared.

"No. What?"

"Dawn looked like she was going to cry when I played that song."

"She did?" He frowns and follows my gaze. "There's something eating that girl."

"What do you mean?"

"The tattoo. The carefree attitude. I don't buy it, at least not one-hundred percent. Something's going on in her life that she's trying to escape. Or she's trying to forget. I'm not sure which."

"Since when did you become Mr. Psychology?" I ask.

He folds his big arms, his biceps straining the snug sleeves. "I just like to understand the people around me. Like you, for instance, enjoy the approval of others."

"Who doesn't?" I say, feeling a little uncomfortable at his scrutiny.

"Dawn keeps people around her at arm's length. It's a protection mechanism."

"She didn't keep you and Joshua and Mitchell at arm's length," I say, confused.

"Sex without connection is about keeping people at arm's length," Jared says.

At that moment, Dawn appears from the bathroom with red-rimmed eyes. She keeps her gaze focused on the floor and heads over to a table in the corner to collect empty glasses and bottles. My heart aches, knowing that the song I chose was one that brought back bad memories for her.

But underneath it all, I find that I want to know everything about this girl who's stumbled into our lives and made such an impact already.

9

DAWN

I busy myself, clearing the unoccupied tables of glasses and bottles, using the cloth I have tucked into my apron to wipe up any mess. Taking deep, controlled breaths, I try to push down the emotion that welled up when Thomas began to play Mom's favorite song.

I couldn't deal with hearing Iris, especially when sung in such a beautiful, acoustic tone. Somehow, the words coming from Thomas's lips were just too much for me to handle. It shouldn't be this hard. Not after so many years. Grief is something that is supposed to hold a person in its clutches for a year, or a couple of years at most. Time is supposed to heal, isn't it? It's an old adage for a reason.

But it doesn't get any easier.

The things that make me remember are the same, and the feelings are just as raw. Maybe there's something wrong with me that I can't get past this. Maybe I'm just never going to be able to hear Mom's favorite songs without breaking down. Maybe it's just something I have to accept.

Thomas noticed. Of course he did. There's no way that he missed the way I reacted. He's a perceptive guy. Most creatives are. And even though I've patted my face with cold water, my eyes are still bloodshot, and my heart is heavy enough to make smiling impossible.

The happiness I usually wear, like a shield, has cracked.

The weight of panic bows my back and leadens my heart.

An image of Mom in her last days haunts me. Hollowed eyes, gray skin. She didn't look like my momma anymore. Holding her hand was like grasping onto a mannequin.

"Can we order?" a woman asks as I pass.

"Sure," I say, forcing a flicker of a smile. "What can I get you?"

"Two Cloud 9's," she says. "And a bottle of water."

"Coming right up."

At the bar, Thomas is talking to Jared, but they pause when I approach. Addressing Lachlan, I tell him the order, and rest the empties on the bar. Logan clears the glasses and tosses the empty bottles into the trash, his eyes lingering on my face a little longer than is comfortable.

There's a quietness about the group that is in stark contrast to the easy chatter of a few minutes ago.

I don't like it, but I don't know what to say.

"You gonna play something?" Lachlan asks Thomas.

Thomas hesitates, not responding as though he wants to delay the inevitable. Over on the stage, he won't be able to watch me in the way that he has been. Maybe he's worried he'll choose another song that will set me off. Everything feels brittle and sharp.

Before he makes his way back to perform, he glances at me with worry. I quickly look away, not ready to face his scrutiny. Not ready to face anyone's scrutiny.

For the rest of the evening, I manage to keep my emotions stuffed down. I find the strength to pull myself together and smile again. I chat with customers, finding some fellow Americans who bring a welcome sense of home to our conversation. Logan encourages me to make cocktails to practice, although I'm certain I got them perfect on the first try.

Thomas finishes his set and Cooper takes his place behind the decks to DJ a more upbeat mix to the rowdier late evening crowd.

Jared and Joshua maintain their easygoing attitudes and Logan flirts whenever I approach the bar. Lachlan is the most reserved of them all, and Thomas, the one who seems to hold on to his concern for me the longest.

By the end of the evening, I'm feeling better, but there is still a lingering grayness beneath the surface.

"You did great tonight," Lachlan says, as I finish wiping the last table at closing time. "If you want, you can take a shift behind the bar."

"If you need me to, I will. But I like talking to customers. I'm happy to do either."

He nods, pleased at my flexibility.

"I'm going to hit the sack," I say.

"Thanks for tonight."

I wave at the group of men gathered behind the bar, wondering what Jared and Joshua are thinking. Do they expect me to invite them back to my room again? Do I even want to?

The sex was incredible, and I really like them, but a repeat of earlier would be dangerous. My emotions are raw, and raw emotions combined with sex leads to feels.

What I need is to keep everything easy and light. Live each day like it could be my last.

When I'm back inside the safety of my room, I press my back against the wall next to the door and take three big steadying breaths. I ball my hands into fists and release them, trying to expel the coiled tension. I close my eyes and think of this morning at the beach and the fun I had with Jared and Joshua. I think of Mitchell and his easy smile and how awesome I felt after our night together. I think of laughing, dancing customers enjoying their night at Cloud 9, a place of fun and happiness.

I remember why I'm in Australia in the first place. Escaping from home was the only way I could deal with the pressure this year brings.

Just as I've finally found some equilibrium, there is a knock at the door.

I want to ignore it, but I can't. Whoever is there knows I'm in here.

When I turn the handle and pull the door open, I find the one person I'm the wariest of facing right now.

Thomas.

"Hey Dawn," he says. His warm brown eyes scan my face as though he's checking for more tears.

"Hey."

"I wanted to check if you're okay."

His directness takes my breath away. "Of course. I'm fine."

"That song," he says tentatively. "It made you cry. I'm sorry."

"I'm fine, Thomas." Taking a step back to put some distance between us, I place my hand over my throat, which has tightened from his words.

"You don't seem fine, and I wanted to let you know that you can talk to me if you need a shoulder. I'm a good listener, and I'm good at keeping secrets."

I swallow down the lump and fold my lips between my teeth before I respond, knowing my words can sometimes come out sharper than I intend them. "Sometimes talking doesn't help," I say, and shrug.

"So, what does?"

Framed by the doorway, Thomas is beautiful. With floppy black curls and eyes as warm as summer, he's like a Mediterranean dream.

He reaches out and takes my hand, holding my fingers so gently between his that tears prick my eyes. "Fucking," I say. "Dancing. Eating. Drinking. Exploring. Friendship. Never staying in one place too long."

"Living for the day," he says, taking a step closer.

"Exactly."

"So, which of those do you need tonight?" he asks. "Exploring and moving on might not be great options, but I make great pancakes and we have enough liquor outside to kill us both a hundred times over. I have a playlist on my phone for dancing."

I notice he leaves out the option of fucking, even though that's what I led with. And his avoidance of the thing he'd definitely enjoy the best makes Thomas even more appealing.

"I'm too full for pancakes," I say. "And I think the smell of alcohol would make me heave this late at night. But we could dance?"

The smile that Thomas gives me is broad, open, and genuine. I take a couple of steps back to give him room to come inside, and he closes the door behind him. The bed looms large in the space, but Thomas doesn't let his gaze drift there. Instead, he focuses on his phone, scanning through what looks to be an impressive music collection before he finds a suitable song.

The first bars of the song play, and he rests his phone

on the edge of a shelf, reaching to take my hand. He's not shy when he pulls me close and wraps his arms around me. My face is at his shoulder, close enough that his fresh, masculine scent is all around me. He leads us with a confidence I didn't expect, and a rhythm I absolutely did, humming along to the song as we move in small circles. Within seconds, I relax in his arms, allowing the notes to wash over me, soothing the coiled tension, and softening my sharp edges. Thomas, in response, pulls me closer. His arms surround me, filling me with a sense of safety. Everything feels simple in this cocoon. Our bodies move easily together, and I close my eyes and dwell happily with this man who cared enough to come to check that I was okay and who offered to do anything to make me feel better.

I wonder about how so many awesome men managed to find each other and set up a business together. It has to be unusual. In my whole life, I haven't found nine women who could do the same.

I think about how content I am in this new place, after such a short space of time, and my mind drifts to the inevitable moment when I'll have to leave, because I will.

"I can hear your mind whirring," Thomas murmurs, jolting me from my thoughts.

"Is my brain that noisy?"

"Absolutely." The smile in his voice feels affectionate. I'm always conscious that I'm not the easiest person to like. I can be upfront and out there, and it's off putting to some. But not this man, it would seem.

He's seen your vulnerable side, my internal voice whispers. *And he's still here.*

Most men run at the first sign of tears in a woman they hardly know, but not Thomas.

"Can I ask you a question?" I slow my feet and look up into his dark eyes, biting on my lip because I'm not sure how it's going to be received.

"You can ask me anything," he says.

"Why Iris?"

"The lyrics," he says, without hesitation. "They've always felt like they were about me."

"That's funny," I say, shaking my head. "They've always felt like they were about me too."

He smiles softly and I notice for the first time that he has one adorable dimple that tugs his right cheek. A dimple I get a sudden urge to kiss. Before I think, I'm standing on my tiptoes and my lips make contact with Thomas's cheek.

To his credit, he doesn't flinch. When I drop down so my heels are on the floor again, our eyes meet. Thomas folds in his lips and releases them, and everything about him seems to become intensified. I'm mesmerized by the size of him, by the gentleness of his clever hands and the way he moves like we're both surrounded by water.

The music continues to play, seeping through my skin and into my bones. In this man's arms, all the pressure that, at the very least, nips at my heels and sometimes threatens to swallow me whole seems far away. Like Mitchell, Jared, and Joshua, Thomas has just what I need to keep me in the moment.

But does he want to be in the moment with me?

We're dancing because he listed it as an option, ignoring the one that's my default.

Sex, my safe and happy place.

The space where my body takes over and my mind and heart can be put aside.

Will he want to do that with me? This tender man with beauty in his fingertips and soul in his voice.

"Dawn," he murmurs, and I sense from his tone that he wants more but doesn't know if he should.

Tears have a tendency to scare men away. They're not good with emotions at the best of times, especially with sadness.

"Thomas," I reply softly, then, before he has a chance to back away, I return to my tiptoes and press my lips to the center of his.

He doesn't kiss me back straight away. It's like there's a war going on inside him. After a couple of seconds, just before I'm going to pull away, his lips move, and I know I've got him.

Our first kiss is as sweet at honey, as tentative as a baby's first steps. My hands ache to stroke all the planes of his muscular body, but I hold back because I don't want to take him out of the moment or make him think too many steps ahead.

I let Thomas lead, and when his hands drift down my body, his touch is as reverent as when he cradles his guitar. I melt against him, wanting more, faster, harder, but understanding that Thomas isn't that man. He's exploratory and gentle, sensitive, and protective. He wants to read my emotions and tune me to his melody.

Beneath my hand, his heart beats a staccato rhythm, and his tongue slides over mine, deep and then deeper, until my back is arched and I'm gripping the front of his shirt for balance. The groan he makes in his throat is long and deep, and between my legs, my pussy squeezes in response.

His hands roam my hips and ass, squeezing gently. Then, out of nowhere, he lifts me so my legs are wrapped around his waist. I gasp and he kisses my neck, taking three steps until my back is at the wall and his hips have pinned me in place.

"You're so fucking sexy," he murmurs against my neck.

"Thomas," I groan, as his fingers trail the straps at my shoulders, easing them down so slowly and tentatively that

69

I want to scream.

"Did they kiss you like this?" he asks, staring right into my eyes, then taking my bottom lip between his teeth and holding it for a couple of seconds.

"Who?" I ask when it's released.

"Jared and Joshua, and Mitchell." His hips press harder against me, the bar of his cock lined up perfectly with my clit. From anyone else, it might sound jealous, but from Thomas, it just sounds curious.

"Everyone kisses differently."

"Does everyone fuck differently, too?"

"Of course. Kissing, dancing, fucking. It's all different depending on who it's with. Even I'm different depending on who I'm with."

"You are?" His hand squeezes my breast, his thumb seeking out the point of my nipple.

"I am." I bring my hands to his cheeks, relishing the scruff of his beard growth and loving the way his eyelids lower at my touch.

"How?"

"I feel the way you like to move, the way you like to touch, and I respond."

"I like the way you touch me," he says, kissing the corner of my mouth. If he wasn't holding me up, I would have crumbled on weak knees by now.

"And I like the way you touch me," I say, letting out a soft groan as his palm makes contact with my bare skin. His fingers are deliciously rough from pressing guitar strings and make me squirm against him.

"We don't have to fuck," he says. "We can just fool around."

"And waste what you have pressed against me? I don't think so."

Thomas's pupils seem to dilate in response, and I grin

70

and squirm against him again so that he's left in no doubt.

Supporting me with one hand, he reaches into his back pocket and pulls out his wallet. I take it from his hands and pull out the foil packet tucked snugly inside.

"How long has this baby been in here?" I ask.

"Couple of weeks," he says. "Don't worry. It's still good."

"Perfect." I tear it open with my teeth and hand him the clear latex ring. "You can put me down, you know, if your arm's hurting."

"Where's the fun in that? Here." He glances between us at the buttons on his jeans, which I unfasten quickly. He adjusts his hold on me as I shove at the thick material, pushing down his dark underwear in the process. With finesse, he slides the condom down his impressive length with one hand, still holding me with the other.

There's no way for me to remove my panties in this position, but I don't care. Yanking the damp fabric to the side is sexier, anyway.

"I'm wet," I say, in case Thomas is worried about warming me up. I'm sure it was part of his plan, but just the thrusting of his hips and the rasp of his fingers is enough to make me ready.

In one hot, dirty thrust, he spreads me open, impaling me on his perfectly sized cock. I close my eyes, relishing the stretch, and he rests his forehead against mine, panting softly.

"Fuck, you're tight." His teeth are gritted as he fights to retain control of his body. I'm so desperate for him to move though, that I used my feet to urge his hips. And then it's a frenzy of lips and hands, grinding hips that's like a perfect movie sex scene. Thomas fucks me with a passion that has me moaning every time his pelvis grinds against my clit. His fingers grip the flesh of my ass, his arms forming a platform beneath my thighs.

He fucks me with enough force that any negative thoughts I might have had this evening are thrust out of me. I get to close my eyes and let his body rule mine until I'm panting and begging because I'm so close to coming it's almost painful.

"Please," I gasp, and Thomas yanks up my right leg until it's high over his shoulder and the depth is exquisite.

"Yes," I shout, not worried about who might be able to hear. "Yes. Yes. Oh fuck yes."

I tip my head back, not caring that it thumps against the wall as Thomas works to tip me over the edge into the sweetest oblivion.

My mind swims, my body arches, and Thomas groans loudly against my neck as he comes with me. I don't know how he continues to hold me up on legs that tremble with release. He's a man of kindness and consideration, but also self-control.

"Jeez," I say on a bubble of laughter.

Thomas is still too lost to speak as his warm breath dampens my neck and his hands hold on to me like he's never going to let me go.

When his head is clear enough to respond, he straightens and smiles at me, his chocolate eyes warm and happy. Then, instead of allowing my feet to drop to the floor, he carries me to the bed, still buried deep inside me, climbs onto the mattress on his knees and lays me down reverently. I wrap my arms around him as his lips find mine and his throat makes a sound that can only reflect contentment. We kiss and kiss, and eventually, Thomas pulls out, dealing with the condom and tucking his cock back into his pants.

But rather than leave, he pulls me close and tucks me against his chest. His breathing evens and I think he's fallen asleep, but then he kisses the top of my head. "I know who you are, Dawn," he murmurs, and the lyrics to

Iris spin around in my head again.

I want you to know who I am.

He thinks that the song is about me.

He doesn't know why I cried.

But wrapped safely in his arms, all I need are those words to banish my ghosts, at least for one night.

10

BRADLEY

It doesn't go unnoticed that Thomas and Dawn appear for breakfast at the same time. We all heard her moans last night and knew at least one of us was having some fun.

Lucky Thomas, I think as I flip five thick pancakes off the griddle. I'm on breakfast duty this morning and pancakes are my specialty. A large stack of them rests on the counter, along with crispy bacon, blueberries, and maple syrup.

It smells just like home.

Bryce inhales deeply from his spot at the end of the counter, and I know he's thinking the same. We love Australia and have no intention of leaving, but we miss our Mom and Dad, and wish they were closer so we can see them more frequently.

Dawn and Thomas walk with relaxed strides and shy smiles tug at their mouths. Thomas is wearing the same shirt as last night, but it's way more crumpled. Dawn is in a denim skirt, black tank and cute hot pink sneakers. Her hair is wet, so at least one of them is showered.

I think if I fucked Dawn last night, I'd want to leave her scent on me for as long as I could. That girl is smokin'.

"G'day," Thomas says, glancing around at the assembled group. For once, all of us have made it out of bed in time, probably assisted by the sex noises that started just before eight am and went on for an hour.

"Morning." "G'day." Eight deep voices boom in welcome accompanied by a few interested grins and a couple of frowns. Lachlan is worried about the Dawn-effect that's sweeping Cloud 9 right now. He thinks that all the fucking is going to lead to bad blood. Maybe he's right, but there's no jealousy being expressed by the four men who've already shared her bed.

Maybe it's a sign that Lachlan shouldn't get involved, if Dawn gives him the chance, that is. Of all of us, he's the one who likes to be in control. I think Dawn and her free way of living might give Lachlan an aneurysm.

"Morning," Dawn says, with a surprisingly shy glance around the room. Mitchell grins with a proud expression on his face, and Joshua and Jared raise their heads in greeting. It's all very friendly and accepting. Weirdly so.

Interesting.

"Morning, darlin'," I say as she approaches the counter. "Help yourself."

"It smells just like home." Dawn says wistfully, eyeing the crispy bacon. She grabs a plate and heaps on two pancakes, four strips of bacon, a spoonful of blueberries and enough maple syrup to make it all glossy and sweet.

"I was just thinking the same thing," I say. "It's my momma's recipe."

"I'll have to see if it's as good as mine." She turns before I have a chance to reply and sits at the long table to the right, facing Lachlan. He shifts in his seat like her proximity makes him restless.

He wouldn't be the only one feeling like that.

I'm not sure what it is about a sexually confident woman that gets under the skin of men. It's like a dream come true to meet someone without hang ups, but at the same time, it's a challenge to the natural order of things.

The stereotype of women not wanting sex as much as men exists for a reason. I'd guess that most women who aren't that into fucking have had terrible lovers and bad experiences. When the sex is good, women can be as horny as men, sometimes even hornier. At least that's my take on it.

As Dawn leans forward to eat, her large YOLO tattoo peeks out between her top and low-riding skirt. I've never seen anything like it on a girl. Mitchell has FOMO on his bicep but only because he was drunk, and young, and stupid. Mitchell claims Dawn got that on purpose because it's her motto. I don't want to make assumptions, but in my experience, people who live like there isn't a tomorrow do so because they're afraid of what the future might bring.

What could Dawn be afraid of? Something back home?

She's made a long journey to be here, and maybe it's just for new experiences. I can understand that way of thinking because that's part of what drove Bryce and me to leave home behind. Seeing new things and meeting new people is exhilarating, and maybe that's all it is. We also left because things were going wrong, and it was easier to move on than face the music.

It's our experience that leaves a nagging doubt in my mind.

Dawn cried last night at a song Thomas was playing. Jared told me about it this morning. If there's one thing you can be sure of in this place, it's that information travels fast. Crying over music is a sure sign of some kind of trauma, but what?

Maybe Thomas knows something. He went to her room to make sure she wasn't still upset, and he didn't leave until the sun had risen. That gave him enough time to dig for the truth.

"Bradley, are you making more pancakes?" Cooper asks, nodding at the now empty plate. While I've been watching Dawn and thinking, all the food has been cleared, as if a plague of locusts has landed.

I pour more batter onto the griddle and listen as my friends talk, or should I say flirt, with Dawn. Her phone is buzzing like crazy, distracting her attention every few seconds.

"Who is that?" Mitchell asks, nodding at the device that rests on the table next to her plate.

"My friend Kyla," she says. "She's teasing me about living with you guys."

"Really? How come?" Cooper asks.

"Well, the last time she got a new job, she ended up in a relationship with the eight tattoo artists she was working with."

"She what?" Cooper says, his eyes bugging out in surprise.

"It's a reverse harem thing."

From my angle, I can't see her face, but I can imagine the smile tweaking at the corners of her full lips.

"Reverse harem?" Bryce asks.

"Yeah. You know. Like a harem, but with many, many gorgeous men."

"Does your friend know you describe her boyfriends as gorgeous?" Mitchell asks.

"Hell yeah. I was the one who got her into that enviable situation. It started as a game."

I flip the pancakes onto the plate and Cooper rises to serve himself.

"What kind of game, Dawn?" I ask.

She swivels in her chair to face me. "Well, Kyla wasn't very experienced in the bedroom." She raises her eyebrows suggestively. "So the very generous men of Ink Factor offered to introduce her to their favorite kinks."

"I bet they did," Mitchell laughs, raising his mug to finish the last of his coffee. "That sounds like the most awesome game ever."

"And they all ended up in a relationship. How?" Bryce asks. Of course, he'd be the one to want to know the ins and outs.

"They all fell in love with her. She's an incredibly special woman."

"She'd have to be to balance the needs of eight men," Lachlan says, his mouth twisting in a thoughtful way.

"She's got it working like a well-oiled machine," Dawn says. "Women are masters of multi-tasking."

"And so, how does it work? Do they each have a day? I don't think I could go eight days between sex."

"No. It's mostly a free-for-all."

"What does that even mean?" Lachlan asks. I narrow my eyes at my friend, shocked that of all of us, he's the one practically interrogating Dawn about her friend.

"It means they all share a bed."

"It can work," Mitchell says. "I've seen many movies showcasing this exact same thing."

"You've seen many gang bang pornos," I say. "Not many loving reverse harem relationships. I'd bet there's a whole load of difference."

"Maybe," Dawn says. "Kyla confided a little before they were official, but now it's all private."

"As it should be," Lachlan says.

"Well, if one of your friends has eight lovers, there's hope for us," Mitchell says.

Lachlan chokes on his coffee and Jared and Joshua laugh like it's an idea they've already considered. I get that. When you have a twin, sharing becomes second nature. But sharing a woman with eight other men would be a few miles further than we've ever gone.

"I'm going to tell her you said that," Dawn laughs, tapping away on her phone. It beeps again and she splutters. "She wants to see a photo of you all, just to check you're good enough for me."

"Didn't you give her your reviews on Thomas, Joshua, Jared, and Mitchell already?" Cooper asks.

"I like to kiss," Dawn smiles, "But I'm not so big on the telling part."

"Kyla's going to be pissed at you if you don't," Logan says. "People in relationships always seem to want to live vicariously through single people with exciting lives."

"She's working in a bar with us," I say. "How exciting is it going to get?"

"Pretty damned exciting so far." Dawn stands, bringing her plate with her to fork the last fluffy pancake. "They're good," she says, "But my recipe has the edge."

"Really?" I say, surprised. I'm a chef by trade, so I'd expect mine to be better.

"A pinch of cinnamon in the mixture," she says with a wink.

"Interesting."

Mitchell's chair scrapes across the tiled floor, and he leans back, resting his hands behind his head. "You could one-up your friend Dawn. There are enough of us."

"Mitchell!" Lachlan exclaims, shocked by the suggestion. Maybe there are only eight of us who'd be up for the challenge. Dawn could at least equal her friend without needing Lachlan to cooperate.

"What?" Mitchell stands, making his way over to

79

Dawn and leaning in to kiss her lips in front of us all. When he comes up for air, Dawn's face is perfectly flushed. "She loves it, don't you baby?"

"I do," she says, grinning and making a point of looking around at all of us so we can be sure she's telling the truth.

"You only live once, right?" Mitchell says, his hand drifting over her tattoo.

"You took the words right off my back." Dawn winks.

"It would be awesome." He tugs her against his chest, and she giggles, struggling to hold her plate level.

"It would be," she says, as he releases her. "Maybe one of you should draw up a schedule."

Lachlan makes a choking sound, and my first instinct is to look across at Bryce. It's funny because it's his first instinct to look at me too.

Would we want to be on that schedule? Is she even serious?

Of course we would.

Not just for the sex, although I have a feeling that part would be mind-blowing. It sounds strange, but I'm used to working with these men. We're used to collaborating on the thing that makes us happiest in life, our business. And there's just something about Dawn, something fun and joyful and carefree that's wrapped around my heart and squeezed.

It's the thing that makes me want to envelop her in my arms and urge her to share all her secrets.

The thing that makes me want to tell her my story.

The thing that makes me want to add a dash of cinnamon to my pancake recipe tomorrow.

Maybe I'll get the chance if she's serious about all this flirty talk, and Lachlan doesn't put an embargo on more of us having fun.

11

COOPER

After the conversation at breakfast, Dawn returns to her bedroom, and the atmosphere between my friends and I crackle with an energy I've never felt before. And that's saying something. With nine men under one roof, and women coming and going over the years, there has been plenty of discussion and disagreements, but we've always found our way through. This time is different.

It's like we're all anticipating the start of something we don't even know is coming.

But first we need to know what happened between Dawn and Thomas. Before I get a chance to grill him, Mitchell steps up.

"Is that your new tactic?" Mitchell asks him, rubbing his beard thoughtfully. "You make them cry with your soulful voice and then seduce them when they're weak and upset."

"Chill out," Thomas says, punching him on the shoulder. "You make me sound like some kind of sexual predator. I was just trying to be a good guy."

"I know," Mitchell laughs. "I'm just playing with you."

"You think she's serious about that conversation?" Lachlan asks, his expression is measured but his tone makes him seem intrigued.

Jared shrugs his shoulders. "If you'd told me last week that a girl would come into our lives who'd want to fuck all of us, and we'd think it was a cool idea, I'd have laughed my fucking head off. But Dawn's special."

"She is special," Thomas says with a softness to his voice that makes me suddenly jealous. I want some of the special. Right now, it feels like four of us have been welcomed into this awesome place while the other five have been left standing out in the wilderness.

"What's so special?" I ask, curious.

"It's just the way she's so authentic," he says.

"Authentic? That's a big fucking word."

"I just mean she's true to herself, and as open as any girl I've ever met…and I don't mean physically…although I guess that's true, too. I mean mentally. She wants to connect. She wants to live in the moment and appreciate whatever that brings."

"Authentic." I nod, getting what he means. Finding people like that is hard. Relationships are complicated because people don't communicate what they really want or feel. For the first few months, most people put on an act and then gradually let the mask slip. By the time you realize that you're with someone who's different from what you originally thought, it's too late. You're connected, and that connection gives you something to lose. I've heard it called a soul-tie. Make too many soul-tie connections and it changes you as a person, apparently. I'm not sure if I believe it. I'm a live and let live, love and be loved kind of person, but part of me craves a longer and deeper connection than I've found so far.

Part of me wants to be seen for the man I truly am.

Part of me also wants to know that no woman will ever come between me and my friends.

It's been weighing on me for the last six months. It's the first time we've all been single, and it's come about because of the issues we've had with dating. When each of us tries to have a relationship, it ends up causing problems. Priorities seem to shift. People set their sights outside the business. More than once, I've worried that people from outside our tight group would bring Cloud 9 crashing down.

I don't want to lose my friends to an implosion like that. I worry especially that if anything happened to disrupt the status quo, Jared and Joshua would return to London. Lachlan to Scotland, and Bryce and Bradley to the US. Half of my brothers - I think of them that way - would be gone. I love Mitchell, Logan, and Thomas, but it wouldn't be the same without the rest. Logan's the only one with family ties to the local area. The rest of us would probably drift back to our hometowns and cities and then Cloud 9 would be just an amazing memory.

I'm not prepared to let that happen.

"Do you believe that story about her friend?" I ask.

Bryce shrugs, running his fingers through his slicked back hair. "Why would she lie about something like that?"

"I don't know. We don't really know her. People can have strange motivations."

Thomas shakes his head, pressing his lips together. "Dawn's not like that, man. You need to spend some time with her, and you'll see. She's as real as it gets."

I study my friend who is known for his soft heart and wonder if he's right or if he's just been duped. Do I trust his instincts?

Maybe he's right. Maybe I need to get Dawn on her own somehow so I can find out the truth. There is too much at stake to leave this situation tumbling like a boulder down the side of a hill.

"I'm going to handle the wholesale run today," I say, addressing Lachlan. "I'll take Dawn."

"Sounds like a plan," he says, nodding. When he holds my eye contact a little longer than usual, I know he's harboring some of the same reservations as me. At least this way, I can confirm if I'm right to be worried or not.

"Coming," Dawn calls through the door as I wait for her to open up. There's music playing loudly inside, and when she finally flings the door open, she's out of breath. "Hey, Cooper."

"Hey. What are you doing?" I peer into her room, wondering if I missed one of my friends sneaking in for round two. The room's empty.

"I was dancing," she says.

"Dancing?"

"Yeah. Don't you ever dance around your room?"

I look down at myself as if to say, do I look like a man who'd dance alone? I hope I don't. These cargo shorts have big pockets at the side, like combat trousers, and my simple black t-shirt is as masculine as it gets.

"No," I say simply, watching her eyes dance with laughter at my response.

"Well, maybe you should. You know, to lighten up."

"Oh, I'm light," I say, grabbing her hand and whirling her into my arms. I dance her into her room, showing her that I have moves that I reserve for when there's a beautiful woman around. "So light I'm practically drifting away. Want to come with me?"

"Where?" she asks, breathless, gazing up at me with wide eyes as though she's seeing me for the first time.

"The wholesaler."

Dawn blinks, surprised, and then bursts into laughter. "That was not what I was expecting you to say."

"Well, I may be light, but I'm also a working man." I stop dancing and allow Dawn to take one step back. Her cheeks are flushed, and her grass-green eyes sparkle with contained amusement.

"Mitchell didn't mention this riveting part of the job." She smoothes her hair like she's worried our dancing disturbed it, and my arm instinctively raises to help her with the task. Before I register how forward it is, I tuck a stray wave behind her pretty ear. For the first time, I notice the little diamond stars in each lobe and the pretty silver heart she has at her neck. Dainty jewelry for a girl who's bold and feisty. I drop my hand, suddenly self-conscious.

"Yeah, well. Mitchell would have said anything to get you to work here."

"Really?"

"Really. You didn't realize he was smitten after you doused him with beer?"

"It's not part of my usual mating ritual," she snorts. "So, what does a trip to the wholesaler involve?"

I shove my hands into my pockets and twist my mouth into a suppressed smile. "It involves sitting next to me in the ute and holding the list while I heft the boxes, and maybe I'll treat you to something small on the way back."

"Something small." She smirks, gazing down at my crotch. "You're selling yourself a little short, excuse the pun."

"I meant ice cream, but if you're looking for something else, I can assure you I have a big scoop."

She grins broadly, biting her bottom lip. "Let's see how things go, shall we?"

Dawn grabs her purse and hooks it across her body, and we make our way to where the Ute is parked, ready for my least favorite journey of the week. She jumps in like we've been riding together for years and grabs some chewing gum from the center pocket.

"So, how come you get the wholesaler job?"

I shrug and then pull the belt across my body. "We're on a rotating schedule. You're just lucky it's my turn."

"Very lucky. How far is the wholesaler?"

"Ten minutes. Just enough time for us to get better acquainted."

"Ten minutes. How about we play twenty questions?"

I turn the key, and the ute rumbles to life. "That's a question every thirty seconds!" I haven't played that game in years. The last time, I ended up having to answer questions that threw a wedge between me and the girl I liked. Truth can sometimes be the death of romance.

"Twenty questions, but I get to go first," she says.

"That's a little risky, isn't it?" I chance a quick look in Dawn's direction. She has her legs stretched out and her arm resting on the ledge of the window and has an expression that can only be described as pure glee. She's loving every minute of teasing me. I'm loving it too.

"Why?"

"Because you could use up all your questions and I might have more interesting ones to ask." I raise my eyebrows in challenge.

"Doubtful," she says. "Anyway, I don't believe in regrets."

I nod, agreeing with her way of thinking wholeheartedly. Living in the past doesn't help anyone.

"Okay. I guess you should go first, but maybe we should cut it down to ten questions or we'll run out of time for me to take a turn."

"Ooohh, ten questions. This just got harder."

"Yep. You have to make the most of each one."

"Okay…what things in your life bring you the greatest pleasure?"

Now that's a great question to start with. "Sex. Food. Sex. Running. Sex. Friends and family. Sex."

"Nice to see you have your priorities in order," Dawn laughs. "What are you most scared of?"

"That's easy. Not finding love that's peaceful." I turn and find Dawn staring at my profile. Our eyes meet and a flicker of something in her gaze sets my heart beating faster. "Or something bad happening to my family or friends. I'd rather it happened to me than to have to watch someone I love suffer."

She nods, and for the split second I can keep my eyes from the road, I'm sure her eyes well with tears before she blinks them away.

"Favorite sexual position?"

I laugh through my nose because this is the one, I was convinced she'd ask first. "My favorite sexual position is my face between a woman's legs." I wait for Dawn to question the truth of my statement, but she doesn't. She shouldn't. There isn't a thing that gives me the ultimate buzz more than tasting a woman between her thighs and feeling her pleasure burst across my tongue. Dawn shifts her legs, and I like the idea that she might be getting horny a little too much.

"Favorite ice cream?" she says.

"All ice cream."

"Favorite place?"

"Here," I say. "Byron Bay, Cloud 9, with my mates. The only thing that could make it better would be a woman who'd keep her legs open for me whenever I want to play."

"You want a woman just waiting around with her legs spread open?" A quick glance reveals that she has one eyebrow adorably quirked.

"Well, I mean, maybe not all day."

"That's good of you…to let the poor thing get up and stretch her legs."

"She can stretch her legs while she's lying down," I say seriously, fighting the urge to laugh.

"I'm only five questions in and I'm scared about where this might go next."

"Don't be scared," I say. "I'm a pussycat who loves pussy."

"Cooper!" she swats me on my upper arm with fake disgust.

"For someone who doesn't seem to have many sexual inhibitions, you're great at pretending to be outraged by my sex-talk."

"I'm not outraged," she says. "I'm intrigued."

"My work here is done." I say. "And you still have five questions."

"Favorite song?"

"That's a tough one," I say. "Who has just one?"

"Okay. A song that you like."

I shrug, trying to mentally sort through my record collection. "Borderline by Tame Impala. It's got a line 'caught between the tides of pain and rapture.' It's the perfect description of most relationships."

"Most relationships that don't involve peaceful love," she says.

"Exactly."

"I'll have to look that one up."

"You should. Is it my turn yet?"

"Nope. I still have four to go. If you could go

anywhere, where would it be?"

"Too X-rated for me to say right now."

"Oh please. You think you can shock me?"

"Between your sweet thighs, baby," I say in utter seriousness. There are many, many amazing places to see in the world. I've traveled and seen a fair few, but nowhere appeals as much as the woman sitting right next to me.

"Wow…now that is a shock, but not for the X-rated reason."

"For what reason?"

"Because it's a big wide world with over seven billion people in it. I can't believe that what I've got between my thighs exceeds everywhere else in the world."

"Right now it's a toss-up between the wholesaler and pulling you into my lap."

"Oh…I see. Forget the rest of the world. My pussy's only competition is the wholesaler."

We both burst out laughing right as I pull up at a red light. "In all seriousness," I say, turning to give Dawn my full attention. "I'd love to wake up to the crack of Dawn."

It takes a couple of seconds for her to register my joke before she splutters and buries her face in her hands. "Cooper, Cooper, Cooper." Her head shakes and I bite my lip at my own hilariousness.

"I'm scared to ask another one."

"How about I ask some, then?"

She twists in her seat to face me, letting her hand rest across her lap. "Okay, Mr. Loverman. You ask the questions. But I'm reserving my last questions until the end."

"How long are you staying in Australia?" It's the obvious first question.

"I don't know. Long enough to enjoy it. Not so long that I get bored."

I frown, signaling into the wholesaler carpark. "What's there to get bored with?"

She shrugs, drumming her fingers on the ledge by the window. "The world is big, Cooper. There's so much to see and so much to do."

"There's a lot to see and do here, too."

"There is. And I intend to make the most of it."

I pull the handbrake and shift in my seat until I'm staring right into Dawn's pretty moss-colored eyes. "What do you want to experience on your trip?"

"Everything that's in the Lonely Planet guide," she says. "And a few extra things."

"Are me and my Cloud 9 mates the extra things?"

"Possibly," she says. "I wouldn't take anything for granted."

"And what do you think seeing and doing all these things is going to do for you?"

Dawn frowns, and her leg begins to bounce. "Expand my mind. Teach me more about the world and the people in it."

"And more about yourself?"

"Is that one of your questions?"

"That depends on if you answer it."

As I expected, Dawn's hand reaches for the handle. "Do we ever really know what we need to discover about ourselves?" she asks, before throwing open the door and sliding off the seat into the warm sun.

Do we? It's a great question. Even though we know things about ourselves, they can be easy to ignore if they're hard to deal with.

"You're either desperate to see the inside of the wholesaler or desperate to get away from my questions."

"It could be a mix of both," she says, bouncing lightly

on her feet.

I lead the way, searching for another question that will help me better understand this girl, pushing the door open into the welcoming cool store.

Dawn pauses at the entrance, looking around with wide eyes. "So this is the wholesaler?" The awe in her voice is forced, but I pretend she's genuinely excited.

"Yes it is." I spread my arms like a game show host, ready to show a new contestant how to play. "You can push the trolley." I grab one from next to us and Dawn takes the handle.

"You know, I never realized how different our language is until I came here. We call this a cart."

"Yeah. You're weird."

"Me personally, or all Americans?"

"That remains to be seen." I pull the list from my back pocket and stride around the store, pulling things from the shelves as quickly as possible.

"You can ask me more questions," Dawn says.

"Favorite sexual position?" I say loudly, drawing the attention of two middle-aged dudes in drooping jeans.

"All of them," Dawn says. "Next."

"Favorite book?"

"The Scorpio Races. You wouldn't know it."

"What's so good about it?" I ask, intrigued that she'd be able to answer the question so quickly. It would probably take me hours to come up with an equivalent answer.

"I don't think it would be your kind of book," she says. "It's young adult paranormal fiction. It's about orphaned kids on an island where they race dangerous water horses. The main characters are so strong and determined and the way they fall in love is just so tender. They see each other...like really see each other for the good and the bad,

91

the flaws and the perfections."

"I'm not sure about the water horses, but the rest sounds good."

I place a box of napkins in the trolley, and we head over to the rack of plastic cups.

For thirty minutes, we gather everything on Lachlan's list until the trolley becomes too heavy for Dawn to push and I've exhausted all but one of my questions.

"Last one," Dawn says, holding up her index finger to illustrate the point.

"Were you serious about what you said at breakfast? About the schedule?"

Dawn grins at me over the huge pile of boxes, her hair tumbling over her shoulders in waves that just ache for my touch. And as I wait for her to answer, I realize that she could have answered anything to my other questions, and I wouldn't have cared. This is the only one that I'm desperate for her to answer yes to. The one that's set my heart into an uncomfortable thudding rhythm.

"Of course," she says in the end. "Who would joke about something like that? Sex is everything. As important as eating and drinking."

I don't know what to call the feeling I get at her answer. Relief. Excitement. Desperation to get Dawn back to her room and taste her pleasure.

All of the above.

I'm momentarily lost for words because I've never been faced with a situation where a girl is effectively offering to share herself with me without the usual conversations about where our relationship is going and what it means to me.

I've never been faced with a girl I've wanted more.

So, I just smile and nod my head, folding my lips in so my grin isn't too overwhelming.

"I think you might be blushing, Cooper."

I think she might be right. "I'm going to make sure I'm next on that schedule," I say, running my fingers through my hair just so that I have something to do with my hands.

"I was hoping you were going to say that," she says.

So, in the middle of the day, I load boxes onto the counter with a hardon straining at my shorts.

Back at Cloud 9, I tell Dawn she's off the hook until her shift starts later. She walks away from the ute with a sway to her hips and looks over her shoulder with a smile, confident that she'll find me checking out her ass. It is a very nice ass.

I use the horn to grab the attention of Bryce and Bradley, who help me unload the boxes until the ute is empty and our storeroom is full.

As usual, I head to the office with the receipt for Lachlan's files. He's a stickler for proper accounting practices, which is a good thing. Without him insisting on professionalism, the rest of us would be doing the fun stuff and panicking at the end of the year.

I find Lachlan and Thomas deep in conversation about Dawn.

"This thing with Dawn is a big risk," Lachlan says.

"She's not like that," Thomas rubs the back of his neck, and leans back in an office chair that looks like it might break from the weight of his big body.

"She's not like that," I agree, drawing both their attention. "And she was serious about the schedule."

Lachlan throws up his hands, exasperated. "You see what I mean? Who the hell is serious about a schedule? It's not even something I can get my head around."

"Free love isn't a new concept," I tell him. "It started in

the sixties."

"Pretty sure the Romans were into it," Thomas says.

"Isn't it what got Sodom and Gomora obliterated?" Lachlan says, shaking his head.

"Dawn isn't like other girls," I say. "She's the real thing."

"Real. Exactly." Thomas meets my eyes and nods. "Your trip to the wholesaler was enlightening, then?"

"It was."

"Good for you," Thomas says. "And good for Dawn. I keep telling Lachlan that all Dawn wants is to get the most out of life."

"Isn't that what we all want?" Lachlan says.

"But some of us want it, and some of us live it. That's the difference." I hand him the receipt and he takes it, scanning over the details.

"And you intend to live it?" he asks me, narrowing his serious eyes that are darker than usual.

"I do. Now all you have to decide is if you want to live it too."

12

DAWN

After making myself a bite to eat for lunch - smashed avocado on toast with tomato salad - I have five hours before the start of my evening shift.

My conversations with Cooper have left me with a funny, bubbly feeling in my chest. I could pretend to myself that it's excitement. He's sexy and fun and there were enough sparks between us to rival fourth of July fireworks. To be honest, I half expected him to have knocked on my door by now. We weren't exactly covert with our flirting. He must still be busy with the purchases from the wholesaler. Either that or he's decided against being the next on the schedule. That would be a shame. I get the feeling we'd be dynamite together.

One of the things I've wanted to do since arriving in Byron Bay is take a walk up to the pretty white lighthouse, and maybe spot some whales or dolphins on the way. It's also Australia's easternmost point, so another reason to tick it off my list of places to go.

I put on my comfortable sneakers and toss a bottle of water into my bag. With my sunglasses on, I stride out into the sunshine, checking my surroundings before I pull my door to my room. I'm disappointed to find there's no one around to invite on my expedition. In a way, I guess it's a good thing. I need some time out in the fresh air to clear my head. All the sexy men around here are distracting, to say the least.

The walk to Cape Byron is beautiful. Craggy cliffs meet turquoise blue ocean topped with white ruffles that hint at the ferocious current beneath. The paths are well laid out, some with wooden slatted floors and wooden handrails, which help with the climb. I'm desperate to spot a whale or a dolphin, so I focus hard on the water whenever it's in view.

The lighthouse is over a hundred years old and painted so white, the reflection of the sun hurts my eyes. It's possible to go inside, but I'm not into maritime history and the view is just too good to miss. I lean against the railing, straining for a fin or a nose, any kind of disruption in the water. The sun beats down against my skin, warming my hair and making my sunglasses slide down my perspiring nose.

I stretch out my arms, not caring that the other tourists around might be wondering why I'm reenacting the iconic scene from titanic. The light wind gusts under my arms and I close my eyes, relishing the tranquility that comes with breathing deep and forgetting everything that's bad in the world.

You only live once, and this is living for me. Coming to a place where I can touch the sky, knowing that I'm as far east as it's possible to go on this giant landmass. I'm dwarfed by the scale of the landscape but at the same time a giant in the world, capable of achieving whatever it is I want to achieve.

Only one thing is tethering me.

One weight rests on my shoulders.

But here, with the scent of salt and sunshine in my nostrils, I can just about shrug it off. That's what traveling does for me. It unties me from the binds of home and the reality that comes with being a person who has to live up to expectations. A person who has responsibilities to other people.

Here, the only person I'm responsible for or to is myself.

And maybe the men of Cloud 9, but I get the feeling they'd forgive me a lot.

It's less than a week until the anniversary of Mom's death passes again. I wish I could forget…actually forget is the wrong word. I wish I could remember her without the dark blanket of her death resting over everything. I wish I could just remember the happy times. That's the saddest part of it. She was such a joyful person, and she'd hate what her passing has done to me and Dad.

She'd hate most of all the pressure he's putting me under and the wedge it's driven between us.

The anniversary of her death this year comes with the weight of a promise I made last year. It's a promise I don't want to keep.

You can't run forever.

Those were the last four words my dad said to me as I packed my bag for this trip. But he's wrong. I've got unending energy and determination to run for as long as it takes. As long as I have.

He'll be angry with me, but it's a bitter pill I'll have to swallow.

Behind me, a family is taking pictures in front of the lighthouse and then towards the horizon.

Their happiness claws at my skin, making everything feel worse. We were like that once. A family who could just have fun and enjoy each other's company. Those memories are the most painful for me to recall.

I start back the way I came, needing the breeze against my skin and the silence of the air around me. I come to the point where I overlook Wategos beach, and spot Jared and Joshua catching the afternoon surf, skimming across the water like pond skaters but with a whole lot more finesse.

The heat of the sun has made my skin hot and my mouth dry. Searching for my bottle, I gulp half of the cool water and wipe my lips with the back of my hand, wishing I could swipe away my troubles as easily.

The beach is long, with perfect cream-colored sand that shifts beneath my sneakers as I approach the water, far enough away that I hope Jared and Joshua won't spot me. At least not immediately. I drop my bag to the sand, slide off my sneakers and socks, relishing the fine grains against the soles of my feet.

I have a bikini top beneath my white tank, but not the bottoms. Still, the water looks too good to miss. I strip off my tank, tossing it on top of my bag and stroll slowly down to the shoreline, letting the water seep between my toes and then over my ankles, up my calves, higher and higher until my denim shorts are submerged. The shock of the cold against my navel takes my breath away, but I don't stop. Instead, I keep the slow striding pace until the water is up to my throat, and even then I don't stop. Taking hold of my nose, I walk deeper, fighting against the tug of the current against my legs and closing my eyes to the spray of the surf. The water churns around me, as rough as the tumble of clothes in a washer.

I hold my breath, relishing the burn of my lungs as I fight the urge to gasp against the cold.

Beneath the water, all the stresses of the world above fade away. It's just me and the ocean. Me and the cold. Me and the push and pull of the tide above.

It's just me and my thoughts. Me and my determination.

Until it's not.

A strong arm hooks around my chest, tugging my feet from the swirling sand and yanking me upward until my face is above water and the wind blasts cold against my skin.

"Dawn," a male voice yells above the waves. A hard chest anchors me. "Dawn."

It's Cooper. Even above the rush of the waves and in my disorientated state, I recognize his voice.

The saltwater stings my eyes, but I force my lids open to look at him, conscious that I might have scared him. "I was enjoying that," I say.

"Are we so bad we've driven you under water?" he asks. His mouth smiles, but I can see the seriousness in his eyes. It's from the worry that he may have just stumbled across something concerning. I know what I was doing might look scary to him, but that's not how it was.

"Yeah. Such bad bosses. Such hard taskmasters."

"I'll get the rest of my asshole friends in line. All you have to do is say the word."

Sweet Cooper.

His questions at the wholesaler are still fresh, the way he was probing to understand the meaning behind the way I live my life. Guys never believe that girls can live differently without it being a sign that she's fucked in the head. With me, it's the opposite. I just see the world clearer than anyone else. The fragility of life, the looming end of it, and I'm not afraid to see everything as an opportunity.

"What word?" I ask.

He wipes errant strands of hair from my salty forehead and presses a kiss in their place. "Any word," he says. "Just say any word and I'm yours."

I beam up at him, clinging to his shoulder as the waves froth all around us. With the other hand I pretend to pull a zipper across my lips, sealing in all my words, and he snorts with laughter.

Any word.

It feels like a challenge, finding exactly the right word to say to make him mine.

Then I know which one to pick. It's never let me down.

"YOLO," I say with a grin.

"Isn't that four words?" he asks earnestly.

"Not for me," I say, pulling against his shoulder so I slide up his body enough that our faces are level. "Not for me."

When I kiss him, I think he understands. At least, I hope he does.

13

LACHLAN

I like my vantage point. Working the bar means I can keep my eye on everything that's happening at Cloud 9. My friends tease me that I'm a control freak, and maybe I am. There are some people in life who are meant to be in charge. People who enjoy the responsibility.

All I know is that I like order and predictability. It keeps the demons at bay.

When Dawn approaches the bar with a long order of drinks, she hands the list over, but doesn't wait for me to prepare it. Instead, she heads over to a recently vacated table and begins to clear it of glasses and bottles.

I was dubious when Mitchell wanted to hire her to work here. Anyone who believes in YOLO enough to have it tattooed on their ass isn't going to be reliable. That tattoo says flaky. It speaks of a person who's ready to drop everything at a moment's notice. That isn't the kind of person we need in our business. It isn't the kind of person we need in our love lives, either.

Except, Dawn has actually been an excellent addition to our team. She's great with people. The customers love her. The tips have doubled since she joined. She picks up everything fast and doesn't try to change things because she feels like it. All my ways of working have been taken on board. Watching her work to my rules does something to me that I can't really explain.

The sway of her hips. The bounce of her hair. The brightness of her smile.

She's the opposite of what I thought I'd want, so much so that the feelings I have for her have unsettled me.

I'm not a masochist, so being attracted to someone who I know has the potential to drive me crazy isn't in my nature.

But attracted to her, I am.

"Dawn, come here a wee minute," I say, when the order's almost ready.

She strides over, balancing a tray which dwarfs her in scale.

"Is there something wrong?"

I take the tray and place it behind the bar, then pick up her handwritten order sheet and pass it back to her. "What does that say?"

"Gin and juice." She glances up at me, and I nod once. "Are you struggling to read my writing? I'll try to make it clearer."

"It's okay," I say. "It might take some time for me to get used to it."

Dawn shifts on her feet, glancing down the bar as though she's not quite comfortable in my presence. The thought that she'd be seeking out one of the others annoys me. Well, it disappoints me. I'm perfectly aware that I'm not the easiest man to get along with. Aware, but not able to do much to alter myself. I am what I am.

I may not have the sunny personality of Cooper or Mitchell or the caring nature of Logan, but I am a good man. A loyal man. A man who wants to give a woman everything she needs to be happy. Most of all, I'm a man who could keep Dawn safe.

The desire to protect her is overwhelming, not because she's incapable of looking after herself. I don't think I've ever met a more confident woman in my life. There's just something in me that senses vulnerability. She may be trying to hide it, but I have a sixth sense for it.

"Here," I say, pushing the tray of drinks to the edge of the counter. "That's everything."

"Okay, thanks," she says, balancing it in her hands without any issues, despite the weight.

As she makes her way across the bar, one of our regulars orders two bottles of beer. And then while I'm flipping the tops off, a man in a suit, who is sitting at the side of the bar, beckons me over.

"I'll be with you in a minute," I say, already feeling annoyed at the way he's acting. Just the haughty way he's holding his head, nose slightly elevated, is enough to raise my hackles. He must be close to fifty-five and we don't usually get customers that old. Thomas plays easygoing music, but it's late in the evening and Cooper's thumping beats are enough to put off the older clientele from stepping over the threshold. I take payment for the beers, then slowly make my way to him.

The man, balding with dark hair at the sides, ruddy-cheeked and one of those bulbous noses that speaks of too many boozy lunches, slides a card over the bar in my direction. His stubby finger remains on it, though. "I'm going to buy your bar," he says, then lifts his hand from the card and stands.

"Excuse me?"

"I'm going to buy your bar. Take a day to think of a

reasonable figure and call me on the number on that card."

I draw my head back, frowning at the sheer audacity of this idiot. I press a finger to the card and slide it back to him. "I won't be doing that, so don't hold your breath."

"We can do this the easy or the hard way," he says with a strange smile that doesn't meet his eyes. "I'd prefer it, and you'll prefer it, if we go for easy."

The rage that bubbles inside me needs an outlet. "Who the fuck do you think you're talking to?"

He narrows his eyes, adjusting his shirtsleeves in his suit jacket, another slow insincere smile spreading across his sneering face. "Be careful, Lachlan."

The shock of hearing my name dropped so easily from his mouth must show. He's a stranger, but he knows who I am. Who the fuck is he?

His smile grows. "You think I don't research who I'm intending to do business with? Now that would just be sloppy, wouldn't it?"

"I think you should leave." I cross my arms over my chest, knowing that it makes my biceps bulge, and my shoulders seem impossibly wide. This asshole needs to get a sense of who he's dealing with.

"Oh, I'm going. But tomorrow, you will call me with that figure. And because of your bad attitude, knock ten percent off whatever you were thinking of proposing. For every additional day, knock off another ten percent."

"Just get out of here," I shout, drawing the attention of Dawn, Jared, and Thomas. My friends start to make their way across the bar, sensing that something is amiss.

"This place is a dump," the man says. "But it's a dump on land that I want."

"You can want it all you like, but you're not getting it," I say with a firmness that sounds like a growl.

"Oh, I will. Everyone sells in the end, one way or

another." He laughs, then. An ominous laugh like some deranged villain from a Bond movie and then takes a step back before turning on his overpriced black leather shoes and walking out.

Out of nowhere, a bubble of rage wells inside me, frustration, a volcano of sheer fury that an asshole like that would try to make me feel so small.

I take three steps back, needing space, needing air, needing to punch something until my knuckles scream and the rage inside me pours out of my fist.

My vision is red, my heart thundering in my ears, and I growl, unleashing a punch to the wall that I don't feel for a few seconds. Then all there is is blistering pain.

"Lachlan," Dawn says, her voice muffled by the rush of blood through my body. "Lachlan. Fuck."

"Lachlan," Thomas shouts, leaping over the bar, his concern twisting his features. When his hand grips my shoulder, I cup my damaged fist in my other palm, and hang my head.

This is not the man I want to be. This is not the man I want Dawn to see.

This is what my father left inside me after years of witnessing his inability to control his temper. I want the ground to swallow me whole.

"His hand," Dawn says, shocked.

My palm is slick with warm blood.

"The first aid kit is there," Thomas says, steering me to the office so customers don't get to watch the rest of this mortifying show. Dawn hurries to grab the pack and follows behind us. I rest on the edge of the desk and stare at my hand, unable to meet Dawn's gaze.

"I'll do it," Thomas says, but Dawn must disagree because it's her small, gentle hands that raise mine to assess the damage. Skin split over bruised bone. It's a mess of my own making.

"I'll do it." I pull my hand back, but Dawn doesn't let go.

She takes antiseptic spray and covers the whole area, using a soft medical wipe to clean the wound. A large pad covers the ruined mess of frayed skin, which she tapes neatly into place. Thomas watches it all, not saying a word. Dawn doesn't comment either. Her silent efforts and gentle touch calm the rage inside me.

"That's it," she says. "I can't tell you it's better, but at least it's clean."

The shame that she witnessed my outburst feels hot on my cheeks, but she doesn't tell me I shouldn't have done it. She doesn't tell me I'm an idiot or that getting so angry is wrong. She doesn't judge me one bit.

Instead, she wraps her arms around me, awkwardly at first, until I widen my legs for her to step closer. She strokes my back and the place on my neck where my hair is short and soft as velvet. She soothes me until my heart rate has settled and my embarrassment has waned.

And inexplicably, I feel better than I have in years.

14

DAWN

Lachlan reminds me of me. That flash of anger that wells up inside like a storm you don't know how to tame. The burst of rage that ricochets outwards until you're hurt, or worse, you've hurt someone else.

It's always there, and maybe I'm better at controlling it than Lachlan seems to be. Maybe I've had more practice at suppressing it. Or maybe I've found better outlets than splitting my knuckles against the wall.

I think of all the times I've swept everything from my bed or thrown a pillow across the room, needing to lash out. I've never hurt myself because of it, but I could have. The lack of control is there and the potential for the unknown a total blur in the red mist that follows.

In my arms, Lachlan is rigid as a board, his expression shame filled and mortified. But under my soothing hands, he relaxes.

Over his shoulder, I meet the eyes of Thomas, who's watching us with a clenched jaw. Concern for his friend rolls from him in waves, but there's more too. I get the feeling he's not used to seeing Lachlan soften for anyone. He's a man with an iron pole for a spine, and a seriousness that imbues everything he does.

But here, in the quiet of this space, Lachlan's posture is different. It's as though he's been peeled from his hard outer casing and allowed a softer middle to show, just for a minute.

Then someone clears their throat and I look up to find Mitchell in the doorway.

"What the fuck happened?" he asks. Lachlan stiffens and is on his feet in a flash, holding his injured hand just slightly behind his back, shielding his moment of weakness.

"That asshole says he's going to buy Cloud 9. Not that he wants to buy it, but that he will buy it and we will sell it."

"What?" Mitchell asks, confused.

"The insinuation is that he's important and powerful enough that we won't have a choice other than to give up our business. I told him where to go, but I don't get the feeling he's going away."

"Who is he?" Mitchell asks. Thomas hands him a card, the one from the bar.

"Jeffrey Barrow?" Mitchell seems unsure, but Thomas shakes his head.

"Jeffrey Barrow is a bigshot property developer. He's always on the news, shaking hands with politicians, signing deals to build monstrosities. Apparently, he has the planning departments in his back pockets. He's a big political donor. Things that shouldn't get approved always seem to go his way."

"Sounds like a prize asshole," I say.

"Sounds like someone we don't want to get involved with," Mitchell says.

"Sounds like someone it's best not to piss off, too." Thomas levels his gaze with Lachlan, who shakes his head.

"You think that keeping quiet is going to help us? Men like that smell weakness and devour anything in their path. Our only hope is that he backs down because there are enough of us to let him know we're a force to be reckoned with."

"Lachlan's right," I say before thinking about whether it's my place to get involved. This is their business after all, and I'm just an employee, not a partner. With all eyes now on me, I decide to continue. "Men like that smell weakness from across the city. They live for exerting power and watching people buckle. I know it's not great to be in conflict with someone who seems so powerful, but men like that don't expect people to stand up to them. If he wants this place, your only option is going to be to take him head on."

Lachlan nods. "Dawn's right. We need to get back out there now. It's busy and we can't take our eyes off the business. But tomorrow morning, we need to meet to discuss our strategy. This isn't going to go away. We have to be prepared."

Thomas and Mitchell nod, and Lachlan strides out of the office. In the doorway, he turns to Thomas. "I'm not going to be of much use with my hand like this. Can you take over behind the bar?

"Sure."

And just like that, everyone goes back to work.

The show must go on.

The whole evening, I'm watchful. I do my job to the best of my abilities, but my eyes don't rest in one place for long. Half of me expects Jeffrey to come back and make more trouble. The other half keeps a concerned eye on Lachlan.

As we're closing up, I find him in the office, resting his forehead in his hand, propped against his elbow on the desk.

"Everything okay?" I ask.

He straightens and nods once. "Aye. I am."

"Do you feel like taking a walk?"

His dark eyes drift to the doorway, considering. "Alright."

"We can go down to the beach, if you like? My feet are hot. They could do with some cool water."

Lachlan nods, almost solemnly, and I let him lead the way because he's that kind of man, but as we hit the sidewalk, he steers me gently with a hand at my back until he's walking nearest the road, even though there's hardly any traffic at this time.

"Thank you, for earlier," he says, glancing from beneath lowered lashes. "I'm sorry you had to see that."

"It's okay," I say, quickly.

"No, it isn't." Lachlan's tone is firm, but he's momentarily distracted by a need to look both ways as we cross the road. "It's never okay to lose it like that. I hate that about myself."

"You didn't hurt anyone," I say. "Only your poor hand."

"Witnessing violence is damaging." His uninjured hand goes to the back of his neck and massages it.

"It is," I say. "But I'm a grown woman and I can tell the difference between a violent bad man, and a man who's frustrated."

"I can't control it," he says, shaking his head. "It's like a flash flood. It just hits me."

"I feel that way too, sometimes."

He glances at me, brow lowered. "You smash walls with your fists?"

"Maybe not smash walls," I say, holding my hands out. "These wouldn't be effective. Too small. I just mean that sometimes, I can't control my temper. I really try, but there have been times when I've said hurtful things and regretted it so badly after. There have been times where I've lashed out and damaged my possessions."

"If I could get rid of my temper, I would."

"That's what makes you a good man, Lachlan."

I don't ask him the questions that bubble against my tongue. Did he see violence as a child? Was he physically abused? Our relationship isn't like that, at least not yet. But I see that in him. A kid who's witnessed too much and who holds life tightly within strict boundaries so that he never feels out of control. A kid who hates that he has a similar instinct to someone who hurt him.

When we get to the beach, I sit on the sand to untie my shoes and slide off my socks. This late, the warmth of the sun has seeped out of the sand, leaving cool dampness in its wake.

Lachlan folds his big body the same way, removing his sneakers and stretching out his long, muscular legs, leaning back on his elbows and gazing at the dark, swirling ocean.

I push up, jogging down to the shoreline, hissing as the chill of the water bites against my skin. I walk in until my calves are submerged and tip my face up to the star-filled sky.

It's hard to feel important when you look around at the world and realize that you're just like a fleck of sand or a spark of light within the infinite universe. It's at moments like this, I chastise myself for dwelling too much on my own problems.

I should help other people. Reach out to the community and play a role in shaping it.

All of that would make me a better person.

I know this, but it's hard.

I glance back to the beach, finding Lachlan watching me. Even in the vast emptiness of this place by night, he's still an imposing figure.

Maybe I am helping people, I think, trying to rationalize my existence. I think of Kyla who's living happily with men I guided her toward. I think of the woman I met at the bar and how a little bit of compassion lifted her spirits. I think of the men at Cloud 9 who are all happier for having spent time in my company.

What would Lachlan be doing right now if it wasn't for me? Blaming himself. Hating himself. Dwelling in a place of fury and frustration.

And now, what is he doing? At least, if he's focused on me, he's not getting lost in self-reflection.

I stretch up to the sky and spin, letting my hair fly in a halo around me, half expecting Lachlan to join me, but he doesn't.

Eventually, I pad back up the sand, and drop down next to him.

"You looked like a wee fairy, out there." There's a gravelly edge to his voice that stirs something inside me. Well, it's that and his soft Scottish accent that licks over my pussy like a hot tongue.

"More like a naughty sprite," I say, grinning at him with my best sassy expression.

"Why are you here?" he asks me. "Why have you come to my bar and bewitched half of my friends? What's your game?"

I turn until I'm facing him, cross-legged, letting sand fall between the fingers of my right hand.

"Why are you here?" I ask, "Sitting on a beach with me in Australia with a busted hand and bare feet."

He snorts, raising his bandaged hand to survey the injury. "That's a good point."

"We're all on a journey, Lachlan. Ours has just brought us here, in this moment, in this place."

"What for?" He frowns as he says it, making his question less flippant and more searching.

"Who knows?" I pick up more sand and start to let it fall, but Lachlan twists quickly and grabs my hand, balling my fingers around the cool grains.

"I think you really are a fairy, sent to tie us all in knots."

"Or maybe to untie the ones already there."

The words settle inside him, and he blinks long and slow. When he opens his eyes again, I'm speared by the heat in them. He brings my hand, still clutched in his huge, rough palm, to his lips and presses a soft kiss there. I inhale quickly as he leans forward, kissing the corner of my mouth so gently it's like a whisper. Then, in a flash, a spark is ignited, and our arms are wrapped tightly around each other, our tongues sliding hungrily, everything clawing and desperate and raw.

Oh god, it's so good. So perfectly passionate that I can barely breathe. I want to murmur his name, but I can't with him exploring every inch of my mouth. I move to straddle him bringing my pussy in line with his cock, needing the pressure of his arousal to fuel my own, but he doesn't like it that way and flips us both until my back is pressed into the sand and Lachlan looms over me. He takes my hands and holds them high over my head, pinned by all his strength.

"I see why they want you," he says, kissing my jawline, letting his words buzz over my skin like the sweetest sensation. "You're intoxicating."

"Like a drug?" I ask, not sure I like the analogy.

"Like slipping into a warm bath."

Now that's better.

"Want to feel what it's like to slip inside me?" I ask.

"More than I want to live," he says, nudging his big, hard cock where I'm aching for him.

"I have protection," I say, tapping the ground to my right where my purse is resting. The moment I find it, I'm scrambling for the condom.

"Here?" he asks, and I snort with laughter at the shock in his eyes.

"Here," I say. "You want to walk back to Cloud 9 nursing that boner?"

He pushes up on his arms and stares at his crotch. His dick looks like it's about to burst through his shorts. "You have a point."

"Glove up," I say, tossing him the foil packet.

He looks side to side, checking we're alone. There's not another soul on this beach, but for how long, I don't know. I guess, the good thing is that anyone who disturbs us will be here for the same thing.

Lachlan undoes the button and zipper on his shorts, pushing the waistband of his underwear down until his cock is in his fist. And what a cock it is.

His hands are huge, but they don't cover even half. Shit.

I squirm, pulling up the hem of my skirt, pushing my panties to one side. Lachlan seems like he doesn't know where to look. His hand fumbles with the ring of the rubber as his attention is dragged to the apex of my thighs. "Fuck," he mutters, working to roll the latex over the top part of his straining cock.

I lick my finger and slick it over my clit, stroking myself while he watches, getting wetter as he works to get himself ready. Without any preamble, he puts two fingers against my entrance and curls them inside me, making me grunt. Oh god, it feels good. He pushes again, once, twice, three times, watching my reactions, adjusting the position of the tips of his fingers inside me. He's working out my anatomy, I think with a start. Checking to make sure he's going to hit the spot. His diligence is something I appreciate massively.

"You're ready," he says, easing his fingers from inside me and licking them lasciviously. The sigh that breaks from his lips is husky and hungry. "Next time, I want time and privacy," he says. "And a little less sand."

Next time.

I'm laughing as he climbs over me, braced on impossibly strong arms, staring at me with eyes that express equal parts amusement and fascination.

But I stop when he notches that big, urgent cock at my entrance and puts all his weight behind it. My pussy stretches around the intrusion, but even though I'm slick, it still burns just a little. Pleasure and pain are close sisters. He feeds himself into me and I take it all until I can't take anymore. Oh fuck. He's so huge.

One big arm scoops my right leg high over his shoulder, and he pulls out a little, like he's using his cock to search for that same spot that made my eyes roll. When he finds it, the little squeaking sound I make amuses him. "You like it right there?" he asks.

"Fuck, yeah," I say. "Just there..."

I arch my back, reaching to shove down my top so I can touch my breast. Lachlan moves slowly at first, rubbing and rubbing the head of his massive cock over that little bundle of nerves that has the power to render the rest of my body immobile. My fingers tease my tight nipple but are replaced quickly by Lachlan's hot mouth and harsh teeth. I groan like a woman possessed, feeling my pleasure building and fearing how big it feels.

"You like this big cock, don't you?" he says, resting his hand around my throat as he sucks my earlobe between his lips.

"Yes," I gasp, shifting my hips.

"Touch yourself," he says. "I want you to come on this cock. Then we'll see who's untying who."

My clit is swollen and sensitive, but I rest my finger above it and the action of his hips is enough to stimulate it perfectly.

Lachlan kisses me deep, his tongue matching the rhythm of his cock and I'm lost in everything this big strong, sensitive, wounded man has to give.

"Mmmm..." I moan, and he speeds his hips into fast shallow thrusts that hit me inside just right. When I come, my pussy squeezing in rhythmic waves and my head thrown back into the cool sand, Lachlan really lets go.

The power behind his movements causes my ass to dig a hole in the sand. I hold him around his broad back, understanding how much it takes him to hold himself to the restrained, controlled person he is in everyday life.

Lachlan is untamed and passionate. He's intense and overwhelming. But behind it all, he's watchful. Because Lachlan's big enough to really hurt me. His cock is so long that if he really pounded into me, it would wreck my insides. He holds back just enough that everything about this interaction is good for me. I just hope it is for him, too.

"Give it to me," I whisper, sensing his restraint. "Give me everything you've got. Fill me up, Lachlan. I want it."

The huge man above me groans like he's in pain and then his body seizes, hips stilling while he arches his spine into an earth-shattering orgasm. I hold him tightly, stroking his back and neck the way I did in the office, feeling his whole body melting beneath my touch.

He doesn't collapse over me, still conscious of his size in relation to mine, even when he's mindless with sensation. Instead, he rolls us so I'm half sprawled over him, sandy and salty and spent.

He stares up at the sky for the longest time and I let the

silence rest between us like a blanket shaken high and released to settle over a freshly made bed.

Eventually, he kisses the top of my head hard and squeezes me into his embrace. I breathe in his masculine scent, wanting to commit as much of this to memory as possible. Because who knows how long the universe will keep us together?

He makes a sound in his throat, and I tip my head to look at him.

"Definitely a fairy," he says. "A wicked fairy who can untie even the tightest, most complicated of knots." And I'm not sure why, but his words make me want to cry.

15

DAWN

Tonight the bar is running a special BBQ night, and my brother and I are grilling as though our lives depend on it. We're always the ones to cook up a storm, but today is something different. Cloud 9 has developed an enviable reputation for food based on excellent quality meat, homemade marinades and a grill that leaves everything smoky and delicious. We've tried our hardest to bring the best of Texan flavors to the Australian market and it's worked. Our latest bestseller is our corn ribs with sriracha mayo and lime. They sell like hotcakes and were even featured in the local newspaper.

Cooper is on the decks playing laid-back music and customers are everywhere, sprawled out on bean bags, hanging in single and double hammocks, and by the bar, swaying to the beat, drinks in hand.

As sweat trickles down the side of my face, I watch Dawn dashing across to serve up overflowing plates to waiting diners. It's been crazy, and she's been rushed off her feet, but after the next five orders are fulfilled, it looks like there might be a bit of breathing space for us all.

I mop my brow on a cloth that I keep tucked in my back pocket, and wash my hands, ready to plate the orders of smoky ribs, creamy coleslaw and potato salad.

"Please tell me we're almost done," Bradley says, his red face mirroring mine. "I need to take a leak, and I've been holding it for the past thirty minutes."

"Go now," I say. "I'll sort this out."

Bradley unties his black apron and tosses it onto the counter, then disappears to the restrooms. Dawn appears, tendrils of damp hair clinging to her forehead and more color on her cheeks than I've ever seen.

"Last ones," I say as she swipes at her hair with the back of her hand.

"I'm so happy," she says. "These plates are so heavy and it's hotter than a sauna in the Mojave tonight."

"It's a humdinger," I say, and she laughs.

"I love that word. You don't hear it much."

"*You* don't hear it much," I say. My momma uses it daily."

"Bless your momma's heart," she says, mimicking the Texan drawl that I know and love. Her small hands grab the edges of the plates I've pushed to her, and she hefts them up.

"When you've delivered those, get your sweet butt back here and I'll fix you a burger."

She sways away and glances back at me over her shoulder. "Sweet butt, huh?"

I drag my eyes up from the Georgia peach we're discussing and raise a brow. "Just calling like it is, darlin'."

To speed things along, I give Bradley the last three plates when he returns from the bathroom, and he makes his way to table seventeen. I grab a couple of beers from the mini fridge beneath the counter, and quickly fix two burgers, setting them onto plates ready for when Dawn returns. Her eyes take in the sight with wide appreciation, and I wonder if that's the way she'd look at my cock. Damn, I'd love for her to look at my cock with that much hunger.

"Come on. Let's blow this joint."

"You sure?" she asks, glancing quickly over her shoulder.

"Lachlan, we're taking a few," I yell. Lachlan nods and I can already see him telling Jared to clear the tables that would have been Dawn's responsibility.

I find a quiet spot and place the burgers on the table, watching as Dawn takes a seat on the chair next to mine rather than across the table. Interesting.

"These look so good," she says, reaching for the juicy meat wrapped in a soft bun, and dripping with cheese and my signature spicy burger sauce. When she takes a bite, the moan she makes sends a shiver of sensation over parts that moans about food usually don't reach.

She lowers the burger, rolling her eyes and then takes her bottle of beer and washes it down with a long drink.

"You don't know how much I needed that."

"I think I do," I say.

"You know, you never told me how you ended up here. It's far from home."

I nod, dabbing my own lips with a napkin and swallowing a mouthful. "Me and Brad had a restaurant back home. BBQ themed, you know. A lot like what we do here but marketed as the best of local food."

"Really," she says. "That must have been hard to leave behind."

"It should have been," I tell her. "But things went wrong. The property was owned by two shady people, and even though we paid good rent to be there, they still treated it like an open house. They seemed to think our business was a great cover for them to operate behind and started dealing drugs out the back. Brad wanted to report them, but I didn't want the trouble. We'd always dreamed of traveling, but our money situation had always been tight. Anyway, when we wrapped up the business and sold everything, we had enough for a ticket here, and we never looked back."

"Well, I guess it shows you that the universe has some interesting ways of nudging people toward their best life."

"I guess it does. So what nudged you in this direction?" I ask.

Dawn blinks, and a fleeting faraway look passes across her face. Then she turns to me and beams. "A craving for adventure and a whole lot of luck," she says.

"A craving for adventure. I like that. Not running from something?" I ask as her clouded expression lingers in my mind.

"Well, maybe the odd jealous boyfriend," she quips. "But what's a girl to do?"

"I can imagine," I say, not believing a word. I mean, Dawn probably has left a trail of broken hearts behind her. She's the kind of girl who could splice open the heart of an unsuspecting man for the very fact that she's crazy confident and doesn't seem to want to form close attachments. She's skipped between my friends like a greedy kid sampling at Costco. I don't have anything against that. We are all young, free and single, and hooking up is the best part of that. It's just that there is something unusual about Dawn. Something I can't put my finger on. Something that makes me feel as though she's hiding something.

I have a trick for that.

"Dawn," I say, leaning forward. "You have something behind your ear."

Before she can reach up to investigate, I pull a coin from her ear and present it to her. For a second, she seems stunned, then she grabs the coin and claps her hands. "How did you do that?" she gasps.

"Haven't you heard of magic?" I'm leaning in close to her, and the scent of her floral perfume tickles my senses.

"You do magic? Seriously?"

"I do magic…"

She takes my hand, turning it over, peering at it as though she's looking for some kind of special pocket. "Magic hands." Looking up, our eyes meet and it's like a zap of static and a swell of warmth.

"Magic fingers too." I raise a brow and she grins, flashing her teeth and spreading those pretty pink lips into a wide, perfect smile.

"Got any other magic body parts?" she asks.

With my other hand, I dip my fingers into the top of her shirt and pull out a tiny flower and present it to her with a flourish. She gasps and I lean closer, whispering directly into the sweet shell of her ear. "I think you'll find I'm magic everywhere."

I know I don't imagine the shudder that passes through her body. I blow softly against her ear, and she shudders again.

"You're a tricky one," she breathes, turning her face to mine. This close I can see little flecks of gold in her iris and a smattering of freckles across her nose.

"You have no idea," I say. The urge to kiss her is strong. The urge to get my hands on her peachy skin and my mouth between her legs is even stronger.

"Bryce," my brother's voice yells from near the grill. "It's getting busy out here again."

Her eyes flick away and then back, and she smiles, licking the center of her bottom lip, a tell–tale sign that she wants to be kissed. "I guess that's all the magic I'm going to get tonight."

"Oh, I don't know. The night is young, and so are we."

When I draw away, it's like she's steel and I'm a magnet. Every part of me craves to be closer. We both sigh and then laugh. I think she feels as startled as I do at the buzz of almost-contact between us.

"Time to rock and roll," I say, reaching for her hand.

As we make our way back to the packed bar and all the work that needs to be done before the night is over, I make a vow that I'll taste Dawn's sweet mouth, and more…a whole lot more…if she'll let me.

16

DAWN

The conversation with Bryce has left me unsettled. He can do magic tricks that send shivers up my spine, but that shouldn't mean he's able to read minds. As I wipe over a table I've just cleared of empty glasses and bottles, a sense that he's picked up the corner of me and peered underneath rests uneasily.

The evening seems to stretch out before me, longer and harder than any other night. I work with a fierce commitment that isn't really like me. My friend Kyla is the kind of person who cleans away her anxieties. The more stressed she is, the more her drawers and cupboards look like something from that film, Sleeping with the Enemy.

I have a tendency to be impulsive, to try to lose myself in another experience so that I can leave whatever's worrying me behind. But I'm already in a place of escape and I can't run again. Not now. Not so soon.

In my pocket, my phone vibrates. I pull it out, finding that it's my dad. I stare at it until it stops, then slide it back to where it came from. Tomorrow, I'll message him with a lie and tell him I was sleeping when he called. I'll give him a long update about what I've been doing that will hopefully pacify him for some time.

Although, it probably won't.

It definitely won't.

I don't know why I continue to kid myself. I made a promise to him and right now, I'm breaking it.

Dad won't be satisfied with news about a trip he didn't want me to take. He wants answers, and the only one I have to give is not the one he wants to hear.

As it gets closer to closing time, my phone rings again. It's dad, and again, I wait until it's stopped ringing, my heart picking up at the image of him standing with his cellphone against his ear, waiting for me to be a decent person, a loving daughter, anything more than I actually am.

When I look up, I find Bryce, standing behind the bar with a glass in hand, watching me. I fake a quick smile, suspecting that he won't be fooled by it. He nods; a simple gesture that makes me feel even more *seen*.

By the end of the evening, my nerves are frayed, and my patience is in tatters. All I want is to be alone. For the first time in a long time, the tightness in my throat feels ready to break into emotion that will be obvious to everyone. All my strategies for pushing my feelings down deep, locking them up and throwing away the key aren't working. As I stride back to the safety of my room, my phone rings again. The urge to toss it at the wall and stomp on it is violent and stupid, but still…

"Dawn." Bryce's voice breaks through the frantic squeeze of regret and panic that's encircled my throat.

Words spill in my mind. *I'm fine. I just need some time alone. I'll see you tomorrow.* But none leave the tightness of my lips

Even if they would, I know Bryce wouldn't let it go. His brows are drawn together, and his eyes narrowed, and they search my expression for answers to his unspoken question. *Are you okay?*

He jogs to make up the distance between us, panting just a little when he's finally close enough to touch. His lips part and that unspoken question threatens to surface. Before it does, I grab the front of his warm shirt and tug him, kissing his surprised lips with a ferocity that shocks me.

Bryce can do magic, but I am magic. Brilliant and bright and full of surprises.

For just a second, his stupor slows his response, but as soon as my tongue touches his, it's like an explosion of molten metal shards that brighten the space between us. Oh god. This is what I need. This is what I always need.

On tiptoes, I teeter against the tall wall of impressive man in front of me. When I moan at his kiss, his fist gathers more of my shirt, tugging me tighter, but then it's like he comes to his senses. Drawing back, Bryce stares down at me, but before he can say anything, I touch his cheek. "Get your brother," I say.

We're standing so close that I notice the moment his pupils blow wide with arousal. "Are you sure that's a good idea…you seem…"

"Horny," I interrupt. Horny is a much better word than upset. "I am horny. And anyway, wasn't this Mitchell's idea? Get a schedule going so that you can all send me to cloud nine, night after night."

"Mitchell sometimes has stupid ideas." Bryce's hand releases my shirt and I feel like he's moving away, inch by inch, slipping through my fingers. I can't let that happen. Tonight, I need him, and Bradley more than I've needed anything in a long time. I step in, pressing my lips to the corner of his mouth.

"Get your brother," I say. "Or I can go find someone who wants me."

Bryce's spine straightens like a snap bracelet forced back to its original form. I don't think it's from jealousy as such. None of these men strike me as the possessive kind. If I had to speculate, I'd say his switch is more about missing out or being replaced. This is his night. His moment in the schedule. His chance to show me what he's made of.

"I'll message him," Bryce says, sliding his hand into his pocket. Pulling out his phone, he quickly taps out a message that I don't see but wish I could read. It would sure give me an insight into his relationship with his twin and maybe into what he's thinking about the rest of our night together. "You're really sure?"

"I'm sure."

Those two little words change everything about his demeanor. We're close to my room, and he stalks me like a hungry panther until my back is pressed against the door, and his breath is hot against my neck. One big hand slides down my hip, tugging my left leg over his hip, holding me tightly to him as he inhales against my skin. "You smell like magic," he says, and I'm buzzed enough to giggle. Buzzed enough to slip my hands up under his shirt and get a feel for what he's got going on. I am not disappointed. Taut skin clings to hardened muscle, and an impossible ladder of abs stretches beneath his belt, leading to the promised land. What he has pressed against my pussy feels very promising indeed.

"I should shower," I whisper, as a trickle of sweat from the humid air and the furnace of his body runs down my spine.

"You're perfect." Nipping my ear, the image of his fingers clutching the coin he found behind there makes me giggle again.

"Perfect? I'm anything but."

127

"Open this door and I'll show you exactly how perfect we are together."

Bold words, and I find I like them. With dexterity I didn't know I possess, I manage to slip the key into the lock and twist, and almost tumble back into the room before Bryce scoops me up like a small child.

Oooh, he's big. A big, brawny hunk of Lone Star steak. A man who knows how to be a man, but still has enough sensitivity to tell that I'm on edge. That's a heady combination.

He'll make a good husband to some lucky girl. A girl who can stick around and be what he needs.

The door is left open for Bradley, but I don't let it worry me, and Bryce deposits me onto the bed and braces his hands by my ears.

"Did anyone ever tell you that you're trouble?" he says, sounding even more southern than usual.

"Plenty," I say. "I take it as a compliment. Trouble is fun. Trouble is memorable. Trouble is…"

"Hot as fuck," Bradley says as his footsteps make his presence known.

"Dawn requested your attendance," Bryce says, never looking away from my face. His golden eyes are still darkened with arousal and his lids are lowered, too.

"She thinks you need backup?"

Bryce bends, nipping my bottom lip. "Do you think I need backup?"

I shake my head. "Nah. I'm just greedy. And trouble apparently."

As Bradley moves closer, he tugs his shirt over his head in a flourish and damn if I don't get an eyeful of swoon-worthy goodness.

"There are too many clothes on people in this room. We need fewer clothes and more nakedness."

I agree with Bradley and start tugging roughly at Bryce's shirt. "Get this off. I want to see how identical you guys are."

"Oh, we're identical," Bradley says, dropping his shorts. In just pristinely white underwear, he looks like a model in an expensive glossy magazine and outlined through the insanely clingy fabric is a very impressive cock.

"You're falling behind," I tell Bryce, as he removes his shirt. I fiddle with his belt and get his top button open with eager hands. He takes over, practically tearing his pants from his body. While he's otherwise engaged, I wriggle out of my shorts and underwear, feeling hungry eyes on my body before I've pulled up my top. The air is buzzing with urgency and anticipation, and I can't wait to be sandwiched between so much man.

Bryce helps me remove my top as Bradley moves closer. "Damn, you're pretty all over," he says.

"You haven't seen her all over," Bryce corrects, then he taps my thigh. "Turn over, horny girl. It's time for you to get what you need."

Ohhhh. I like a bossy man.

I scramble over until my ass is high and I'm resting the weight of my upper body on my hands. Bryce tells his brother to get on the bed. "You take her mouth. I'm going to make her come."

Before I have a chance to think, Bryce's hand is resting on my spine, over my tattoo, and Bradley has his cock in his hand. "My brother has ideas," he says. "You agree with those ideas?"

Bryce chooses that exact moment to flick his tongue over my clit and I almost collapse face-first onto the bed. Shit. In this position, with everything spread wide, I'm so sensitive.

"Yes," I gasp and keep my mouth open in readiness for the thick cock Bradley's stroked into a rigid bar. He's going to need some restraint because there's no way I'm deep throating that. But when he slides it thickly over my tongue, I wish I could. After a night of work, he still smells fresh and tastes good.

"Slowly, baby." Bradley touches my cheek with rough fingertips, easing back. "I'm not in a rush. We've got all night."

"Dawn doesn't," Bryce murmurs against my thigh. "She's going to come in record time."

Bradley hums in agreement. "There are no limits on orgasms. At least not for a willing woman."

Bryce's tongue explores the folds of my pussy before pushing deep into my opening. The depth he reaches is such a surprise that I grunt, amusing Bradley enough to make him laugh. "Whatever you did just then, she really liked," he tells his brother, but I think Bryce knows. The fact that my pussy clenched in his face most likely made it very obvious!

I close my eyes, focusing on the push and pull of having one man in front of me and one behind me. As Bryce's clever tongue does its magic, the warm tension that pools low in my belly eventually spills, and I gasp, letting Bradley's cock slip from my mouth while I arch my back from the pleasure.

"You did that in record time," Bradley says, sounding proud of his brother. I'm proud of Bryce too. He almost caused the top of my head to explode!

When I've stopped panting and manage to find the strength to tip my face up, I find Bradley slowly stroking his cock, smiling down at me. "You ready for more, or do you have something else in mind? It's the lady's choice."

"That's what I like to hear," I rasp past a tongue that suddenly feels too big in my mouth.

"So, what's it to be, baby?" He cups my cheek with his big, warm hand as Bryce kisses slowly up my spine until his cock slides against my slick pussy. Oh god. Just that long, slow slip of hard flesh against soft skin is enough to make me squirm.

"I want you both," I say, desperate for that intense feeling of surrender that comes with being sandwiched between two big, powerful bodies. One in front, one behind, and I can disappear to a place beyond real life where everything is out of my control. Powerlessness feels totally intoxicating when life is at the point of dragging me down.

Rising, I kiss Bradley, and he moans into my mouth. Maybe he can taste himself. Bryce moves closer, fisting my hair and twisting my head, kissing me deeply too. I move between them, kissing, touching, the transitions between their mouths so quick I lose the sense of who is who and who is where.

Hands squeeze my breasts and tease my nipples with sharp pinches that make me gasp. Fingers probe between my legs, teasing me until I'm hot and needy again, ready for whatever kind of sharing they might have in mind. "Come sit on my lap," Bradley says, "but face away."

I don't get what he means until I go to straddle him, and he pats my thigh. "Other way, baby. I'll hold you tight. Don't worry."

I rotate to straddle him reverse cowgirl style and wait as he slides a condom down in a flourish. He's so big that I anticipate a burn as he pushes deep, but I'm so wet, I stretch easily. Maybe it's because I've been having so much sex lately. The thought fills me with heat and longing for the other men who've shared my bed.

"Fuck," Bradley says. "You're tight. Rest on your feet and lay your back against my chest. Bryce is coming in too."

Bryce's intense eyes meet mine as he slides a condom over his cock. He licks his lips that must still taste like me, and eyes me up like I'm Little Red Riding Hood and he's the big, bad wolf. "Make the magic happen," I say as he climbs closer, his eyes fixed on my spread pussy and his brother's cock lodged deep inside.

"It's not going to be me who makes the magic happen, baby," he says, kissing the inside of my thigh. "It's all you."

I'm certain the actual mechanics of this sex act would be easier if I were lying face-down on Bradley's chest, but I can see why Brad chose to do it this way. When one of his arms wraps across my chest and the other tugs my right leg high, the control he can have from beneath becomes obvious. "She's wet," he says. "She's ready for you."

Ready for them both.

This is only the second time I've been with two men, and it's already less daunting. I know my body can deal with the physical pressures. As Bryce braces over me, rubbing his nose against mine and smiling, tears well behind my eyes. "You're amazing," he says huskily, and my throat becomes molten lava.

"Fuck me," I tell him. "Make me feel it."

For a flash, his expression darkens with uncertainty, but as I strain against Bradley's grip, rising just enough to kiss his mouth, any apprehension is lost.

Two men work together inside me, slipping and sliding, rutting deep and hard, and I close my eyes, hanging on like a rodeo rider, wishing I could stay between them forever.

Muscled chests and abs work to deliver my pleasure. Skin burns with exertion and grows slippery with pleasure. "That's it," Bryce says, as I spread my legs wider. I wish I could see Bradley's expression, but from the noises he's making and the frantic shifting of his hips, I can tell he's close.

I want them to come together. I want to feel these two gorgeous twins release at the same time, gripping me frantically between them as they tumble into oblivion. It's a lot to ask, I know, but a girl can fantasize, especially when she's created her very own fantasy vacation experience.

"I'm close," I gasp, sounding surprised, but I'm not really. It would be impossible not to come with a man as sexy as Bryce gazing down at me with awe in his eyes. A flush spreads across his cheeks, his hips moving jerkily. "Let it go," I order. "Fill my pussy."

As I hoped, my words have a triggering effect and suddenly, Bradley lurches up, his arm tugging me so tightly against his chest that I lose my breath. Bryce seizes too, every muscle on his ripped chest rippling as he comes inside me. My own orgasm hits me like a whip as Bryce collapses over me, effectively pinning my small body between his and his brother's.

"Oh god," I gasp, finding Bradley's hand to hold in mine, and stroking Bryce's big, strong arm.

"I don't think he can help you," Bryce mumbles.

We all laugh, and they both slide from inside me with a sound that makes us laugh even harder. I think I must drift off into sex-induced la la land because, when I stir, I'm facing Bradley who's breathing softly and evenly. Behind me, Bryce makes a contented humming sound, pressing the long, hard line of his body against my ass and thighs. "That was something else," he murmurs into my hair.

"It really was," I whisper.

The sheets rustle as he rolls away, and I feel the soft press of his fingers as they begin tracing the letters of my tattoo. It's shiver inducing. "There's something you should know about me, Dawn." I swallow hard as he pauses. "I like giving you what you need, but in exchange, I like to understand why you need it."

"There's nothing to understand," I tell him, replying with speed that sounds immediately defensive. He makes a light tsking sound and rolls closer again.

"I know you're running from something. I get that it's

your business. But I wouldn't be a friend if I didn't tell you that I'm here for you whenever you want to stop and face whatever's behind you."

I blink into the darkness, aware of the ticking clock and my own fast beating heart. "Once you're running, it's so much easier to keep going than it is to stop," I whisper.

He kisses the back of my head, draping his warm arm around me as though he wants to shield me from all the bad in the world. What he doesn't realize is that by running, I've become bad too.

17

LOGAN

I rise early so I can make the most of my visit with my mum today. I try to see her as much as I can, and make it over at least twice a week, sometimes three, when we're not busy at the bar. I dress in casual clothes that I can work in. There are always things to do at Mum's, and I like to get stuck in and not have to worry about dirt.

Stepping outside into the fresh morning air fills me with a sense of wonder. It sounds stupid, but when you've faced the possibility of no more mornings, each one that you get to experience feels so much sweeter.

As I make my way through the communal area, I find Dawn curled in a hammock, staring into space. For a second, I wonder if she's asleep with her eyes open, but then she turns to look directly at me. "Hey Logan." Dawn tries to sit up and the hammock sways, causing her to grip onto the sides. "How come you're up so early?"

"I could ask you the same question?"

"My bed is filled with twins," she says. "They're too hot

and big for me to sleep in between. I felt like I was going to melt."

"Good reason!" I say. "I'm going to see my mum."

"Really. This early?"

Shrugging, I slide my hands into my old jean shorts, widening my stance. "I like to make the most of my visits. She needs my help."

"How come?"

"She's disabled. Independent as they come, but even so, there are things she can't do. I pick up the slack."

"Son of the year." She smiles and fiddles with her hair as though she's worried she isn't presentable.

"What are you doing now?" I ask her. "Planning to sleep some more?"

"Nah. That ship has sailed. I don't know. I'm a free agent today."

"Why don't you come with me? Mum loves company. No pressure."

As soon as I've made the offer, I immediately feel like an idiot. Why would Dawn want to hang out with my mum who's a complete stranger to her? But instead of rejecting my offer, Dawn's face lights up. "Really? You serious?"

"Yeah. Of course."

"Help me out of this hammock."

Holding the edge of the fabric, I take the weight while Dawn swings her legs, straining to get her feet on the ground. Even with my help, her dismount is still a catastrophe, but rather than being embarrassed, she doubles over with laughter. "You think I'll get better at doing that before I leave?" she asks.

The word *leave* hits me more than I thought it would. I don't know Dawn that well, but over the time she's been working here, we've had fun. It would be great if she could

136

stay awhile. I know there are more than a few of my friends who'd like her to stay, too.

"So where does your mom live?" she asks as she slides her feet into flip flops.

"It's mum in Oz," I smile. "And she's only five minutes from here."

"Right. Mum. It sounds so formal!"

We start to walk to where the ute is parked. "Mum's anything but formal," I tell her. "And she's going to love you. Just wait and see."

"I'm very loveable," Dawn says, beaming. In her pink Minnie Mouse t-shirt, and soft black shorts, she's the picture of cute.

"You are," I say, and when she links her arm through mine, my heart does a funny little squeeze.

I have a key to Mum's house, which I use to open the door. The radio booms from the kitchen, playing the eighties music that she loves so much. Mum's voice can be heard intermittently, singing along in a tone-deaf way that makes me laugh out loud. What an introduction Dawn is going to get.

Realizing I probably should have called ahead to warn Mum that I'm bringing a visitor, I stride quickly into the kitchen, praying that she's dressed and ready to receive a guest. We find her at the large oak table, peeling apples.

"Hey Mum." I bend to greet her, kissing her warm rosy cheek, inhaling the comforting scent of her face cream. "I brought a friend to keep you company while I tackle your list of jobs."

Her eyes flick to Dawn, and as soon as she sees who's there, her whole expression lights up.

"Not just a friend," she says. "A pretty girl."

"She's a woman, Mum." I reach out to snag a piece of apple and Mum swats my hand playfully.

"If you keep eating it, there won't be enough for the pie."

"You're making apple pie?" Dawn says. "Wow."

"I'm not sure it's going to be a wow pie," Mum says. "More like a good enough pie."

"This is Dawn, Mum. And your apple pie is perfect. Don't let her fool you."

Dawn smiles and takes a seat at the table. "Is there anything I can help you with?"

"Sure." Mum passes her the peeler and the bowl of apples. "You peel and I'll chop. And Logie can make us a nice cup of coffee."

Groaning at her use of my pet name, I fill the kettle and rustle up some basic coffees using instant and whatever milk is in the fridge. I'm sure it's not barista level, but it'll wake us all up.

When I place the mugs on the table, Dawn reaches for hers and cups it in both hands, making a humming, appreciative sound.

"I'll leave you two," I say. "I'll be outside."

Dawn gives me a parting wave, and as I open the sliding rear door, the sound of her and Mum chatting follows me into the messy space that is crying out for my taming hands.

An hour later, when I've worked up a sweat and my mouth is as dry as the outback, I kick off my filthy boots on the deck, and swipe away the sweat and dirt from my face with the hem of my shirt.

Inside, the music is still playing, and I discover Dawn sitting next to Mum, with a ball of wool and knitting needles clutched like weapons, and Mum desperately trying to stifle her laughter.

"I can't do it," Dawn says. "Look. I think I've dropped another stitch."

"Be patient," Mum says. "It doesn't matter. You're not making Logie a jumper."

"You really want to keep calling me that in front of Dawn?" I sigh, making a show of my exasperation, while mum's responding laughter is filled with glee. She loves teasing me, and it seems she loves it even more when it's in front of a pretty woman.

Dawn's eyes meet mine and they are filled with panic. "Seriously. I'm terrible at this. If there was ever an apocalypse that wiped out all the machines, my family would have to walk around naked!"

Mum waves her hand dismissively. "You've been trying for five minutes. No one learned anything worth knowing in five minutes."

"Stick around," I say, coming up behind Dawn. "Mum is about to unleash all her words of wisdom." I rest my hands gently over Dawn's and take over the movement of the needles. "Just follow me. In, around, through and off. In, around, through and off."

With my help, Dawn successfully manages three stitches, then I let go. "Right. Just do the same."

She manages one stitch and squeals. "I did it. I did it." Then she lowers the needles to her lap and stares up at me. "Wait. You know how to knit?"

"I do." Running my hand through my hair, I glance at mum who looks like she wants to explode at my embarrassment. It's stupid to feel that something like knitting isn't for men. It's a skill like any other, and I'm certainly not an expert. At a push, I could knit a blanket or a scarf. Basic stuff. Mum insisted on teaching me all kinds of life skills. It's why I can cook, prune roses, lay insulation, and change a plug. The list is endless. But I guess my ability has blown Dawn's mind because her mouth is still open.

"That is awesome!"

"Dawn made cakes," Mum says, tugging on my arm, urging me to twist and see. Next to the sink is a tray of chocolate cupcakes with creamy frosting.

"You made those?" I ask, already striding across for a closer look, with a watering mouth.

"She didn't even need a recipe."

Mum is glowing with pride on Dawn's behalf, which doesn't surprise me at all. Dawn, on the other hand, blushes and shifts in her seat as though she's not used to hearing and accepting compliments.

I grab a cake and a glass of water and sit at the table, smiling as Dawn screws up her nose in concentration, mouthing the words in, over, through and off, with every stitch. Mum tells me her news and we spend another thirty minutes in contented company.

When Dawn has managed an inch of very rough looking knitting, she lowers it again. "It doesn't look good, but I'm so damned proud of myself."

"You should be." Mum rests her hand on Dawn's arm. "It's not easy, and you tackled it with determination."

"We should probably go," I say, glancing at my watch.

"Can I take this?" Dawn asks. "I want to keep practicing, but I promise I'll send the needles back with Logie!"

Mum's eyes sparkle at Dawn's use of my nickname. "You keep them. I have plenty."

I stand and clear the table of mugs and plates, washing them quickly and stacking them on the draining board. Dawn offers to dry, but Mum insists we let nature do the work.

With knitting in hand, Dawn bends to hug my mum in such a gentle and tender way that I have to swallow to clear the burning sensation in my throat. "It's been so nice to spend the morning with you," she says.

"The pleasure's all mine. You come back anytime you want."

As we walk down the hall, Mum follows to show us to the door, the wheels of her chair squeaking against the wood. I open the ute so that Dawn can get in, but jog back to the door when Mum calls me back. When I'm close enough to hear a whisper, she says. "That girl's a keeper, Logie. You better hold on to her."

"We're not even dating," I tell her, wondering if she'd still think that way about Dawn if I told her what's been going on at Cloud 9 since she joined our team.

"Well, you better change that. Women like that don't come along often, honey. She's got a light inside her that can never be snuffed out, a spine of iron, and best of all, she's funny. You know I don't like to get involved in your personal life, but this time I am. It's time *you* had some fun. Let the past go." She reaches to take my hand and I give hers a squeeze.

"Okay, mum," I say. "I'll think about it."

With one arched brow, she tells me thinking isn't enough.

On the way back to Cloud 9, we pass my favorite coffee shop, and with Mum's words still ringing in my ears, I decide we should make a stop.

"Are we going somewhere?" Dawn asks when I pull over.

"Yep. For the best coffee in town and a surprise treat."

"Is it a lamington?"

I groan, realizing that I'm late to this party and my friends have already had opportunities to share good things about Byron with Dawn. "Ah shit. Did someone get there first?"

"Yep, but don't worry. I'm not lamingtoned out."

I throw open the car door. "Anyway, these lamingtons are the best in town. No competition."

Dawn follows me and we find a free table outside, grateful that it's shaded by a broad white parasol. We order flat whites and a lamington each because they are just too good to share, and I ask Dawn about her life before Cloud 9. She talks about her dad and her friends back home, her green eyes sparkling with every funny story she tells me. She even has a story about meeting international popstar Luna Evans and helping her get a tattoo. It would sound farfetched from anyone else, but not from Dawn.

But notably, she never mentions her mum.

When the cakes are delivered, we take our time eating each delicious bite and I observe Dawn watching a middle-aged woman and her teenage daughter who are sitting a few tables away. It's like she can't take her eyes off them.

When we get back to Cloud 9, we have a couple of hours before our shifts start. "Well, thanks for entertaining my mum," I say.

"Thanks for taking me. I had fun."

"Time for a shower". I run my hand through my messy blond hair to illustrate the point. Dawn reaches for my other hand.

"I could use a shower too," she says and without any preamble, leads me away from the door to my room, towards hers.

Mum's words ring out in my mind. *That girl's a keeper.*

Maybe, in an ideal world, we'd take the time to get to know each other better. In some ways, Dawn is so open, but in others, she's like a rosebud; closed up tight around all her secrets. I wish I didn't have questions rattling around in my mind. Why's she here? When's she leaving? What's she hiding?

Maybe only time will provide the answers. Or maybe, getting closer, I'll find out some more about this beautiful woman, whose soul seems to sing the sweetest melody to so many ears.

She leads me into the bathroom and turns on the water before beginning to remove her clothes. For a couple of seconds, I'm frozen in place, watching as inch by inch of her soft skin is revealed. As she holds my eye contact, it's like a ribbon of electricity forms between us, and before I know it, I'm tugging off my own shirt and removing my shorts, socks, and shoes in record time.

Usually, there's an element of uncertainty in undressing in front of someone new, but not with Dawn. She seems totally at ease with herself, and with me. Rather than feeling exposed, I feel a sense of purpose beyond the carnal.

"Let me wash you," she says, stepping into the steaming water and allowing it to cascade over her hair and face. I join her, leaving just a sliver of space between us, shivering as her warm hands begin to explore my chest and stomach. A touch so gentle and searching, it feels like she's reading my story in braille, passing over the scar on my abdomen, and lower until her hand wraps around my cock.

A hiss of breath escapes my lips as she slowly moves, squeezing and rotating her fist into a rhythm that makes me want to rise up on my toes. I take her mouth in a searing kiss that has us both moaning and clawing to get closer. Oh god, the feeling of her ass in my hands makes me want to press her against the cold tiled wall and fuck her until she screams. Her breasts are warm and soft against my chest, her hand a tight ring of pleasure.

"Fuck, Dawn," I mutter against her neck as she arches her spine. When I take one of her tight little nipples into my mouth, the rush almost knocks me off my feet.

"Logan," she moans, grinding her pussy against my thigh.

The water streams over both of us, making everything hot and slick. I hitch her leg over my hip and my cock notches at her entrance, like it instinctively knows the way to paradise. In the frenzy of the moment, with Dawn squirming against me, I'm suddenly balls-deep inside her. Our eyes meet, our lips are parted, and everything is suddenly so real that my head spins.

"I'm clean," I say. "I've had more blood tests than any person should ever need."

"I'm clean too," she says. "I've never fucked anyone without protection, and I'm on birth control."

She shifts and white-hot pleasure courses up my spine and licks over my balls. Is this stupid? Should I just carry her to the bedroom and put a condom on?

"You're sure you want to?" I ask, too buzzed to care about the details. In a moment of primal realization that is so unlike me, the idea that I'll be the first man to come inside this woman makes me forget everything.

"Yes," she gasps, and that's it. I'm lost.

The first thrust is like nothing I've ever felt before. Dawn's tight and so slippery, we fit together like it was always meant to be.

"Oh fuck," she gasps, tipping her head back, fingernails almost puncturing the skin of my shoulder. "That feels so good."

"You have no idea," I growl, burying my face in Dawn's neck as my hands grip hold of her so that we don't fall.

All I want to do is make her feel good. All the small moments when I've noticed her expression become more somber flash through my mind. This might be the only chance I get to wipe some of those moments away for her.

And as she comes, crying out like she's in pain, gripping onto me for dear life and begging me not to stop, I know I'm never going to want to let go of her.

I don't finish in the shower. The opportunity to make this perfect day last longer is just too tempting. I carry Dawn through to the bedroom, snagging a towel on the way. I dry every inch of her, except between her legs. I want to taste her arousal and know what it feels like when she comes on my tongue. I lower myself onto her and slide back inside her.

It's different in the comfort of her bed. Different because we're eye to eye and the weight of my body pins her beneath me. Different because our eyes are open as I move inside her. When I come, I root deep, letting every pulse of my orgasm fill the deepest part of her. And after, I stay in her slick wet heat for the longest time, knowing I'll never forget this moment.

When I eventually withdraw, I cup my hand between Dawn's legs, feeling my cum leak from inside her. A primal instinct makes me push it back inside her, and she hums with satisfaction.

"I think you ruined me," she says. "I'm never going to want to use condoms again."

"If you stay here with us, you won't need to. We're all clean."

She curls into my body like a satisfied cat resting in the sun. "Stay with you?" she whispers.

"Yeah. You know. The opposite of leave."

She makes a small noise that definitely isn't an agreement with my suggestion, avoiding any discussion about the permanence of her presence, tracing over my scar again. I expect her to ask what happened to cause it, but she doesn't. Then, I realize it's probably because she doesn't want me to ask personal questions either.

My fingers find the tattoo at the base of her spine, and I trace the word YOLO, even though her back is turned away from me so I can't actually see it.

What inspires a person to live each day as if it's her last? Maybe she was sick like me. Maybe she is sick?

The thought is like a knife to my heart.

Dawn Mitchell might be holding herself as tight as a rosebud, but I'm going to find out the truth, whatever it takes.

18

DAWN

Jeffrey Barrow is back at the bar, wearing a suit and looking completely out of place. As soon as I notice him, I grab Mitchell's arm and turn him until he's facing the right direction. "Look."

"Oh fuck," he says, immediately sprinting to where Lachlan is currently talking to a customer at the other end of the bar. He whispers something into Lachlan's ear, which causes his spine to straighten and head to swivel. Mitchell clasps him by the shoulder to fix him in place, then strolls to the end of the bar as though he doesn't have a care in the world.

I inch closer so that I can hear what's going on and because I'm worried that the situation has the potential to explode.

"What can I get you?" Mitchell asks smoothly. He takes a cloth and wipes the bar in front of the man, looking exactly like a saloon owner in a western, just waiting for the gunfight that's about to erupt.

"Whisky."

No, please, and no thank you either when it's poured and pushed across the bar. I glance at Lachlan, who's folded his arms over his chest and is watching everything with a menacing stare. His hand is bruised and scabbed from his last encounter with Mr. Barrow, and I'm not letting him lose it again.

The man tosses a large bill onto the bar and rises, pulling a crisp white envelope from his suit pocket. He rests it on the bar and pushes it so it's within reach of Mitchell, but he doesn't let it go. Not immediately. "This is the offer I discussed with your friend. Read it. Accept it."

He steps back, and his face spreads into the creepiest smile I've ever seen. "I'll be seeing you."

Mitchell retains his composure, but I know inside he's vibrating with the urge to smack this asshole in the face. I know because I am too, and it isn't even my bar that's in jeopardy.

When Barrow has left, Mitchell takes the letter and shoves it into the back pocket of his jeans. Our eyes meet and he shrugs. "We've got work to do," he says. "And nothing that asshole says is important to me."

When he walks behind Lachlan, he pats him on the shoulder. In a flash, Lachlan has the letter in his hand and tears it open with his index finger.

"Leave it, man," Mitchell says, trying to retrieve it. "It's not worth it. Not right now when we've got shit to do. We can read it later."

"You want to know what that fucker is offering us?" Lachlan says a figure which I think sounds small but I'm not knowledgeable about Australian property values, so I'm not sure. But when Mitchell splutters with laughter, I get the picture.

"He wants us to accept that?" Mitchell doubles over with laughter, clutching his stomach. "Who does he think he is? Don fucking Corleone?"

"I think he thinks he has a lot of power in this town and we're going to find that intimidating."

"Well, I think he's a piece of shit who needs to go fuck himself."

Lachlan crumples the letter into a ball and tosses it into the trash unceremoniously.

"What are you going to do?" I ask.

"Nothing." Lachlan says. "This is our bar. End of. No suit-wearing prick is going to come in here and think he can force us to sell up our dream."

"You need to tell the others what's happened," I say. "You need to share the burden and come to a joint decision about how to act. And you should take that letter out of the trash and keep it for evidence."

"What do you mean?" he asks.

"My friend's boyfriends had an issue with their business. They ended up under investigation. This guy obviously isn't a fair kind of person. There's going to be trouble. He isn't going to go away quietly. You need to plan and carefully consider a strategy."

Lachlan nods thoughtfully.

"Dawn's right," Mitchell says. "It's not all on you to take this on. There are nine of us here. We're strong because we're a team."

"Okay," Lachlan says, bending to pick up the letter and smoothing it against his trousers. "We'll talk later."

It's obvious from the stiff way he changes course that Lachlan isn't used to asking for help. He's used to relying on himself, a lone wolf. But none of us is an island. We all need help sometimes.

Even as I think it, I feel like a hypocrite. My friends and family have all given me advice and I've chosen to fly across the world to avoid it, sure that I know better. Or at least, sure that I don't want to hear what they have to say, even if it comes from love.

Later, when the bar is closed, everyone gathers around the outdoor tables, nursing cold beers. Thomas yawns, rubbing his hand over his face, and I catch his tiredness, yawning too, snuggling closer to Jared, who has his arm around my shoulder.

Lachlan sits opposite with his legs spread wide, his hands behind his head. His eyes are on me, but not in jealousy. At least, I don't think he's jealous. It's more a possessiveness that's lingered since we were together at the beach. But he's stood aside for his friends, and that shows me how much he loves them. It shows me that he can control his temper when he wants to.

"So, this asshole has come back with an offer. It's so low, it's insulting, not that we ever planned to entertain it." Lachlan shifts, pulling the letter from his back pocket and tossing it onto the table in front of him. He slumps back against the chair and watches as Bryce picks it up, reads the short paragraph and passes it to his twin with a grimace. As the letter works its way around, there are more growls of insult and anger.

"Who the fuck does he think he is?" Bradley asks.

"He's as dirty as they come, but he's also influential, and he has connections." Logan rubs the back of his neck, shaking his head.

"You know this?" I ask.

"I did some research on him."

"So, we play dirty too," Cooper says passionately, tossing the letter back to the table. "We play him at his own game."

"I don't think you understand what dirty means. We're not the kind of guys to do illegal shit to defend ourselves, are we?" Bradley says.

"I don't know about you guys, but I'd rather not get into anything messy," Logan says. "I have my mum to consider."

"You won't need to, Logan," Bryce says.

"If he's so influential and has so many contacts, why is he threatening us? Surely, he could influence his way into getting what he wants."

"Maybe he thinks intimidation will get him what he wants more quickly, or more cheaply," Logan says.

"We can handle this," Bryce says.

"As a first step, I think you should call a lawyer for some advice," I say. "They can prepare you for the kind of evidence you might need if things get bad. Maybe wearing a wire to get him to implicate himself?" I say.

"Yeah, that sounds good," Thomas agrees. "And maybe it's time to install some CCTV around the place. I know we looked into it and couldn't justify the expense, but I think this changes things. I still have the card from that guy, Adam, who came to quote last time. He gave us the best price."

"Aye, look into it," Lachlan agrees.

"The main thing is that we keep our eyes open," Joshua says. "Anything suspicious, no matter how small, we need to share with everyone. He could have people scoping the place. He could have people out to sabotage our business. If we don't have customers, it'll make it easier to get us to sell."

"Good point. I know that none of us like to live this way, dragged down by suspicion, but I don't see that we have much choice." Lachlan stands, his shoulders bunched with tension. Our eyes meet and I nod slowly, acknowledging his frustration. Just that small action seems to help him relax.

For the first time since I arrived at Cloud 9, the

atmosphere is somber. The men I've grown to care about so much aren't their usual happy, funny selves. As the meeting disperses, I make my way back to my room alone.

In the quiet of my room, a space I haven't yet gotten used to inhabiting by myself, I pick up my phone and call Carl. Of all of Kyla's many men, Carl reminds me the most of Lachlan. He's the one who's taken on the serious side of the business. He handles the parts that require strategic thinking and organization. He does the hiring and the firing like Lachlan. I know he'll have a perspective on what is happening here. He went through a lot with the tattoo franchises when they were used as a cover for other more nefarious business activities.

Usually, I'd feel weird about calling my bestie's boyfriend, but Carl owes me. I was the one responsible for Kyla taking the admin job at Ink Factor. I was the one who encouraged the game they played with her that made them all fall in love. If I don't get a mention in the wedding speech, I'll lose my shit.

The dialing tone is that weird international one that sounds so foreign, but Carl is quick to answer. "Hello." His voice is gruff and abrupt, as though he's expecting me to be a cold call or one of those scammers who tries to get you to transfer money out of your account.

"Hey Carl, it's Dawn."

"DAWN," he shouts. "How's it going down under?"

"Awesome," I say. "I'm on Cloud 9."

"Kyla told us," he says. "Good for you. About time you got to have the kind of fun you coaxed your friend into."

"My thoughts exactly. Anyway, I'm not calling to discuss my sex life, as fascinating as it is. My friends here are having some issues with their business."

I spend the next five minutes pacing and outlining what's happening with Jeffrey Barrow, and Carl makes disgusted noises every time I pause for a breath.

After I've relayed the details, I perch on the edge of my mattress to hear his response.

"Bad businessmen are the worst," he says. "It sounds like your friends are in a bind. They need to play things very carefully. You gave them good advice about the attorney. They need to know their legal position and also keep records of every contact he makes and the details of what happened during that contact. Get the CCTV installed and be vigilant about who comes in and out of that place. I'd also recommend they contact their local political representative with concerns about the suit dude's business operation. Record the meeting so they have it logged. They should also speak to other business owners in the area in case anyone has heard anything. What he's proposing is going to change the town significantly. Smaller hotels will get put out of business. With a network of supporters, they'll be more likely to be able to resist, and they'll have other people looking out for anything suspicious."

I breathe out a long, frustrated sigh. He's absolutely right. Of course he is. But it sounds like so much work and we're already working at capacity. "Okay. That's great, Carl. Thank you so much. I knew you'd be able to help."

"Anything for you, Dawn. I owe you a debt that I'll never hope to repay."

"You don't owe me a thing," I say, smiling. "As long as you look after Kyla like the queen she is, we'll always be even."

"That's a commitment I'm more than happy to make."

"Is my bestie there?," I ask.

"Err…not right now." Carl suddenly sounds a little hesitant.

"Is she okay?" I ask quickly.

"Yeah. She's fine. She just can't come to the phone

right now."

His statement strikes me as weird. If she was in the shower or out somewhere, wouldn't he be specific?"

"Okay. Can you tell her I called? Tell her I miss her."

"I'll tell her."

We say our goodbyes, but the pang for home doesn't leave me.

Later, as I slide between the sheets, I think about how happy I've been since arriving at Cloud 9 and wonder if this is how Kyla felt when she started working at Ink Factor. Happiness is great, but it won't last for me the way it has for Kyla. I'll get restless, searching for that thing beyond the horizon that I never seem to be able to grasp. And when I do, I'll have to leave these men and this place behind.

I will let myself enjoy every minute, but all the while keeping in mind that there's no point in getting too attached.

19

DAWN

I lie awake, the events of earlier churning in my mind. I picture Lachlan struggling to sleep too as he shoulders the burden of worry for this place.

They don't deserve the stress Jeffrey Barrow is bringing into their lives.

They don't deserve the stress you're going to bring into their lives, my mind whispers.

At least with me, there's pleasure involved. And maybe they won't be that bothered when I move on. They were fine before me. They'll be fine after.

My phone vibrates on the nightstand, and I reach for it, wondering if it's Kyla. When a message from Dad flashes up, I drop the phone without reading it. I know what it's going to say, and facing the words again gets my heart racing.

I can't go back to the US, at least, not until I'm ready. Where can I go next?

New Zealand. Bali. Singapore. Maybe even on a tour of

southeast Asia; Thailand, Vietnam and Cambodia would rock. Kyla showed me some pictures taken by one of the other women in the reverse harem ladies' group. Natalie is a photographer, and she's traveled the world documenting some of the amazing sights she's seen.

I should be filled with excitement. My imagination happily devours the options, but my heart struggles to imagine packing my suitcase, setting off into the world and never seeing these men again.

I try to think of one thing about each of them that I will fix in my memory. Mitchell's laugh, Cooper's smile, Logan's gentle touch, Lachlan's dark watchful eyes, Thomas's musical fingers, Bryce's quick magical hands, Joshua's sense of adventure, Jared's playfulness, and Bradley's warm heart.

They've each managed to imprint themselves onto my heart in a way I wasn't prepared for. Would I have it any other way? No. Everything about our time together has been too special and even though it's probably time for me to leave before they get any closer, I can't just pack up with this awful situation banging at their door.

The truth is, I don't want to. I want to discover more about what we could be like together. I want to feel exactly what Kyla has, even if it's just for a brief time.

The rumble of masculine voices outside my room carries through the door, and I scramble out of bed and towards the noise as quickly as I can.

In the hallway, all nine men linger, talking quietly amongst themselves, before they head to their rooms for sleep. I guess, after I left to call Carl, they must have carried on drinking and talking.

"Sorry, Dawn," Logan says, spotting me first. Eight other heads swivel to face me. "Did we wake you?"

"I couldn't sleep."

I look down, suddenly conscious that I'm standing in

front of them in a tight white tank which does little to conceal my breasts beneath, and a pair of white cotton panties. Nine sets of eyes rake over my body, and I'm warmed by the intensity of their stares.

"You need someone to help you get to sleep?" Bryce asks, his Texan drawl making his half-innocent words feel sinful.

Folding in my lips to moisten them, I take time to look them all over with the same approving gaze they're giving me. And damn, I don't think I've ever seen such a fine group of men gathered together. Or such a good group of men.

I imagine describing them all to Kyla and her friends and am pretty certain what their reaction would be. I'm sure they'd tell me to do all the things that've been on my mind since the day I came to apply for the job and I got to meet them all.

Yes, sex in ones and twos is awesome, but sex with nine men? What would that even be like?

Would they even want to find out?

Kyla's quite private about her love life, but she was kind enough to answer a few logistical questions that I asked in fascination. With three men, I get what each of them might do. Four or five is still easy to imagine, but nine? That's a lot of men just standing around waiting for their turn, isn't it?

Would that be so bad?

My cheeks heat at the thought of vocalizing what I'm thinking, but isn't this what living by my mantra is all about? When will I ever get another chance to experience this with nine men I care for and who care for me?

Never, that's when.

So, if I want to know what it's like, and store away the memory for a time long in the future when I'm old and in need of something incredible to reminisce on, I have to do it now.

The phrase I live by, you only live once, is what moments like this were made for.

"I need all of you," I say softly, resting against the doorframe.

Oh god. Just asking them sends a shiver of sensation up my spine and over my scalp. When my nipples tighten, at least four sets of eyes notice. Lachlan stands straighter, as though he wants the decision for what happens next to rest with him, but knows that it won't. Maybe he won't be comfortable with fucking in the same room as his friends? Maybe sharing me will become more difficult for him when he can see it rather than just imagine it.

Mitchell's eyes seem to dance with anticipation. Cooper licks his amazing lips and Thomas shifts on his feet. Seconds tick past and I know I've really shocked them. The thought of nine men stunned by my indecent proposal makes me want to giggle.

Eventually, Joshua steps forward and rests his warm hand on my hip, bending to press a soft kiss to my lips. "I don't know what you fuckers are waiting for."

In a flash, he scoops me off my feet, encouraging me to wrap my legs around his waist as he carries me to the bed. He kisses down my throat and between my breasts, pushing the thin fabric of my tank down with his chin. The sound of the door shutting punctuates the air, but I have no idea who crossed the threshold and who decided to remain outside.

It's probably just Jared who's joined his twin. They're used to each other, so this situation wouldn't prove to be a challenge. Maybe Bryce and Bradley. They're also used to sharing, but when I open my eyes, my mind is blown. They're all there, standing around, watching Joshua do filthy things to me. All waiting to make my fantasy a reality.

My phone buzzes on my nightstand again, but I reach out for Jared's hand, pulling him close. He kisses me while his brother feasts on my nipples, then kisses lower and lower, pushing my panties aside.

There's a collective sigh as my pussy is bared to the room. Lachlan climbs onto the bed, sliding his hands beneath my arms and pulling until I'm lying more centrally. Of course, he'd be the one to deal with the organization of my placement. I smile up at him, and he lowers his head to kiss the tip of my nose. "You sure about this, ma wee bonnie lass?"

"I'm sure," I say firmly, smiling at the way his Scottishness seems stronger when he's feeling passionate. Bonnie lass is just the sweetest endearment.

I close my eyes as more men step forward to touch me, and I try to focus on each hand, each mouth, each finger as it explores my body. Someone drags my panties over my thighs, impatient to remove the last flimsy barrier. I don't know who is who, and I don't care. I know each of these men will treat me with respect and handle me with care.

Hands softly squeeze my breasts and tease my nipples. Lips kiss my calves and my ankles and then the insides of my thighs. I'm so wet between my legs, so desperate and needy that my hips writhe, seeking more contact.

When a tongue flicks against my clit, my hips buck. "Sensitive," a gruff voice observes. It's Bradley, I think, but I don't open my eyes to find out.

Locked in the darkness behind my lids, I don't need to consider the logistics of how this is going to work. I just need to be.

"Damn." There's a chorus of hisses and growly throat noises as someone pushes their fingers deep inside me. What must it look like to observe something so raw and sexual? Hot, I think. Maybe a little frustrating that it's their friend's fingers exploring my most private of places.

A finger traces the seam of my lips and I open my eyes to find Lachlan kneeling next to my head, his cock held rigid in his fist. "Ready for me?" he asks.

I answer yes, but I feel as though I'm telling a lie. I don't think I'll ever be fully ready for what Lachlan has to offer, but I'll give it my best shot just to see his eyes flutter shut with sensation. Just to witness a few moments of him coming undone by my mouth.

As he traces my lips with the head of this cock, I open to lick him. The hissing sound that emanates from his throat is exactly what I need to hear.

"Lick her," Lachlan instructs. Someone takes the instruction, running their rough tongue up the seam of my pussy, probing my entrance and flicking at my clit in a crazy rhythm that has me moaning around Lachlan's cock.

"My turn," Cooper says, moving closer on the opposite side of my head.

This is what sharing is about. Patience. Taking turns. Relishing others' pleasure but not being afraid to seek your own.

As I let Lachlan's cock fall from my mouth and turn to Cooper, I take a moment to fully appreciate the nine men around me. They're all in varying stages of undress, as though they grew too distracted to finish the job. Most of them are shirtless, and the sheer number of muscled, tan torsos on show makes my pussy clench. I lick my lips, feeling close to coming just from looking at them and thinking about what their bodies can do to mine. Flashes of our time together one, or two on one, come to mind, and I shiver from the memories alone. Logan is the one between my legs and our eyes meet, both burning with the intensity of intimacy and passion.

Cooper touches the side of my face, eager to feel the hot, wet heat of my mouth. "Ready?" he asks.

"Yes." One little word for an avalanche of pleasure.

I open my mouth, hooking my hand around his ass, staring up past the impossible ridges of his abs to his defined pecs and intense face. He folds his lips in, moistening them, or maybe trying to stifle the noises he wants to make. He tastes sweet and salty, and smells masculine, with a hint of clean soap that makes me want to lean in, take more, swallow him as deep as I can.

Two mouths latch onto my nipples, sucking in alternating pulses that make me squirm against Logan's mouth. He pushes two fingers inside me, curling them up and fucking into me, until I'm coming in a blinding flash. For a moment, I lose control of my body, slipping from Cooper's straining cock, locking my eyes shut so I can drift in the flashing lights of orgasmic oblivion.

Then, before I can fully get my breath back, the rustle of foil, the tear of a pack, and the slick sounds of a cock being sheathed fills the air. At least, I think it's one, but maybe it's more.

Through barely opened eyes, I see Jared and Joshua naked and ready. Joshua lies on the bed next to me and pulls my limp body across his. "Don't worry," he says, stroking back my unruly hair. "We're going to handle this."

I moan loudly as he presses against my hips, spearing my swollen pussy with the iron bar of his cock. I moan even louder as Jared presses against the back of my neck, forcing me to bend over his brother, because I know what's coming next and how amazing it will feel. I know how undone I will be when he forces his cock inside me alongside his brother's, stretching my pussy wide, opening me like a flower in full bloom.

When Jared moves, I groan, and beneath me, Joshua grits his teeth, fighting for control in a situation that feels wild and unbound. Cooper is there, tipping up my chin, bringing his cock back to my lips, filling me to the point of impossibility. Fingers play with my nipples, gripping my breasts as they shake with each thrust. Someone kisses me in the middle of my spine, and it's so gentle, so unbelievably tender, that I cry out.

"That's it," Lachlan says. "Give it to her." The slick sound of him palming his own cock, jerking off to the sight of me being fucked by his friends, is so hot. I'm sure the others who aren't inside me must be doing the same.

I want to wriggle, but I can't. Jared has me fixed in place, using his big hands to hold me firmly against his brother's body.

In my mouth, Cooper's cock seems to swell impossibly large and then, with a groan, he's coating my tongue with his cum, holding me by the hair at the back of my neck to prevent me from stimulating him anymore. I swallow, staring up at the majestic ripples of his body as he experiences the greatest physical high. He flops back onto his heels, cupping his dick in his palm, staring at me as though I just revealed the answer to the universe's greatest question.

On the nightstand, my phone vibrates again, and panic wells inside me. I gaze up at Lachlan, pleading with him to take Cooper's place because when I'm giving these men pleasure, my mind is clear and my heart is full. There's nothing in the world that can break through their shielding presence.

He seems to understand, just from the look in my eyes and moves closer, coating my bottom lip with the slickness on the head of his cock. "You want more?" he asks. "You're a hungry wee lass."

Jared, watching everything, speeds his thrusts, crushing my clit against his brother's body and with a surge of heat, slick with sweat and filled with a desperation I don't fully understand, I come again, just as Jared and Joshua let go too.

Inside me, two cocks pulse, and I wish there were no condoms between us so I could drip their arousal. Lachlan holds me firmly in place, using my mouth to chase the oblivion his friends are currently groaning through.

"You see how good you make us feel," Joshua murmurs, stroking over my back. Jared withdraws from inside me, just as Lachlan grunts his release. He doesn't come in my mouth, though. Instead, he pulls out and coats my arm and shoulder with ribbon upon ribbon.

"You see how amazing you are?" Thomas says, sounding so proud of me, tears singe the back of my throat.

"She does," Logan says, soothingly. His fingers tuck my hair behind my ear, and he gazes down at me, softly. "She knows."

Even though they must all be impatient for their turns, I'm left to relax, with soft strokes to my body and even softer kisses pressed over my skin. Jared and Joshua move away, leaving room for Thomas and Logan to take their places.

"Do you want us to use condoms?" Logan asks, the memory of our night together as fresh as if it happened just an hour ago.

"You don't have to," I whisper.

"Fuck," Thomas mutters, as he pushes his thick cock into my curved fingers, gripping around my hand to show me the pressure he prefers.

Logan, who's lying in front of me, touches my cheek. "Tell me what you want," he urges.

"I don't want to think," I reply, the admission making my throat burn. All decisions weigh on me, even the little ones.

"Hold her hands," Logan instructs Bryce. "Hold her legs." This time, it's Bradley and Cooper who take instruction. Suddenly, I'm pinned beneath Logan, unable to move. He kisses my jawline, slowly tracing my face with his fingers and lips. "We've got you," he says softly. "You don't need to worry about anything."

My phone buzzes again, and I want to scream. I need this so badly, but it's being ruined. "Joshua, could you take my phone and shut it in the bathroom?" I ask. "And Thomas, could you put some music on? Something sexy."

There's no hesitation. My requests are fulfilled, and I'm lost in the dulcet soulful tones of Thomas's playlist. I can slip away from my thoughts and away from any responsibility. I can let these men control my body because ceding all control is what I need to escape.

Logan moves inside me with slow determination, grinding against my clit and thrusting up in a perfect way that makes me close my eyes with sensation. After a few minutes, with Thomas's encouragement, he rolls us to our sides. Thomas presses his body against my back, and his cock slides between the cheeks of my ass.

"We can both be inside you, if you want," he says. His fingers explore in ways that feel filthy and forbidden and I understand what he's asking.

"Do it," I whisper.

Silence spreads in the room as Thomas rolls on a condom. The lubrication will help, but it's not the first time I'll have a cock in my ass. It *is* the first time I'll have one in my pussy at the same time, though.

With experienced fingers, he gradually prepares me, and Logan holds still inside me, his breath raspy with excitement. I shiver with anticipation when his fingers are replaced by the head of his cock. Can I do this? Will my body do what it needs? I hold my breath and bear down, wincing at the breach even though Thomas takes it slow.

"Relax," he whispers. "Your body is mine. It belongs to me. Let me inside."

Goosebumps flair across my skin as his fingers play with my nipples, teasing and pinching with a rhythm that makes me crazy with lust.

"Fuck," someone says from a distant vantage point as

Thomas begins to move slowly in and out. Logan groans as he shifts inside me, and I close my eyes so that I can drift in this safe space between two powerful men who are owning me so thoroughly. There is something so raw about what they're doing to me, about being pinned in place and observed by so many eyes.

Logan tips my chin, urging me to open my eyes, and when I do, I see such intense feelings in him that my heart accelerates. It's not right for him to look at me as though he loves me, but that's how it feels. I stare back, panic surging through me.

Don't love me, I think. *Don't even care about me.* Liking me would be fine. One day, remembering me with fondness would be okay.

But not love.

"You're beautiful," he says.

"Perfect," Thomas agrees.

"You feel so good," Logan breathes, kissing my mouth as Thomas speeds his thrusts.

And oh god, I do feel good, primed and ready to come, powerless to stop what these men are doing to me.

But also too powerless to stop the inevitable bonds that are developing between us.

20

MITCHELL

Watching my friends with Dawn is like an out-of-body experience. I feel disconnected from myself, almost able to feel what they're feeling even though it isn't my hand that touches or my mouth that kisses.

When Logan and Thomas come, leaving Dawn in a boneless, disorientated state, those of us who haven't been involved step back, understanding she needs time before we take our turns.

It feels like an eon since I was with her the first night she started working here. Since then, I've watched each of my friends experience the same heaven that I did, not jealous but craving more for myself. I've grown to care for Dawn in a way that has felt inevitable, from our first interaction where she doused me with drink and set me on fire with a smile.

I've grown to appreciate the way she brings out the best in each of my friends and the way she's bonded us even more as a group. Most of all, I love her sense of humor and the way she can make me laugh over the smallest thing.

Logan lingers the longest, stroking her arm and kissing her hand like he senses she needs affection and care. When he eventually steps aside, I move forward to take his place.

"Dawn, baby," I whisper, kissing her forehead. "Are you ready for more? If not…if it's too much for you…just tell us you're done."

"I'm not done," she says. "I won't be done until the end."

There are still three of us who haven't come yet. Three huge men to wreak havoc on her already satiated body. Does she really want more, or is it simply that she feels she owes us? Or maybe this is a challenge she's set herself?

It's a challenge alright.

"Are you sure?" I roll Dawn onto her back and gently ease her legs open. I expect to find her sore between her legs, and she is swollen there, but seems fine other than the mess my friend has left behind. "Shall I clean you up?" I ask, stroking her hair from her face. She blinks slowly and a flicker of a smile teases the corner of her mouth.

"Does it bother you, because it doesn't bother me?"

"No," I say, meaning it. The men in this room are like brothers to me. There's nothing about sharing this woman with them that worries me in any way.

"I always knew you were a dirty boy." When she winks and bites her bottom lip, the urge to take her hard is overwhelming. "Kiss me, Mitchell," she says. "Like you did that first night."

She remembers.

Even with everyone around us, it still feels just as searching and intimate to move my lips over hers. There's just a small chunk of history between us, but it's enough to make everything feel warm and familiar.

That first night, I went with her favorite sexual position, but tonight, I want something different. I want to watch Dawn move on me. I want to give her control and see her expressions as she builds to orgasm. Most of all, I want to be sure that if she's hurting between her legs, that she can stop when she needs to.

Rolling us both until I'm on my back and Dawn is splayed over me, I push her hair back from her face with both my hands, cupping her cheeks and focusing her attention on me. "I want you to fuck me," I say. "But only if it feels good. If it hurts, stop, and we can find other things to do."

"Feeling lazy?" She swats my pec and then bends to kiss me, capturing my lip between her teeth and holding it. Then, before I have a chance to prepare myself, she shifts so that my cock slides inside her.

Oh god, it feels good. So warm and slippery and tight. I arch my back, gritting my teeth as she begins to roll her hips. I'm not a man who ever has a problem lasting, but with Dawn and everything I've watched my friends do with her, I'm already close.

She arches her back so that her breasts are round and high, and Bryce, too tempted to wait for his turn, moves behind her. When his big rough hand cups her softness, teasing her nipple with sharp pulls, Dawn groans. And when his other hand slides down her belly until his finger is pressed against her clit, she seems to lose control. Slow rolling becomes bucking as her hips piston on my cock. Bryce whispers filthy things in her ear. "That's it. Fuck my friend's cock. Give him that pretty pussy. Let him watch me touch you until you come, then he'll get to feel it, won't he? He'll get to feel that sweet pussy clamping down on his cock."

Dawn groans and mutters expletives under her breath. Her eyes fix on mine for a second and it's like a bolt of lightning, then she tips her head back to the ceiling and cries out loudly. Bryce is right. I do feel it. I feel her pussy rippling so much that I can't hold on anymore.

Coming inside her is like nothing else I've ever known. The instinct to push my cock deep against her cervix is overwhelming.

If Bryce wasn't holding her up, I'm sure Dawn would have fallen against my chest by now. Instead, he grasps her by the hips, pulling her from me until she's sitting on his lap, impaled on his cock. Her eyes widen and glaze with surprise. "That's it," he says. "You don't need to do anything. I'll do it all."

He holds her in place, thrusting from beneath like a jackhammer. With her legs spread, I can see every explicit detail; his cock moving in and out of her pussy, my cum and Logan's dripping from inside her, her clit so swollen it looks painful. Her nipples are red tipped and erect as Bradley crawls in front of her, latching his mouth on to tease them some more.

Dawn's moaning is almost continuous now, as though she's slipped out of conscious reality and into another dimension of white hot pleasure. "Fuck," Bryce gasps. "Fuck."

He comes, pumping Dawn full, gripping her around her chest and stomach, totally possessing every inch of her. And then, in a gesture of pure twin love, he lifts her off his cock and onto Bradley's waiting erection.

Bradley has the compassion to wait for Dawn to catch her breath, kissing her forehead, then her cheeks, then her lips in a cross of affection. With her eyes closed, her expression is relaxed, almost blissed-out. Eventually, she blinks her eyes open, staring first at Bradley, and then twisting to look at us all around the room. I shift until I'm closer and so do Logan and Cooper, sensing that maybe she's had too much. Bradley won't mind. None of us is *that* guy. That's what makes this whole thing work. Our trust for each other. The knowledge that we'll always put

Dawn's first.

"Are you okay?" Logan asks, placing his hand over Dawn's tattoo. The reasons behind it are still a mystery that's driving me crazy. As Dawn nods, I rub my FOMO tattoo, recalling the bite of the needle and my drunken laughter.

The tattoo is a clue. Of that, I'm sure. A clue to a secret. Maybe even a clue to Dawn's heart.

Dawn's hands rest on Bradley's shoulders, and she starts to shift her hips. Her movements are slow, as though she's drunk on what we've done together, but Bradley more than makes up for it.

Watching Dawn's body move makes my cock thicken, ready for more, except there won't be more tonight.

I wonder, if she stayed with us, would she grow better accustomed to so much sex, and be able to handle us all for two rounds? Would a night like this be just for special occasions or every time? I think I'd enjoy a mix of both group, and one-on-one time. This has been the sexiest night ever, but I love the intimacy of being with Dawn and not having to share her.

"Oh god," she groans, grinding harder in Bradley's lap. Is she going to come again? That's got to be a record, or a superpower, or something.

"Shit," Bradley says, as Dawn arches her back and then snaps forward, collapsing against his sweat-slicked chest. Thrusting from beneath, he finishes inside her, clinging to our girl like he's worried she's going to blow away on the breeze.

Our girl.

The words form in my mind so easily, and I wonder if my friends are thinking it too.

I know reality is so much more complex.

As Bradley rests back on both his arms, his chest heaving with exertion, I scoop Dawn off his lap and into my arms, cradling her close.

I kiss her damp forehead and her closed eyelids, savoring the sweet smell of her hair and the raw scent of her skin.

Mine, my mind whispers, and I clear my throat, not wanting to accept the stupidity of my possessiveness. She isn't mine. She isn't even ours.

All of this is just a mirage, moments that will feel like a dream when whatever is temporarily tethering her here comes loose.

"You did so good," I tell her, glancing around the room at my friends. "You did so good."

She makes a soft humming noise and then clears her throat. "I don't suppose any of you happen to have a burger and fries in your back pockets?" And then, like perfectly timed punctuation, her stomach rumbles loudly.

It's a moment of lightheartedness after so much intensity and the effect is magic. Laughter ripples through the group, and Dawn's face is alight as she takes in the effect she has on us.

"I can rustle one up," Bradley says, patting her affectionately on the ass.

"How about rustling up ten?" Lachlan says, and we all laugh again, including Dawn.

Half an hour later, we all sit around in various stages of undress, stuffing our faces with juicy burgers and crispy French fries, laughing, and joking without a care in the world.

But that all changes in a flash.

21

COOPER

The sound of glass splintering, and a loud thud interrupts our middle-of-the-night feast. Me and Lachlan are the first to react, sprinting towards the noise, and looking frantically for the source. The office window is shattered. Lachlan unlocks and bursts into the room, swearing loudly and grabbing for the brick resting in the center of the floor, the implement that caused the damage, picking it up before I can tell him to leave it where it is as evidence.

"This is Barrow," I spit. "It has to be."

"Gutless bastard," Lachlan growls, resting the brick on the desk and shuffling the glass aside with the toe of his foot.

"It's a message."

"Aye. Cooperate or else."

Dawn is next to reach the scene, closely followed by Mitchell and Jared and the rest. "What the hell?"

Lachlan looks up and as his eyes meet with Dawn's, his shoulders lower and his expression relaxes just a fraction.

She has such a calming effect on him and it's a big relief to us all. The last thing we need is him lashing out and damaging his hand again, or something worse. We need to keep our heads while this situation is playing out. If not, we won't have a chance of getting through it. "We need the CCTV," he says.

"Fuck" Mitchell growls, taking a seat behind the desk. "If we had it fitted, we might have the evidence we need to implicate Barrow."

"We need to get this window repaired," I say. "I'll organize that."

"What, so someone can toss another brick through it?" Jared snarls.

"We're going to need to take shifts to patrol the property," Lachlan says. "Now we know Barrow is going to use threatening tactics. We can't risk being caught out again."

"We can do that," I say. "There are enough of us."

"Maybe you should go in pairs," Dawn says, her eyes scanning the group as her brow pulls into a concerned frown.

"We'll work it out." Lachlan takes a seat on the corner of the desk and runs his hand over his face. "We need to meet with the lawyer. We can't put it off anymore. I didn't want to have to pay when none of this is our fault, but we're going to have to."

"Yeah. Don't worry about the money for now. We have to defend our business. Whatever it takes." Mitchell rises from the chair and claps Lachlan on the shoulder. "That's the benefit of there being nine of us. Nine against the world."

"Ten," Dawn says. "At least for now."

All of us turn to face the girl who made our hearts soar for just a moment before dropping us back to earth.

"Ten," Mitchell says, ignoring the last part of her

statement.

She smiles, and it's warm, but her eyes seem sad, like she knows something we don't. Maybe she has a return ticket and hasn't told us? Maybe there's a date already set in concrete and we're just oblivious, falling deeper and harder for her.

"I'll go get the broom," she says, resting her hand gently on Lachlan's knee as she passes. I watch her walk out the door, feeling as though each step she takes is leading her out of our lives and not just to the cleaning cupboard.

"For now," Mitchell says, shaking his head. "Those are not the words I wanted to hear."

"Nothing's happened yet," Lachlan says, his hand curling around the edge of the desk, gripping so tightly his knuckles are the color of bone.

"We have to focus on the business," I say. "But not at the expense of the rest of our lives."

Dawn returns before he has a chance to reply, but I know he understands what I mean.

I take the broom from Dawn even though she objects and begin to sweep the sharp shards of glass into a pile. Mitchell brings a bag to collect it all, and between us we make quick work of the cleanup.

We find tape and a board to secure the window until the glazing repair man can come in the morning.

I don't sleep well, even though I know Mitchell and Lachlan have stayed up to patrol Cloud 9 like it's Fort Knox. When the sun rises, I groan, throwing my arms behind my head and arching my back into a stretch. I imagine Dawn somewhere beyond the walls of my room, curled up asleep, her hair spread across her pillow like an angel fallen from heaven. Did she sleep peacefully, or did she lie awake worrying about the brick and what Barrow might do next? Did she spend time imagining leaving this place?

I tear the sheets from my body and stalk to the shower, hating the idea of her room being empty and what the bar will be like when she's no longer bringing laughter and joy to everything we do.

I scrub the dirt from my body and try to slough the worry from my mind. There's still time to make Dawn see that this place is her home, not just for vacation, but forever. There's still time for her to realize she doesn't have to travel the world to make good on her tattooed promise.

At breakfast, we all talk about the incident and who has done what since.

"The glass guy is coming out around three pm," I say.

"Me and Logan have time with the lawyer at one pm," Lachlan confirms.

"The police are coming this morning," Mitchell says. "They couldn't give me a specific time."

"We're going to have to get really organized before shift today." Lachlan bites at his finger, his nerves showing through. "Jared and Logan are going to patrol, so we'll be two down."

"I have a friend coming tonight, but she won't be a problem. She's been going through a tough time and just needs to get out and be amongst good people, so I told her to come here," Dawn says.

"What's your friend's name?" Bryce asks.

"Chantelle. She's from here." Dawn nods.

"Ah…a fellow Aussie," Thomas says with a smile.

"Yeah, be kind because she needs it."

Despite the stressful situation we're all living in, conversation moves to lighter topics. I sit back and watch my friends discuss anything and everything, and marvel at how easily Dawn manages to keep up the conversation. I start to imagine what it would be like if she stays and these mornings all together become our every day. It's an idea that takes root inside me, one that I know I shouldn't keep to myself.

Dawn's tattoo flashes into my mind. YOLO. It's such a stupid saying, but I get it. I'm still a young man, but I can feel life speeding up. The last year has passed by in a flash. It feels easy to let days go by, and then all of a sudden, find that I haven't really noticed or marked the time at all.

I don't want Dawn to become one of the people who passes in and out and I need to know how my friends feel about her, too.

When the food is all eaten, Dawn returns to her room, and I take my opportunity.

"I really like her," I say, scanning the faces of each of my friends for their reactions. There are nods of agreement all around, which only confirms the rightness of what I want to say. "I know this isn't a regular situation…all of us with one girl. But I think it could work. We all get on great and run this business without any issues. Everyone warned us at the start that financial commitments can ruin friendships, but we didn't listen. We were confident that we could work together, and I'm confident we can handle this too."

"I am too," Bryce says, running his hand over his chin. "If the rest are, the main issue I think we're going to find is with Dawn."

"Yeah," Logan says. "I don't think it's in Dawn's plans to settle down. She's here temporarily, and she lives her life one day at a time. I think she'd run at the first hint that we're thinking about this thing between us as anything other than a short-term fling."

"Logan's right," Mitchell says. "She's a butterfly. Her presence here is only temporary. We just have to make the most of whatever time we get."

"That isn't good enough for me," I say, frustrated. It's not that I don't agree with my friends. They're reinforcing my existing doubts. I'm not the kind of man to give up before I've even tried. Love is important to me. It's the reason for existing. If I have to fight for it, I will. If I have to work to convince Dawn that this is where she's meant to be and we are who she's meant to be with, I will.

If I have to do it on my own, I'll do that too.

But I'd rather have my friends with me. I want us to do this together.

"She knows it can work," I say, when no one responds. "Her friend is already in a poly relationship."

"Yeah, but knowing it can work for someone else and believing it can work for you is something totally different," Thomas says. He leans forward in his chair, tearing pieces off a napkin and piling them neatly in front of him. "If she doesn't want it, we're not going to be able to make her. She's too stubborn for that."

"She is," I smile. "It's one of the things I love about her."

I don't miss the surprise in the eyes of some of the men gathered around me. Love is a big word and not one that any of us has spoken for a long time, if ever. "We won't have a chance if we're not firmly united in trying," I say. "She has to know that we're rock solid. Even a hint of uncertainty will only reinforce her reasons for moving on."

"I want her to stay," Lachlan says, in a surprising outburst of emotion. "It was good before her but it's better with her here."

"Are you sure you think this can work?" Bradley asks. "I mean, I can see it being something good in the short term. But can you see it long term? If she agrees to stay, and that's a big if, she'll want kids at some point. She'll want to get married because that's what people do. What will happen then?"

"Not everyone wants to get married," I say. "And kids won't be a problem. At least one of us will be up to the job."

There are snorts of laughter from around the group as we all remember the other night and what it was like for all of us to be with Dawn at the same time. Without latex barriers and oral contraception she'd get pregnant in a flash.

"What if she misses home too much?" Bradley asks.

"You miss home," I say. He nods, running his hand over his chin. "But you choose to stay because you love it here more."

"It's not an easy choice," he says. "It's not easy to accept that you're going to feel torn your whole life."

"It's not easy to leave something great behind either," I say. "And this thing between us is great. Better than I ever could have imagined."

Bradley nods, and settles back in his chair, tipping his face to the sky and inhaling a deep breath. I guess I didn't realize how much him choosing to stay here has been a challenge. In a way, that's what will make this relationship between us all so much stronger. Having lots of different perspectives will mean we're always able to focus on what's important and proactively face off any issues before they become serious.

"So, we try?" Lachlan asks hopefully.

"We try," I say, breathing out in relief.

Later that night, when Cloud 9 is buzzing, I take over from Thomas's relaxed live set to play the more upbeat music our bar is known for. It takes a lot of concentration to blend music seamlessly, but I've been doing it for enough years that I'm confident with my abilities. I don't need to focus one hundred percent of my attention, so I watch as Dawn welcomes her friend and settles her at the end of the bar. Chantelle is pretty but doesn't draw my attention from Dawn. It makes me realize just how much I feel for her, even after such a short time.

Dawn has to work, but while she's waiting for Lachlan and Jared to fulfill orders, she laughs and jokes with her friend. Jared keeps Chantelle company when Dawn is serving tables, and it seems as though she's having a good time.

At the end of the evening, as the bar is emptying out, I notice a man walking past the bar and looking in. For a second, I don't think anything of it, but then I remember what's been going on and my senses are alerted. It's late for someone to come to Cloud 9 from work. It's late for that kind of business attire.

I squint, trying to make out if the man is coming into the bar or just looking from the outside. I wave at Dawn to get her attention, pointing to where I'd last seen the man. She glances back at me with wide eyes. "It's him," she mouths.

Pointing to the bar, I indicate that she should tell Jared before Lachlan, but by the time she makes it through the gathered customers, the man has already taken a seat at the end of the bar. I put the music on auto-play, not caring that the tracks won't mix. After the brick, Lachlan isn't going to be able to hold his temper and we can't risk being on the wrong side of the law with this man.

I rest my headphones onto a hook, and I sprint over to the bar, watching as Jared tries to get around Lachlan. I manage to get behind the bar as Jared tells the man that he's not welcome. Lachlan, noticing what's happening, moves closer just as I get my hand on his shoulder. He whirls to me, but I hold firm.

Dawn is on the other side of the bar, standing next to her friend.

"I'll take a whisky," the man says.

"I told you, you're not welcome."

"What kind of bar is this?" the man sneers. "The kind of bar that needs to be closed down for poor service."

"The service is great," Dawn says. "For customers who aren't assholes."

"You should reign that bitch in," Jeffrey Barrow says, jutting his chin at Dawn. My blood pulses in my temples, a hot flush of rage surging over my whole body.

Dawn's friend places a hand on Dawn's shoulder, turning her away. I think it's because she doesn't want Dawn to do anything stupid, but there are tears in her eyes.

Dawn seems confused, but leans into her friend, asking what's wrong.

I swivel, finding Jared leaning across the bar, telling Jeffrey to leave.

His smug face splits into an amused smirk that makes me want to pound his flesh with my fists until all that's left is a bloody, fractured pulp. How is this the way that people do business? Is it seriously the men who act like this who get their way in the world? It's a depressing thought.

Jeffrey backs away from the bar slowly, his face still twisted into a grin that sends a shiver of awareness over my skin. Dawn has pulled her friend into a hug that I don't understand. Did something else happen that I didn't see?

I rest my hand on Dawn's shoulder and lean in to ask her if everything's okay. She draws back from her friend, her expression grave.

"Chantelle used to work for Jeffrey Barrow," she says quickly. "He sexually assaulted her and then threatened her when she said she planned to expose him."

"He did what?" My head snaps back to the last place Jeffrey was standing, but he's gone. Before I can run after him, Dawn's hand fixes on my shoulder.

"Leave it, Cooper. For now, at least."

When I turn and find Chantelle with her head buried in her hands and her hair hanging to conceal her face, I understand. She's too distraught and Dawn wants to find out more. The only way to do that is to give Chantelle time to calm down.

For a second, a swell of hope that this piece of information could be enough to get Jeffrey off all of our backs floods my mind. But then I realize that it's Chantelle's trauma, and maybe she'll never want to face the repercussions of taking on a man like Barrow. Maybe it's another sign that we don't have a hope of trying to resist him.

If he has his sights set on Cloud 9, maybe it'll be impossible to protect it.

22

DAWN

I lead Chantelle out of the bar to the chill-out area at the back. She's still trembling, even though Barrow left the bar over fifteen minutes ago. "He's gone," I confirm again, trying to reassure her as she slumps onto a bean-bag chair and swipes at her tear-streaked face.

"I can't believe he's the one who's trying to ruin your friends' business," she says. "I wish I could give you better news, but Barrow just doesn't give up. He's like a shark with razor-sharp teeth. He'll do anything, and I mean anything, to get his way."

I take a seat on the beanbag opposite but lean forward and rest my hand on her leg. "He shouldn't be able to keep getting away with it," I say. "He shouldn't get to walk around doing whatever the hell he wants and damned the repercussions on anyone who gets in his path."

"He shouldn't," Chantelle says, rubbing the back of her hand across her blotchy cheeks. "You don't know how many times I've tried to convince myself to go to the police about what he did to me. But I'm not brave enough. For all I know, he could have the local police in his pocket. If you have money, you have influence and control. I don't have money. I'm a nobody, and Jeffrey Barrow is friends with so many people in high places...and low places too."

"Maybe if you just talked to someone at the station, off the record. There might be other people who've done the same. If there's enough smoke, maybe they'll try looking for the fire."

She shakes her head. "I'm too scared, Dawn. I'm not brave like you."

My throat swallows involuntarily because I'm not brave. I'm scared, just like she is. Scared to face the possible truth. Scared to find out if my life might be heading in a direction I'm not strong enough to deal with.

"It's okay," I soothe. "You don't have to do anything you don't want to do."

Although it would help us all at Cloud 9 if Barrow was pulled up on sexual assault or harassment charges, I'm not going to push Chantelle to do anything she isn't comfortable with. That would make me as bad as Jeffrey. I wouldn't want that man's wrath directed at me, so I can't expect Chantelle to shoulder the risk, either.

But something has to be done.

My phone vibrates in my pocket and when I pull it out to see who's calling, I find three missed calls from my dad. Just the sight of his name and what it represents is enough to have my heart skittering. The longer I avoid talking to him, the angrier he's going to get, and I don't blame him. I made a promise and I'm breaking it with every day that passes.

All it would take is one little phone call. I'd get dad off my back in less than five minutes. But that five minutes could change my life forever. I know he's only hassling me because he loves me. I understand that, but I'm not ready to know what he wants me to find out. I just need more time.

More time for what? I hear the words in Dad's frustrated voice and go cold all over.

To live my life unburdened. Is that even what I'm doing?

I need to escape. I need oblivion and that's what I have here. Nine men to take me to another place where I don't have to worry about my dad's frustration or my avoidance of the burden of truth.

I understand Chantelle's desire to just put all her troubles behind her, safely tucked up in the bed of the past. I understand her avoidance of potential repercussions. We're not all brave enough to head into every problem headlong and without concern for the consequences.

"Do you need to call someone back?" Chantelle asks softly, and I blink up at her, realizing I drifted away on my own reflections.

"No," I say. "Not right now."

She smiles a sad smile. "I just wish life was simpler. I wish there weren't problems or people like Jeffrey. I wish I didn't have to *adult* all the time."

I snort, leaning back in the beanbag chair and staring up into the starlight sky. "Adulting sucks balls," I say loudly, and we both burst into fits of emotion-laden laughter, wobbling on the precipice of crying for different reasons.

Tonight, when the bar is closed, I think all my men will need the escape of sexual oblivion. They'll all need a chance to feel powerful and strong, and I'll revel in feeling owned by nine gorgeous men. Between them, they can erase all my worries, and maybe, for a time, I'll be able to erase theirs.

I chill with Chantelle, exchanging stories, until the bar

is closed and the men who are going to take me to the cloud nine in the sky all appear. They're tense and worried, evident in the bunch of their shoulders and furrowed brows, but they still greet me with relieved smiles. Logan arranges a cab for Chantelle and when I've hugged her goodbye and she's making her way safely home, I lead nine men into the comfortable safety of my room, and we all get lost in a place the rest of the world can't touch us.

23

DAWN

I wake feeling used in the best possible way. I can't even count the ways the nine men in my life gave me pleasure. It involved more than nine orgasms. I managed to keep track of that part, at least.

I open my bleary eyes and find Thomas' arm across my naked belly and Logan's leg anchoring mine. God only knows the state of my hair right now, and I stink of sex.

Everything feels bruised and sore, even my heart.

There was so much care and affection in their touch, as well as passion and desire. I lost count of the number of times I felt tears well behind my eyes because of the tender way they treated me. I've seen enough gang bang porn to know how awful and used nine men could make a woman feel. But my nine men know exactly how to please me, and exactly how to make me feel treasured.

I shift until I manage to get out from Thomas and Logan's limbs, and head to the shower for a quick freshen up. When I emerge smelling of strawberries rather than cum, I find the boys are still sleeping.

My stomach growls, demanding food after so much physical exertion, so I decide to head to the kitchen area to rustle up some breakfast. Nothing, apart from hot, filthy sex, satisfies a man more than good food.

When I tiptoe out of the room, closing the door quietly behind me, I spot two huge suitcases resting next to an occupied hammock. Did someone arrive in the night and Lachlan forgot about their booking? That wouldn't be like him at all. Then again, with all the distraction and stress from last night playing on everyone's minds, nothing would surprise me.

When I get closer, I see familiar looking hair spilling over a familiar looking sleeping face.

"Oh-my-god…KYLA!"

I scream the last part, the shock of seeing my friend so far from home exploding out of me in a rush. She jumps, her limbs scrambling in a comical way that tips her half out of the hammock, and I have to catch her before she face-plants.

"DAWN!" she yells, wobbling as I drag her to her feet. We fall into each other and hug like it's been a lifetime apart rather than a few weeks.

"What the hell are you doing here?" I squeal into her hair. She smells good. Familiar. Of happy memories and more fun than I could ever recall.

We jump up and down, still hugging and squealing like crazy people. By the time we disengage, still clutching each other by the arms and staring with wide excited eyes, Joshua, Jared, Thomas and Logan have all appeared in different stages of undress.

Kyla's eyes bug out at the sight of bulging muscles and tan skin. "Who are they?" she whispers conspiratorially.

"My fuck buddies," I laugh.

"Four of them?" Her surprised eyebrows make me

snort with laughter. From anyone else, I'd accept the surprise that I have four lovers, but not from Kyla.

"Nine," I say, nodding my head proudly.

She swivels her head quickly to take them in in more detail. "Of course you'd have to one up me."

"It was not my intention, but it turns out the bar is named after the men."

"Of course it is."

"I'm okay," I call out. "This is my best friend from back home, Kyla."

They all nod, and wave, then look down, realizing they're standing in the open in their underwear. "Go dress," I say. "I'm making breakfast."

"You sure you want to tread on the B twins' toes?" Jared asks.

"Absolutely," I confirm.

"The B twins?" Kyla asks, as I lead her to the outdoor kitchen.

"Bryce and Bradley from Texas," I say.

"Seriously. You're banging two southern boys?"

"And two London boys. And a Scot. And five Aussies."

She shakes her head. "Only you, Dawn. Only you."

"Why the hell didn't you call me when you arrived?" I ask, running my hands down her arms, still not quite believing she's really in front of me.

"I wanted to surprise you, but my flight was delayed and then my transfer took forever, and by the time I arrived it was the middle of the night, so I just hung out in a hammock."

"I love those hammocks," I admit, leading Kyla to the kitchen area. She looks around, taking in the bench tables and the long stainless steel counter where Bryce and

Bradley make their magic. I reach into the fridge to pull out eggs and milk. These lucky boys are going to be fed with my momma's pancakes today. "I can't believe you're actually here."

Kyla takes a seat at the counter and watches me crack eggs into a huge mixing bowl. "Me either," she says. "I think it's going to take me a while to clear my foggy head of jet lag. How many pancakes do you need to make?"

We both stare at the epic number of eggs I'm about to crack. "Enough to sink a small ship," I say. "These men put away so much food. It's a constant battle to keep up."

"Yeah. I bet they need more after you've worn them out."

I toss some flour at my friend, and she ducks, missing the worst of it but still ending up with a white powdery shoulder.

"This is coming from the girl who met her life partners through a giant, kinky sex game."

"Encouraged by you." She points at me, aghast.

"It was still you who did it." I shake my head. "Bad girl."

Rather than denying it, Kyla grins and nods. "Yeah, that sounds about right. It's good being bad. Isn't it?"

"Hell, yeah! It's the best."

I start to whisk the batter until it is smooth and creamy, adding salt and a good measure of cinnamon at the end. The rounds sizzle when they hit the hot buttered surface, and I watch as bubbles begin to rise to the top.

"I haven't had your mom's pancakes in years," Kyla says softly. "Have you made them for the boys before?"

"No," I say, meeting her eyes and seeing cautious sadness there. She wants to talk but is worried it might hurt me. "First time I've made them in years."

"That's good," she says brightly. "Good, that you're

189

ready to remember the good stuff."

I nod, realizing she's right. For whatever reason, I've taken a small step forward to being able to remember Mom without clamming up or withdrawing. I'm able to share something nice about her with others.

Flipping the pancakes, I reach for a platter to lay them on when they're done. By the time I've prepared the first batch, Jared, Joshua, Thomas and Logan are back, this time showered and wearing appropriate clothes to meet someone new. I formally introduce each of them to Kyla, stifling a giggle as she looks them over like prime beef.

"So this is *the* Kyla?" Jared asks, eying her with one raised eyebrow. To an outsider, Kyla doesn't appear like the kind of woman who'd be interested in having a harem of men. Even though she slept in her clothes, she's still so neatly put together in her beige slacks and cream linen blouse that she'd fit in better at the country club than in a tattoo parlor with eight lovers.

"This is *the* Kyla," I confirm, and Jared reaches out to shake her hand.

"Can I just say a big thank you for being the one to pioneer the one-woman-many-men relationship? We are very grateful that Dawn is following your example."

"I'm sure you are." Kyla winks at me as Jared pumps her hand up and down enthusiastically. "And you should probably thank a woman called Natalie Monk because she was the first woman in the Reverse Harem Ladies Club. That's how me and Dawn found our original inspiration."

"There's a club?" Thomas asks, opening the fridge door and pulling out a huge bowl of blueberries. Logan finds plates and silverware and Joshua hunts for the maple syrup. The men are stabbing pancakes and heaping them onto their plates so fast, I can't keep up.

Logan, being a total sweetie, fixes Kyla a plate and slides it down the counter.

By the time the rest of the Cloud 9 crew emerge from their bedrooms at the sound of chatter and laughter, everyone is sipping coffee and devouring breakfast.

Bradley and Bryce follow the scent of pancakes and peer at the new batch. "Is this your recipe?" Bradley asks.

"It sure is," I reply. I wish I could tell him it's Mom's. I may be ready to use her recipe, but I'm not ready to talk about her openly with people who never knew her.

"They smell so good," he says, inhaling a lungful of scented air.

"You can have the next batch," I laugh as he wraps his arm around my waist and kisses me like an overenthusiastic puppy. I love that he doesn't point out that my pancakes aren't all exactly the same size or shape. He doesn't brag about his cheffy skills, just appreciates my efforts. When he takes a bite and his eyes roll in ecstasy, I want to hug him so tight. Mom would have loved him. She'd have loved them all. She probably would have questioned the sanity of sleeping with so many men at once, though.

Just thinking about her smiling face makes me sad. At Christmas, she'd make these pancakes but decorate them like a grinning Santa head with strawberries for his mouth and hat, whipped cream for the snowy trim and beard, and chocolate drops for his eyes. She did so many amazing things for me when I was a child. Things I wish I could remember without wanting to bawl.

"You'd better flip those," Kyla says, and I realize I've been frozen for a while, lost in my memories, ignoring the task at hand.

I flip the slightly overcooked pancakes, just as my phone begins to ring and vibrate against the counter. Before I can ask Kyla to pass it, she's picked it up and answered it.

"Hi Mr. Mitchell," she says, happily, meeting my eyes.

"Yes, I got here safely. I'm with Dawn right now. She's busy flipping pancakes."

For the few seconds she's talking to Dad without a care in the world, my chest caves in. My breath is trapped in my lungs, and my hand forms a claw around the utensil.

"Thanks. Yes. It's going to be awesome. At least it will be once I get over my jetlag…I'll pass you over."

She holds out my phone to me and I stare at it like it's a vial of deadly disease. I stare because I don't know what to do. I can't face Dad. Not now. Not when I don't know what to say. Not when anything I do say will only make him mad.

I don't want to face his questions surrounded by these men. I don't want them to see me vulnerable and upset. Our relationship is all about fun. Seizing the day. Taking the chance to live our best life.

Not facing up to our greatest fears. Not arguing with our one surviving parent. Not being an awful selfish person.

I drop the turner and it clatters when it falls.

I don't realize I'm running until I'm halfway to my room and everyone has stopped talking.

Tears stream down my cheeks and I fumble to open the lock so I can hide away and deal with this embarrassing breakdown.

I slump onto my bed and cry harder than I have in a long time.

24

JARED

As Dawn runs away, Kyla immediately pushes back her chair to make after her. Before she can fully rise, I grab hold of her arm.

"Kyla, what's going on?"

Her hands fly to her mouth as though she's suddenly realized something or recalled a previously forgotten piece of information. "Nothing. I just..." she stutters, staring at me and then after Dawn as though she has no idea what to do or who she should be speaking to.

"What's going on with Dawn? Who was that on the phone?"

"I can't..." she starts, staring at my hand where it's still gripping her arm. I let go, even though I don't want her to leave yet. This feels like a pivotal moment where we could find out whatever it is that's making Dawn live each day as though it's her last.

"You can," I say. "If you know something, you should tell us, for Dawn. She's hiding something. We know that much. We care about her, and we're worried about her. We can't be there for her if we don't know what's happening in her life."

"You care about her?" Kyla slumps back into her seat, rubbing her hands over her weary stressed face.

"We care about her. We want what you have. We want that with Dawn, but she's running from something. She pastes on a smile to cover her true feelings because there's something going on," I continue.

Kyla scans the expressions of the rest of my friends, as though she wants to check I'm really speaking for them all. Whatever she finds on their faces must be enough.

"It was the anniversary of Dawn's mom's death a few days ago," she says softly, worrying at a hangnail on the side of her ring finger. Her dad called...she promised him that she would do something...she hasn't done it. I shouldn't have picked up the phone."

"What did she promise to do?" I ask, not interested in the politics of whether picking up someone else's phone is right or wrong.

"I can't tell you that," she says softly. Her eyes seem to implore me not to ask more, but I'm persistent when I want to be.

"You can tell us," I say. "You need to tell us."

"If Dawn wanted you to know...if she trusted you to share...she would have told you everything. I can't make that decision for her. Not about something like this."

"Please," I say, knowing I'm losing the battle but needing to try everything before I give up.

"I can't." She blinks her soft brown eyes at me, folding in her lips apologetically, effectively ending our conversation.

"You should go after her," I say eventually, wanting Dawn to have the support of her friend if she can't have our support. I grip the arm of my chair, frustration bubbling through me. Dawn won't tell us. Kyla won't tell us. Dawn is slipping through our fingers, and we can't do a thing about it.

When Kyla is out of earshot, I lock eyes with my twin. Joshua's face is as grim as mine. "She's running from something," he says.

"Something to do with her dad."

Logan looks thoughtful, gnawing on his bottom lip. "All you guys should understand the need to get away," he says. "Isn't that why you all ended up here? None of you planned to stay in Byron. You were all just passing through. Even I ended up joining with you guys to open this place because I needed to move out of home. We should all understand the desire for a fresh start. We might want Dawn to be a part of our group, but it has to be what she wants, not just because she's trying to escape from her real life."

His words hit the group hard enough to render us all silent. I do understand the need to get away. I understand the need to explore and become an adventurer, if only for a while. This place is my home now and I'm settled, but there is still a part of me that wants to wander and see new things. Maybe Dawn's the same. Maybe she'll never be happy resting her hat in one place.

Logan might be right.

But I'm not a quitter. I believe that life can become something we shape rather than something we sit back and allow to form.

Dawn might not want to share what she's avoiding, but I will find out. Whatever it takes, I'll find out.

25

DAWN

Kyla doesn't immediately search me out, which I'm grateful for. I don't want her to find me in a blotchy, tear-stained heap. But I know it probably means that she's talking with everyone, most probably talking about me, and that I don't like.

The boys will definitely want to know why I'm upset, but will Kyla tell them? I doubt it. She knows how private I am about my personal life. She'll figure out they don't know about anything serious, and she'll make excuses. She'll keep my secret because that's the kind of friend she is.

Eventually, when I've wept until there aren't any tears left and I have a pounding headache, I sit up, head to the bathroom and wash my face. As I'm drying it on a comforting soft white towel, there's a knock at the door.

"Who is it?" I call out.

"It's me," she says. "Let me in."

As soon as I open the door, Kyla barrels in and pulls

me into a fierce hug. "I'm so sorry, Dawn. I'm so sorry. I didn't realize. I'm so dumb, I just didn't think about the timing. I didn't put two and two together."

"You mean, you didn't figure out that I'm in Australia to avoid my dad?"

She shakes her head. "I thought you were looking for some adventure. I've been so wrapped up in my own complicated life that I just didn't think. I'm so sorry." Pulling me tighter against her, she pats my shoulder. "You know, you should talk to me about this stuff. I'm always around, even when I'm on the other side of the planet."

"I know," I say. "But I've been okay."

"Okay?" She pulls back, studying my face. "You mean you've been okay while you've had your head firmly in the sand?"

"The sand is very soft," I say. "I like the sand."

Kyla shrugs, brushing her hand over her arm and trying to avoid eye contact with me. "You can't run forever, Dawn. You know that, right?"

"Running's fun. Haven't you heard? It helps to keep us fit."

"Very funny."

I take a step back and perch on the edge of my mattress, my muscles and bones feeling suddenly weary and weak. Rubbing my hands over my face, I grimace at the puffiness left behind by my tears. What must Kyla think? It's her first day here and before I've even had a chance to catch up on her news, I'm having an emotional breakdown.

She takes a seat next to me and rests her hand on my leg. "You know, you should be honest with those men out there. They obviously care about you a lot, and yet you're hiding this important thing that's happening to you."

"I can't," I whisper. "That's not how things are between us. We're just not on that page."

"I think you are," Kyla says, squeezing my knee. "At least, I think *they* are."

Turning my head to look at her, I blink in surprise. "You think they are?"

"Yeah." She nods to emphasize the point and I really look at my friend, feeling like I'm seeing her for the first time. Gone is the shy, insecure Kyla. She's been replaced by a self-assured woman, ready to give me difficult advice without worrying about the consequences. Advice is usually my area of expertise. "They're worried about you, honey. They're ready to shoulder some of your troubles."

"It's just sex," I say.

"Really? That hug you got didn't look just like sex to me. I saw all the lingering looks they gave you, and the small affectionate touches. You all move in sync, anticipating each other's moves. It's how I am with my men."

I shake my head, denial coming easy. "Your situation is totally different, Kyla. You wanted to fall in love. You were looking for a relationship. I couldn't be further from that place if you tossed me into space."

Kyla folds her lips and raises her eyebrows. My friend doesn't believe me, but that's okay. It doesn't matter. It won't change anything at all. "If you don't want to talk to them, at least let me help you. I can stay with you while you call the doctor."

I don't want to fight with her, but that's what's going to happen if we continue any further down this road. "You know what? We should spend the day at the beach today. I'm not needed here until later. It's really beautiful."

Her pretty chocolate colored eyes search my face, but I stand quickly before she can make any assessment. "Okay. Sure. That sounds good."

"Drag your suitcases in here. You can stay with me."

"Lachlan offered me a room in the hostel," she says

198

quickly. "I don't want to disrupt your time here…you know…be the world's biggest cock-block."

I snort, shocked at her quick turnaround to humor, and grateful too. "I'm sure if I need some cock, I can go to someone else's room."

"As long as it's not right next to this one, that'll be fine with me."

"You don't want to hear the grunting and groaning of more than ten orgasms?" I ask.

"Believe me, I have that shit ringing in my ears already."

We both double over with laughter, but even though I can have this happy moment with my friend, it does nothing but paper over the burden I'm currently carrying.

Spending the day at the beach with Kyla is so much fun. We sunbathe in bikinis, gossiping and eating chips and candy. I get a chance to forget about my worries, forget about what's happening with Cloud 9 and Barrow, and just be a lucky woman on holiday with a friend.

"Who's the brooding one?" Kyla asks me.

"You mean, who's most like Carl?"

"Yeah."

"That would be Lachlan."

"The Scottish one?" She lets the white sand trickle through her fingers, staring into space as though she's thinking about Carl back home and missing him.

"Yeah. He actually reminds me of Carl a lot."

"Does he spank you?" Kyla asks, blushing when she realizes she's revealed a little more about her relationship with Carl than she intended.

"Yeah. How did you know?"

"The bossy controlling ones seem to like a little

199

spanking."

We giggle and I roll onto my front, resting up on my elbows so I can scan the beach. "Mitchell reminds me of Noah."

"Do you have a matching man for each of mine?"

"Probably." I poke the sand with my finger, making a hole, before smoothing it over, wishing that real life troubles could be so easily mended. In the distance, I spot Jared and Joshua, heading down the beach with their boards. "Oh, and I have one spare."

"Oooo…A different one. Which one's that?"

I swat my friend's arm, watching as she follows my gaze. "I don't know. I haven't compared our boyfriends one for one. Is it just me who's finding this conversation weird?"

"Lex has a thing for food. Does Bradley?"

"And Bryce. Jared and Joshua have a hard-on for surfing."

"Yeah, I don't have any men like that. Mine have a hard-on for tattoos and me!"

We laugh as I watch Jared and Joshua jog into the water with their boards under their arms. In their wetsuits, their muscular bodies are perfectly outlined, leaving nothing to the imagination.

"Did you manifest all this?" Kyla asks me, frowning at the horizon where more surfers gather waiting for the perfect wave.

"Manifest?"

"Yeah. You know…the huge trend for positive thinking. You imagine yourself getting everything you want, and the universe sends it to you. Like a magnet attracting pins and nails."

"You think I jetted halfway across the world and imagined gathering a harem of nine men and a bar?"

"I don't know. That's why I'm asking. It seems like a huge coincidence that this would happen to you too. An amazing coincidence," she adds quickly. "Although, a home-grown harem might have been better for the long term, you know, for when you come back."

"I wish life was so easy," I say, sitting up and hugging my sun-warmed legs. I find Jared, or maybe Joshua, standing on his board as a wave pushes him toward the shore. It's as though he's floating over the water, a master over nature. His brother follows almost exactly mimicking his movements, and I remember how they were with me the first time we were together. Like two sides of the same coin, always in sync with each other.

"You wish you could manifest the things you want?" Kyla moves to sit like me, her gaze following mine.

"The things I want seem to come easy to me," I say. "It's me who isn't easy."

Kyla's silent for a while and I know she's working hard to find the right words. She's cautious where I'm forthright, kind when I'm no nonsense. "They're really good at that, aren't they?" she says, eventually.

"They're really good at a lot of things."

"I'm happy for you," Kyla says softly. "Maybe you didn't manifest them. Maybe the universe sent you exactly what you needed."

"If the universe thinks I need a fuck ton of great sex, I'm happy to leave myself in the universe's hands." I grab two big handfuls of sand and toss them towards the lapping ocean, and Kyla does the same.

"The universe definitely thinks I need a fuck ton of great sex," she says. "In fact, I'm enjoying having some time to myself. I mean, I love those men, and I'll never get tired of all the ways they make me feel good, but it's nice to have some time to myself, and nice to spend it with you. I've missed this."

We grin at each other, and memories of our friendship over the years warm my heart.

I needed this time with my bestie, and I wonder if Kyla's right. Did I manifest her? Did the universe send her to me exactly when I needed her? However she ended up down under, I'm happy.

We chill at the beach together, soaking up the sun, enjoying the waves and mostly laughing in each other's company.

When Jared and Joshua leave the beach, Lachlan appears. He keeps a respectful distance, waving as he runs into the water, his big, muscular body cutting through the frothing surf and disappearing beneath the waves. He swims out to the horizon, almost disappearing from sight, and I watch him worried, trying to focus on Kyla's news about her job at Ink Factor, and failing. Eventually, I spot him swimming to the shore and he reappears with a heaving chest and water dripping from his dark hair. He smiles briefly in our direction, and raises his right hand in a quick wave, then he dries off and leaves the beach.

Around thirty minutes later, Bryce and Bradley stroll past as though they have nothing better to do than walk the beach in the middle of the day. They say hi but don't linger, disappearing almost as quickly as they appeared, and my heart hurts because it's so obvious that they're checking up on me.

At around midday, Kyla's phone rings and she spends half an hour on FaceTime with her men. They're so nauseatingly sweet to each other. It's so obvious how much they miss her. She has a place in the world where she belongs and I'm so jealous, I'm swamped by the feeling. I'm tumbleweed, caught up in the desert wind. But how can I build a future where everything outside of today fills me with terror?

26

LACHLAN

As each of us returns from the beach, we share the little we've managed to glean about Dawn and Kyla.

I notice that Dawn's eyes seem sad. Bryce and Bradley report that her shoulders seem higher and tighter than usual. Jared and Joshua saw her laughing, which is a relief. None of us wants her to be upset.

But none of us knows how to reach her.

I feel it in my bones that she's going to leave when Kyla returns home. As much as I wish we were an anchor capable of keeping her here, I know it's wishful thinking. Dawn is adrift and something is keeping her from struggling to the shore. She's flighty, like a bee that moves from flower to flower, never quite finding a place to rest.

How do we get her to see that letting roots grow is what's best for her?

When I'm showered, I head to the office, glancing at the newly installed glass, still raging inside that Jeffrey fucking Barrow thinks he can damage our business and face no consequences. When we find a way to get him to back off officially, I'm going to make it my mission to seek the only kind of revenge that will satisfy me.

Logan is sitting behind the desk holding a letter, his face grim.

"What's that?" I ask, slumping into the chair opposite. He slides it across the wooden surface. With only a quick glance, I can tell it's from Barrow. Snatching it up, I scan over the text. It's the same offer letter as before, except the offer has been crossed through with red ink and reduced by twenty percent.

Very funny. Fucking hilarious.

Barrow has a fucking death wish.

This is it. No more.

"I'm calling the police," I say.

"We have a crime number," Logan says, reaching into the drawer for a folder. "It's from the report of the brick through the window."

"Okay," I say, as he passes it across the desk. I look up the number for the local police station, and when I eventually get through to a human being, I take my time to describe what's happening. To say the police sound uninterested would be a huge fucking understatement, and I know I don't imagine the clearing of throats and change of tone when I mention it's Barrow.

"Leave it with me," he says and hangs up without confirming my number.

Logan, who watched the whole conversation, shakes his head. "We're getting nowhere."

"Nowhere," I agree.

"At least it's logged."

"You think they're actually writing down the details of our complaint?"

"Probably on a slip of paper and then disposing of it as

soon as he's off the phone."

We both sigh and I ball up a piece of paper I wrote the details of the report on and toss it at the wall. Logan reaches to the floor and picks it up, smoothing it out. "I know it's frustrating, but we just need to keep our heads. Men like Barrow try to provoke a response. When they don't get one, they get bored."

"You think he's going to get bored and walk away from a multi-million-dollar deal?"

"I think there are many multi-million-dollar deals out there for a man like Barrow. We need to hold out for long enough that he finds another easier option to pursue."

"Maybe," I say. "It's probably worth typing out those notes and sending them in an email. The police can deny a phone call ever happened, but an email is proof of disclosure."

"Exactly," Logan says with a brief smile.

I leave him to deal with the email, glancing up at the newly fitted CCTV, and wonder if it will make any kind of difference. Then, I head to the bar to restock the fridges. We're opening soon and it's going to be a busy night.

I fulfill a large order and take my opportunity to speak to Kyla, who's perched at the bar sipping on a Cloud 9 cocktail. Dawn is working and there's no one waiting for my mixing skills, so I pour two shots of tequila and hand one to Kyla.

She stares at it dubiously. "I haven't drunk tequila in years," she says.

"Me either," I admit. "But tonight feels like one of those nights."

She eyes me as I knock back the bitter liquor, and grimace as it burns its way down my throat. I expect her to leave the drink, but she copies me, coughing and spluttering immediately after she swallows it.

"How was Dawn today?" I ask, then kick myself for not working my question into some lighter conversation.

Kyla's eyes flick to where her friend is wiping over a table that's just cleared, then return to me, assessing. "She's okay," she says. "Better now she's working."

"Better with a distraction?"

"Maybe." She shrugs, reaching for her cocktail to wash down the tequila's aftertaste.

"You know you can tell us what's going on. We only want what's best for her. We want to help her."

Kyla's lips stay sealed, pulling back as she widens her eyes and shrugs. "Like I told Jared, it's not my story to share. Dawn isn't in a place where she wants to be open about what she's dealing with. If I told you, she'd probably leave, so she wouldn't have to face your questions or concerns. Believe me, I'm doing you a favor by keeping you in the dark."

"She's going to leave, though, isn't she? Whether you tell us or not."

Kyla's eyes scan my face and I wonder what she's looking for. Is she trying to work out if I'm genuine? Is she pondering on the truth or fiction of my words?

"She's going to leave because that's what Dawn does. She lives for each day, until it becomes too difficult, then she finds an easier place to live for each day."

My fists ball, hidden by the bar, and I'm glad Kyla can't see how angry and frustrated her statement has made me feel.

I'm powerless to resist Barrow, and powerless to hold on to the only girl who has ever made me want to think about a future. Everything feels as though it's slipping through my fingers.

27

THOMAS

After a busy night, everyone returns to their rooms to sleep without pausing to chat and drink and wind down like we usually do. Dawn and Kyla retreated to Dawn's room without a backward glance, and after that, the rest of us accepted that nothing was going to be accomplished by rehashing the same conversation we'd been having all day.

For a while, I try to sleep, but there is so much uncertainty buzzing around in my brain that I just can't relax. Eventually, after twisting my sheets into a tangled knot, I decide the only way I'm going to get any sleep is to head outside. I grab a blanket, even though I probably won't need it, and head out to the hammocks.

Kyla is sleeping in Dawn's room, but I know Dawn. When she can't sleep, she always comes outside to look up at the stars, so I take a hammock, hoping I'll get some sleep, and hoping even more that I'll wake if Dawn appears.

Getting time alone with her is difficult when there are

eight other men in competition for her affection. Now that her friend is here and we're battling other issues, it just feels overwhelming.

The hammock swings gently when I climb in, and the stars blink down at me for as long as I can keep my eyes open. The sounds of the night eventually lull me into an easy sleep.

I don't know what time it is when a hand rests on my shoulder and squeezes. I crack a dry eye and find myself gazing into the tired face of Dawn.

My wish came true.

"Can I get in?" she says softly. "I can't sleep."

"Sure."

It's a weird and awkward process to get into a hammock with another person. There's no preventing the tangle of limbs or the vigorous trembling of the cloth that is the only thing supporting you. By the time she's successfully wedged in next to me, we've laughed and gasped and succumbed to more than a few bumps and bruises.

"I'm going to miss this place," she says softly, sadly.

Her words spear my fucking heart, but I don't want to let her know how much. I get the feeling that any kind of pressure is enough to send her running.

"This place will miss you," I reply, calmly. I want to tell her she can't leave, that I'll miss her too much, but keeping my feelings to myself is the right thing to do.

"Do you know how lucky you are?" She snuggles against my chest, wrapping her arm around me.

"Lucky?"

"Yeah. To have a place to be where you feel at home. To want to stay somewhere for good."

"You've never had that?"

"Not for a long time."

I kiss her gently on the forehead, hating that I'm aware of the longing in her voice for something that every human being should have. "What about your hometown, where you grew up? Don't you have roots there?"

"My dad is still there, but it doesn't really feel like home anymore."

"What about where you were living before you went traveling, near Kyla?"

"It was okay for a while, but it wasn't home." She sounds wistful and a little bereft, as if admitting her feelings causes her even more hurt.

"Sometimes it's not the place that doesn't feel like home," I tell her. "Sometimes it's us. When you're not content with yourself, you become like a rolling stone."

"I was never into rock," she says, and we both shake with laughter that we struggle to suppress. Everything seems louder with the blanket of darkness overhead. Everything seems more intense with our bodies pressed together and so much left unsaid between us.

I stroke her arm, and lace our fingers together, gently swaying our bodies so we swing back and forth just a little. She slides her foot between mine, shifting closer. If we were in a bed in a private room, maybe we'd get hot and heavy, but I'm glad we're outside and we can't. I want this moment to stay innocent and sweet. I want our closeness to be based on something other than sex.

For a while, I wonder if she's fallen asleep. Her breathing is even and her body slack, so when she speaks, it makes me jump.

"Will you sing that song, Thomas? The one from the first night."

"Iris?" I ask, surprised. The last time I sang it, she cried. Why does she want to hear it again now?

"Yeah."

"You sure?"

The nod of her head is almost imperceptible against my chest, but it's enough to confirm what she's asking of me.

When I start to sing the words, she holds her breath, listening intently by angling her head. Her hand tenses in mine, and we clasp our fingers tightly together, so tight that I can feel the bite of her nails into my skin.

When her shoulders hitch, I stop, but she urges me on with a squeeze of her hand. Feeling her cry against me, her tears seeping through my shirt from barely repressed sobs breaks my heart, but she needs this. She wants this.

So I sing on until the end.

Until all the words have floated away on the soft night breeze.

And when I'm done, I don't ask her any more questions. I tell her about my favorite place, the beaches of the Whitsunday Islands, with crystal clear blue ocean, blindingly white sand, and the manta rays that swim there with no fear. I tell her about my best friend Jordy who got married at twenty and moved to Germany and who I miss every day. I tell her she has to travel to the center of Australia and see the big red rock of Uluru at sunrise.

I give her other things to think about that gradually form layers over whatever sadness she has until the tension leaves her.

She listens, asking no more questions, and eventually falls asleep wrapped in my arms.

28

JOSHUA

I awake to frantic shouting; a man's voice and a woman's. It's one word that makes me fly from my bed and through the door, with Jared a second behind me.

Fire.

On bare feet, I run through the central chill-out area, finding Dawn and Thomas scrambling in the outdoor kitchen for a bucket and water. A tail of smoke licks through the office window, and a smoky yellow light bleeds into the night.

Lachlan appears from his room, roaring when he sees the damage to our property and the fire that's set on further destruction. Before anyone has a chance to hold him back, he smashes his fist into the nearest wall. Dawn runs over, resting her hand on his back as he hunches over in pain, cradling his hand. The shame in his eyes and defeat in his clouded expression is obvious to us both.

When Mitchell and Cooper arrive with half-cracked eyes and sleep mussed hair, they rush behind Thomas to unlock the office door.

"Get the extinguisher and the fire blanket," he yells, shoving the door open. The heat from the fire can already be felt in the air around the office and the smoke is acrid with chemicals from man-made furniture and flooring.

Thomas throws the bucket of water, dampening the inside of the office, but it's not enough to put out the flames. Dawn gasps, her hand clasped over her mouth, shock widening her pretty eyes.

Logan uses his phone to call the emergency services. Bryce has woken Kyla, and Bradley steers Dawn away from the danger and to a group of chairs on the far side of the outdoor area. She pulls Lachlan along, tugging at his shirt until it's over his head and she can wrap his bleeding hand in it.

I run around the side of the bar, eyes frantically searching for anything out of place, the person who most likely did this, or worse, a fire in another area of our business. Jared follows me, and we weave back and forth, scouring for anything that's not right. There's so much to burn at Cloud 9. The wooden bar, the wicker chairs, the hammocks and cotton weave cushions, and bamboo decorative paneling. Everything is made of natural materials. It could incinerate in a flash.

All our dreams and the discussions we had when we were putting together an idea of our business, flash through my mind.

It could all go up in smoke so quickly.

"I don't see anything," Jared yells from over by the bar.

"I don't see anything either."

"Keep looking." He disappears through to where the toilets are, and reappears, as I head around the other side of the bar, to the separate access to the hostel rooms. It's clear. No one lurking. No fire burning.

If the only damage there is tonight is to the office,

we're lucky.

Jeffrey Barrow is still looking to scare us, not to burn us to the ground.

"It's all clear," I yell as we make it back round to the office. Bracing my hands on my knees, I pull in deep breaths to calm my racing heart.

"The fire's out," Thomas says. He has a smudge of ash across his face and he's kicking a sooty brick across the floor.

"Another brick?" Jared asks as a siren pierces the quiet of the night, getting ever closer.

"Another fucking brick." Thomas shakes his head, staring at the charred remains of the brick with so much hatred I fear it could explode. He bends, touching it with his finger. Then, he uses a piece of paper to protect his hands from the latent heat, picking it up and staring at it. When he sniffs, he wrinkles his nose in disgust. "This time it was wrapped, doused with accelerant and lit."

"Did you see anyone?" Cooper asks.

"No. By the time Dawn and I made it out of the hammock, whoever started it was long gone."

"You were in a hammock with Dawn?" Logan eyes Thomas with a raised brow.

"We were sleeping," Thomas says. "She didn't tell me anything new."

Although we're all focused on the fire, the news that Thomas took no forward steps with Dawn when he had a chance is disheartening.

As the siren reaches almost deafening volume, it's flicked off and the rumbling of the firetruck's large engine disrupts the conversation. Firemen run forward, eyes scanning for the fire. "It's out," Thomas says. "It started with this." He hands the brick over to a stocky fireman, who's weighted down with his sturdy uniform and helmet.

"You found it inside?"

"Yeah." Thomas leads the fireman into the still smoldering office; Cooper and Mitchell follow. The police aren't far behind, their investigations lasting for an hour while we sit around, waiting.

Bradley ushers Kyla back to Dawn's room, agreeing to wake her if anything else happens. Dawn finds the first aid box and deals with Lachlan's rage wounds again. She's so calm with him, and so accepting, as though his actions don't bother her at all. It pains me to see him hurt, but it also enrages me. A man should be able to control his temper. If we can't control ourselves and hold on to our inner peace when everything around us is turning into shit, what hope do we have?

When she's done, I follow Dawn to the door of her room, and lightly touch her on the back. "I'm worried about what's going to happen," she says, rubbing her palm over her face, sighing, and resting her hands on her hips. "He's going to do something stupid. I can feel it."

"Don't worry about Lachlan. We'll keep it together. There are nine of us. We've built something great and kept it together. We know what to do."

She nods, her eyes searching mine. "You did build something great," she says. Then she rests her hand on my shoulder and leans up to kiss me on the corner of my mouth. Every part of me wants to fall into her, to scoop her close and keep her safe. I want to wrap her inside this thing I've built with my friends so that she's a part of it, a brick in our wall. Joined and impenetrable to the outside world.

I want life to be simple again, to know most of what's coming tomorrow and not fear any of what's unknown.

"Goodnight."

I watch Dawn open the door and disappear into the darkness of her room, closing it softly behind her. It's only then that I allow the rage from what's happened tonight to surge inside me.

Jeffrey Barrow isn't going to get away with this.

We'll find a way to break him, if it's the last thing we do.

29

DAWN

I don't sleep well. The charred scent of burning clings to my skin, but I'm too tired to shower. Kyla sleeps beside me, restless with exhaustion and jet lag, twisting the covers around her limbs and sighing like the world is resting on her shoulders.

Inside, I'm restless too.

Caught up with the dangers that lurk outside Cloud 9. Caught up with the dangers inside me.

I blink in the darkness, remembering the way it felt to fall asleep in Thomas's arms. To hear him sing Mom's song. To cry and accept the sadness rather than fight it.

I think of Lachlan and his hand that won't heal without leaving scars.

I remember Chantelle's tears when she saw Barrow, and the fear in her trembling hands.

My mind swims with too many disparate thoughts, becoming a tangled mess of images and feelings that wrap around me like the tentacles of a mythical sea monster.

Eventually, that monster drags me down into the depths of a fitful sleep.

In the morning, I find Jared and Joshua with shadows coloring the hollows of their handsome faces, keeping watch. I slump down onto the bean bag opposite them and shake my head.

"Have you been up all night?"

"Yeah," Jared confirms. "Bryce and Bradley are going to take over at 8 am."

I pick at a hangnail on my finger, wondering if I should say what's been brewing in my mind.

"I think Chantelle is the key to taking down Barrow, but she's scared. I keep wondering what I can do to try to convince her to report what he did. If there's enough coverage of his actions, I think other women will come forward too. I suspect there'll be a trail. Sometimes, it just takes one person to stick their head above the parapet."

"You really think she'd report it? What about the risks?" Joshua asks.

"Her main concern is her safety. She lives alone. She doesn't have family in the local area. It's a big step to take without a network of support."

Joshua straightens. "We can be her network. We can support her. She could come and stay here."

"You'd do that?"

"Of course," he says. "We're already in the shit with Barrow. I don't have any concerns about adding to it. We have room. She could help out around the place for something to do if she's not working."

I nod, already seeing the possibilities in what Joshua is saying. I don't know Chantelle well, but maybe, just maybe, there'll be a chance that she'll go for it. She's scared of Barrow, but she's also angry. If there's a way of getting him to face consequences for what he did, she might just take it.

In the back of my mind, I imagine her taking over my place here, giving me the chance to walk away. Maybe, with Chantelle as a replacement, Jared, Joshua, and the rest of my lovely boys won't feel the loss of my presence. I know I'd feel better knowing there's someone around to brighten their days.

She could replace you in more than just waitressing, my mind whispers. *She could replace you in their beds and in their hearts.*

The thought curls in my stomach like a thick, black snake, jealousy an ugly emotion that I don't have a right to feel. If I give them up, I can't hate the woman who comes after me. I can't resent them for seeking comfort and warmth and love in someone else's arms.

But I would. I know I would. I'm not a good person. I'm a selfish woman who wants it all, even though I can't handle it.

Standing quickly, I smooth my shorts and make my excuses. "I'll call her and ask. I'll let you know what she says."

"We'll be sleeping until this evening," Jared points out. "Tell whoever's awake. We need to get onto this quickly before Barrow has a chance to rearm."

"I will," I say.

On the phone, Chantelle listens to what's been happening, reacting angrily to Barrow's continued assault on Cloud 9. "Your friends don't deserve this," she says. "They're all so nice."

"They said the same thing about you," I say. "I hate to have to ask you this again, but I have to. Will you consider going to the police with the information and evidence you have against Barrow?" Before she has a chance to say no, I continue. "The guys at Cloud 9 have offered to support you through the process. They've even offered for you to come live here, so you feel safe."

"They offered for me to live at Cloud 9?"

"Yeah. They have space, and they want you to be safe. The best place for them to ensure that happens is here with them."

"That's crazy nice."

"They're really great people, Chantelle. They'll do anything to keep you safe while you're under their roof."

"I just...I'm scared that he'll do something bad, Dawn."

The fear in her voice makes me pause for a second. "I know. I get it. But even if you keep your mouth shut, there's still a chance that he could turn on you, isn't there? Isn't it better to deal with it? At some point, people have to get together and draw a line in the sand. Bad men like Barrow need to be stopped before they get so powerful that there's no taking them down."

"Isn't he already that powerful?" she asks. It's a good question and one I don't really have the answer to.

"If he was that powerful, he wouldn't need to carry out his business using bricks as threats. He doesn't have all the people he needs in his pocket or what he's trying to do with Cloud 9 could be accomplished easily."

"True." She nods and her expression softens as though she wants to believe what I'm saying.

"Just think about it, okay? That's all I'm asking."

"It could be fun, coming to live with you guys and I'm going to struggle to make rent this month." She says the last part as an afterthought, but it's pretty fundamental. Maybe that will be the tipping point.

"See. It's like it's meant to be," I say.

Am I being a good person? I think I am. I really believe that Chantelle will be better off with Lachlan and the boys at Cloud 9 than out there on her own. And if it saves her having to return home with her tail between her legs, it's even better.

"Can I come over and talk to them?" she asks. "I think that would help me decide."

"Sure," I say, surprised that she's moving faster than I anticipated. "Can you come now, before things get busy with the bar?"

"I can. I'll see you in an hour."

When Chantelle arrives, I've already briefed Thomas, Cooper and Mitchell about the possible arrangements. They give her a warm welcome, offering her a drink and some homemade cookies, encouraging her to sit on a comfortable rattan sofa and nodding attentively when she's speaking. They do their best to make her feel safe, which I know comes naturally to them. It's how they make me feel whenever I'm in their company.

"But are you sure about me moving in here?" Chantelle asks, her gaze flicking between the three men.

"Of course," Cooper says. "We have the space, and it will make things easier. None of us would want to worry about you being across town by yourself, especially when coming forward is more of a risk to you than it is to us."

Chantelle smoothes her hands over her white linen trousers and exhales a long breath. "I'll be honest and admit that I don't know if I'm doing the right thing. Maybe, in a week, I'll kick myself for sticking my neck out. Maybe everything will explode, but I haven't slept well for weeks. I just keep turning over what happened with Barrow in my mind. I can't seem to let go of it. And if I never confront him about what he did, maybe it will always stay with me. I just want to get past it and this feels like a way to do it."

"Okay," Thomas says, shifting forward in his seat. "We can help you move your things today, if that works for you. And you're welcome to stay here until everything is legally resolved."

"Until it goes to court?"

"Yes." Cooper says the word firmly, but I can see he's forcing a sense of confidence. Who knows if it will even get that far?

"It works for me then." Chantelle looks to me as though she wants confirmation that I'm okay with the plan.

"I'll help you pack up," I say, resting my hand on her knee. "And my friend Kyla can help, too."

"I have one other thing I need to do before we head back. Are you okay to wait here for a little while?" I ask Chantelle.

"No worries," Chantelle says, as I rise from the seat next to her and nod at Cooper, Mitchell and Thomas. "I'll be back."

I walk around the front of Cloud 9, staring up at the big blue sign, and the white neon cloud behind it. In the day, it doesn't have much impact, but at night, the way it glitters and shines is eye-catching.

I know it's late back home, but I want to try my friend Allie. She's a journalist and is always working into the night, dealing with crazy deadlines. If she's awake, she's awake. If not, I'll leave a message.

"Dawn, do you have any idea what time it is?" she says, as soon as the call collects. Her voice is husky from tiredness but light with amusement. I do have a tendency to get in touch at unsociable hours, not only since I arrived in Australia.

"I do, and look, you're awake!"

She snorts and takes a noisy sip of a drink. "I'm awake only because I'm mainlining espressos. I swear my boss is trying to kill me."

"More stories about the best ways to fellate a one-night stand?"

She snorts derisively. "Tonight's gem is a write up of how many men were unable to identify the position of the clitoris in a recent survey."

"Depressing stuff," I muse. "How many years did you study in college for this opportunity?"

"Don't. Seriously. I keep telling myself that I'll do it for one more month and find something else, but every time I look, nothing pays as well."

"It's a deal with the devil," I say.

"It really is." Allie sips her drink again and the rustle of clothing in the background creates an image of her reclining against her office chair. "So what has inspired this call today?"

"Can't a girl check in on a bestie once in a while?"

"A girl can check in on a bestie whenever she wants, but I have a feeling this is about something else."

"Your reporter's intuition is uncanny," I say. "To summarize quickly, so I don't keep you away from your blow job stories, I'm in Australia. I'm having an awesome vacation romance with nine gorgeous men. They're being harassed by a powerful man who wants to buy their bar. I met a woman who was sexually harassed by the same man. She's agreed to tell the police about the sexual harassment to try to help my nine gorgeous fuck buddies…"

"Hold up, Dawn. What the fuck? I've drunk six espressos today. My mind is made of coffee grounds right now. Slow down. Nine men?"

"Yep. You know me. I like to go big."

"Bigger than Kyla," she snorts.

"It's not a competition. It just worked out that way."

"And the sexual harassment?"

"It's a man named Jeffrey Barrow. He's a big shot on this side of the Pacific."

"And you're telling me all this, why?"

"You have a contact in an Australian newspaper. I remember you mentioning it when you got the blow job job."

"I do. Crystal. A woman I studied with went to work in Sydney."

"Bingo," I say, smiling up at the sky. "Would you be willing to send me her details? I want to run my crazy story past her, leaving out the fuck buddy aspect, of course!"

"Why spare her the good stuff?" Allie asks. "That's probably the part she'll want to run with!"

"Because she's not one of my besties."

"Good answer. I'm sending you her details right now. When are you coming home?"

I spin on my foot, her question sending a rush of restlessness up my spine and over my scalp. "I don't know, Allie. I like it here a lot, but my feet are already itchy."

"You mean those nine sex gods are getting too close?"

"I'm hanging up now before you turn to psychoanalysis."

"Behind blow jobs, psychoanalysis is my second expert subject."

"TMI," I laugh. "Speak to you soon, and thanks."

Armed with the name and phone number of Allie's journalist friend, I search out Lachlan and find him hunched over a laptop. When he looks up and notices me, he drops his bandaged hand beneath the low table in front of him.

I shake my head. "You don't need to hide it, Lachlan. I bandaged it for you, remember?"

He nods once, then his eyes drift back to the screen.

"I have the number of a journalist in Sydney, a friend of a friend. Maybe we can make this whole thing with Barrow into a story she might be willing to look into more?"

"A story?" He sounds doubtful but I think that's just Lachlan's first approach to everything. All he'll need is a little convincing.

"Yeah. Why not? It's got everything. Ruthless corrupt asshole. Nine sexy bar owners. A woman standing up to sexual harassment. A development that's going to crush small business owners. If she takes the story, it could really help get someone to look at Barrow."

"I'm just filling out the insurance forms for the fire damage," he says. Then, shaking his head, he reaches to the chair next to him and pats it. "They can wait, though. This sounds like it could be something good."

For the next hour, Lachlan and I refine the story about what's happened at Cloud 9 and to Chantelle. I put a call in to Crystal, the journalist, relaying the information as best as I can and providing her with contact details for Chantelle and Lachlan. She agrees to call me back once she's had a chance to think about it and do some digging.

After, Kyla and I head back with Chantelle to begin the job of packing up her life.

So many changes are happening around me. So many people seem to need me, and I'm not good at being needed. I'm not good at being an anchor for myself, let alone anyone else.

By the time we get back to Cloud 9 and Lachlan and Bryce help Chantelle move her things into her new room,

I'm frazzled.

I pull Lachlan aside and before I can say a word, he wraps his big, strong arms around me and squeezes tight. "I know all of this is weighing on you."

"I just...I'm so worried about you guys and the business, and now Chantelle is wrapped up in this too. I just need to make sure she stays safe."

"That's not your job, Dawn," he says firmly, still not letting me go. "Chantelle is stepping in to help us, not you. That makes her our responsibility."

"But she's my friend."

When Lachlan squeezes me again, and presses a kiss to my forehead, I know he understands what I'm saying. "She's your friend, lassie, but not your burden to shoulder. Let us look after her. We'll make sure Jeffery doesn't get to touch even a hair on her head."

The relief that he's going to look after Chantelle lifts a concrete block from my shoulders. I know it's selfish to feel like I have enough on my plate, but it's how I feel.

I don't tell Lachlan that, though. I don't want him to know that running from all of this drama is exactly what my feet are itching for.

"You know, I'm thinking about where to go on my touristy trip," Kyla says, as I get ready for a night of waiting tables and worrying about the men in my life.

"Whitsunday Islands," I reply, without hesitation. "Thomas was telling me about the crystal-clear waters and white sands, and the manta rays and other ocean life. It sounds perfect."

Kyla taps something into her phone and makes an approving hum. "Look." She faces the screen to me, and the images that she scrolls through are idyllic. "You should come with me. I mean, I know you're enjoying it here, and you have nine men to make your time more than interesting, but it'll be fun. Just you and me. I don't have a lot of time and I want to see as much as I can."

"That sounds awesome," I say, even as a pang of guilt twists its way through my chest.

You want to leave, my internal voice whispers. *You want to leave all this behind before your heart gets roped in any deeper.*

My heart is not involved, I argue back, but even my own internal debate sounds hollow and uncertain. The way I felt snuggled in Thomas's arms, and nursing Lachlan's hand wasn't nothing. The way they all treated me when we were together, touching me gently, holding me close, kissing me softly, prioritizing my pleasure wasn't nothing. Logan's tender words and their genuine concerns about my state of mind can't be brushed away. There's more here than I can happily concede. More than I need.

You don't know what you need.

The truth is a bitter pill to swallow.

"Come with me," Kyla says. "It'll be the trip of a lifetime. Something we'll remember when we're old and gray and sitting on my porch back home."

"Not the porch argument." I wave my hand in dismissal. "Seriously. You want to drag that one out?"

"Every time."

"You're an evil woman, but I can't resist your emotional blackmail."

My bestie squeals happily and jumps around, punching the air. "Yes. Yes."

"I'll need to ask Lachlan," I say. "He might say no."

"That man would do anything for you," Kyla says, already sorting her clothes as if we're bound for ocean blue pastures immediately.

Would he?

Would I even want him to?

"I hope so," I say. But there's only one way to find out.

30

DAWN

Kyla was right. Lachlan agrees to our trip without argument and before I know it, I'm packing a small bag and booking a sailing trip and bus transfer. Kyla and I are ready to make our escape.

Chantelle settles into her room in the hostel and offers to help with tasks to contribute towards her stay. I'm not certain whether Lachlan is grateful for the help or if he realizes that she needs something to do to keep her mind from everything.

"Don't worry," he says, as I check in on the status of everything before I depart. "Crystal called to say she's interested in running the story. The final say will be with her editor, but with Barrow being such a high-profile figure, she's ninety nine percent confident that it'll be printed."

"Seriously?"

"Yeah. She discussed the angle with Chantelle who provided the name of a witness. It turns out the cleaner has also been fired and is happy to back up her story."

"And she's going to mention what's happening with Cloud 9?"

"Yeah. This isn't the first time Barrow has tried to bully people into giving up their property."

"Just the first time anyone was prepared to fight against him."

"That I don't know." Lachlan runs his hands through his dark hair, and folds in his lips, both signs of the pressure he's shouldering and trying to minimize so that I don't worry. "Just go and have some fun with Kyla and don't worry about anything. If we need to get in touch, we'll call."

I reach out to wrap my arm around his middle, squeezing him in a sideways hug that he quickly turns into a bear-like embrace. I inhale against his blue shirt, finding happiness in the familiarity of his scent. "I'm going to miss you, my sweet girlie," he whispers, warm against my scalp. I'm going to miss him too. So much. But I can't tell him. It's not fair.

"I'm only going for a couple of days. I'll be back before you know it," I say breezily, easing myself from his arms.

It shouldn't feel this hard to say goodbye to the Cloud 9 crew. I'll be back in no time, so why does my heart tug as though it's been pierced by a fishhook and bound to the men I'm leaving behind? Why do tears burn in my throat as I hug them one by one, breathing in their scents like it's the last time I'm ever going to be this close?

As Kyla and I walk away, I don't risk turning around because I don't want to see longing in their expressions or for them to know that my eyes are glassy with tears that I don't have the right to shed.

This is my fault. I've let it go on for too long. I've pretended too much.

As we board the bus, Kyla is gushing with excitement. I

try to wrap myself into her bubbling enthusiasm so that I can leave the sad black shadow I have trailing me on the sidewalk, but it follows me up the steps and to my seat, and doesn't leave me, even when we board the tall ship that's going to take us on our tour.

"Check out our cabin. We're in the bow." Kyla pushes open the small wooden door until it swings open, revealing a compact cabin with two small bunks which angle in at the end. "We can play footsie," she laughs, dropping her bag into the small space on the floor.

"Keep your piggies to yourself."

"Did you see those guys out there?" Her eyes drift to the door.

"Which ones? The annoying jocks from Ohio or the nerds from New York?"

"All of the above. Did you book us on an American tour or something?"

I shake my head, taking a welcome gulp of water from my metal bottle. "No. It's just our bad luck to end up surrounded by people we wouldn't even hang out with at home."

"They don't seem so bad." Kyla raises her eyebrow and looks me over. "You'd see that if you weren't in such a grumpy mood."

"Me? Grumpy?"

"Yes, my usually upbeat friend. You!" Her expression softens as I scowl. "Ever since you left those fine men behind, you haven't been your usual jovial self."

I turn, pretending to unpack my clothes when really, I just need a moment away from Kyla's scrutiny. She can see through me like a fishbowl. "I'm just worried about what's happening to them all. It's a lot."

"It's more than that." Her voice trails off. "You remember when I panicked? When I was packing up my things to move home?"

"Yeah. You were being an idiot."

She chuckles lightly. "I prefer to think of it as having a crisis of confidence. I didn't know what I wanted or how to even reach for what I needed. I didn't believe I was worthy."

"I know. You were being an idiot."

"Forgive me in advance for this, Dawn, but you're being an idiot."

I swivel around, dropping my spare denim shorts on the bed. "I am not being an idiot, Kyla. I know what I want, and I go for it."

"And then you drop it like a hot potato and sprint away in the other direction." She arches a knowing eyebrow and my frustration builds.

Outside our door, the boom of male voices passes, and feet noisily ascend the stairs to the deck. We shouldn't be down here right now, having stupid debates about my idiocy or lack of. We should be up there watching as we set sail off on our adventure.

"We should go up," I say. "I don't want to miss a moment of what Thomas told me about. He painted a picture in my mind. I want to see if it matches."

"Sure."

We gather up the things we need in silence, packing smaller bags of snacks, phones, towels, and sunscreen. As we climb the stairs, I tip my face to the sun, soaking up the warmth but still feeling the drag of that shadow.

As I lay my towel out on the bench and watch as the crew sails the ship away from the harbor, I can't help my mind drifting and imagining what each of the men I've left behind are doing. Mitchell will be laughing at something. Of that, I'm certain. Probably Cooper. Those two have a vibe. Lachlan will be bent over a spreadsheet or legal document, discussing it with Thomas and Logan. I glance at my watch and wonder whether Jared and Joshua are cutting through the waves as I am now. Bryce and Bradley will be at the butchers, collecting the meat they cook with so much heart. I'm not there, but their world will keep on turning and that's how it will be when I leave Byron Bay for good.

Kyla's hand on my shoulder makes me jump. "Let me put some cream on your back, sweetie," she says softly. "The sun is like Satan's BBQ."

I let my friend protect me from the elements, and while she smooths cream into my skin that smells of summer, she talks about each of her men back home and how much she misses them. She mentions something that each of them does for her, that makes her life better. Lex makes sure she eats well, focusing on nutrition to reduce her monthly pains. Carl takes care of everything money related, explaining it all so she doesn't have to worry. Noah makes her laugh, even on days when she's feeling blue. Dex pushes her to experience new things. She goes on and on, and for each of her men, I find myself drifting into a fictional time in the future and a me with a similar life. I imagine what each of the men in my life would do for me, and what I could do for them.

Lachlan would ensure all my affairs were in order and in return, I'd keep him calm and nurse his wounds.

Mitchell would make me laugh, and I'd bring the jokes too, so we'd always giggle together.

Cooper and Logan would care for my mind and my heart, reminding me of all the things that are possible.

Jared and Joshua would encourage me to take adventures, and I'd be the anchor to inspire them to keep one foot grounded.

Bradley and Bryce would always remind me of home, and I could be their safe haven.

Thomas would sing to me whenever I was feeling sad, and I'd happily provide him with an outlet for his talent and inspiration for his songs.

Together, they work as a great unit, but with me, it could be so much better.

The ocean swells gently around us, lapping against the varnished wood of the boat, frothing up in its wake. In the distance, islands beckon like glossy green hills surrounded by sugar white cupcake frosting, peeking through the glassy turquoise water. The breeze whips strands of my hair, and strands of Kyla's, tangling them together behind us.

She's my best friend, and I know she's only talking about her life because she wants me to believe that I can have what she has. She's trying to do for me what I did for her. To help me find my place in the world. Encourage me to reach for my best life and cling onto it with both hands.

But there's a significant difference between us. Kyla believes, like most people, that she has years stretched out ahead of her. She can imagine a gray-haired, wrinkled version of herself, sitting on that porch swing with a glass of iced tea and a crossword, and eight men who love her.

I know that I most likely don't. The image of a gray-haired Dawn has been erased from my mind. All I can picture is the me I am right now. Anything else feels like a false promise. A cheap hope. A betrayal of my mother's memory.

"They love you, you know," Kyla says softly.

"Love is a weighty word that is often overused," I say, even as my heart picks up speed in my chest.

"They do. You need to know that because I know what you're doing. You're trying to convince yourself that they don't need you. That they'll be better off without you. You're trying to convince yourself that it will never work and that it's time to move on before anyone gets attached."

"Mind reading. We need to add that to your list of skills on your resume," I reply, as her words curl like barbed vines around my heart and squeeze, causing tiny beads of ache to form on the surface.

"Can you take a photo of us?" one of the guys from Ohio says. He's cute with a broad, straight white-toothed smile and blond brows, but not a patch on any of my men.

"Of course."

I take his phone and find a good place to stand so that I can make the most of their pose and the mind-blowing view behind them. I force myself to really look at him and his friend.

They're good-looking guys. Probably a whole heap of fun, too. There are so many people and places in the world to experience and I never made any promises to the men at Cloud 9, just as they didn't promise anything to me. We had fun. I'll carry the memories of the time with them for as many days as I'm gifted.

I need to move on to whatever destination the universe will send me to next.

You don't want anyone else, my internal voice whispers. *You only want them.*

But I can't listen to the truth when it has the power to destroy.

With the salty breeze in my hair and the sails of the ship billowing behind me, I make the decision that it's time to leave.

But in my chest, my heart rests heavy with the weight of all the lies I tell myself.

31

LOGAN

"Logan!" Dawn's voice rings out over the music, and I swivel, finding her and Kyla dragging their small suitcases, sunkissed and beaming as they make their way into the bar. Dawn waves and then lengthens her strides until we're face to face. Without thinking, I pull her into a bearlike embrace, inhaling the scent of her hair and soaking up her warmth. "Wow," she giggles. "I was going to ask if you missed me, but I guess I know the answer."

"You have no idea," I say, meeting Lachlan's eyes over Dawn's shoulder and finding him watchful and still. He has a lot on his mind, but for all the stress and strain of what's happening with the business, I know my friend is worrying about this.

Worrying about the impact on our friendship.

Worrying about Dawn and what she's hiding behind her bubbly exterior.

Worrying she's going to tell us she's leaving.

Worrying about what she'll leave behind.

I feel the same. All I want is to know that this beautiful, vivacious woman wants to stay and live with us. I want to know she's committed to this unconventional relationship we've built. But wanting and getting are on two totally different sides of the coin.

"Dawn," Jared yells, placing the tray he's carrying laden with dirty glasses onto the bar, and spinning her out of my arms. He plants a passionate kiss onto her lips, taking his greeting one step further than me. Dawn laughs as he spins her again, and her cheeks grow flushed with excitement and embarrassment.

Behind her, Kyla smiles broadly at her friend.

"Welcome back," I say to Kyla as Dawn is passed from man to man, receiving kisses from Thomas, Cooper, Joshua, and Bryce. She has a smile on her face that doesn't feel genuine, as though she pasted it there to cover her true feelings. Eventually, Lachlan leaves his place behind the bar and tugs Dawn into a fierce hug.

"It's good to have you back," he says, squeezing the life out of her. Dawn seems a little winded, and maybe a little shocked at the fierceness of his reaction to her return. Lachlan's not good at showing emotion and when you spend time with him, you come to expect and accept a level of reserve in his interaction. This is anything but.

"Wow. I should go away more often," Dawn says brightly. Behind her, I catch Kyla pursing her lips.

"How was your trip?"

"It was great." Kyla rests her case against the bar. "Really great."

"Kyla loves it so much she doesn't want to go home." Dawn perches on a bar stool and surveys Cloud 9 as though she expects to see changes. Nothing's different. Cooper's still DJing. Bryce and Brandon are finishing up the grilling. We're all in the same place we were when she left. Only Dawn seems different.

"When are you going home?" I ask.

Kyla reaches into her pocket, pulling out her phone. "I've lost track of the days," she says. "I've got just over a week."

"A week?"

I glance at Dawn, who suddenly won't meet my eyes and I know what's made her tense and different. She's planning to go back to the US when her friend leaves and she doesn't know how to tell us.

Well, fuck that.

"Are you sure we can't encourage you to stay longer?"

Kyla shrugs. "I'd love to, but I have eight men at home who are desperate for me to get back."

"Yeah, that's got to be an incentive."

Her attention switches to her phone, and then she smiles broadly. "They're messaging me right now...look at them."

She flashes me a picture of eight tattooed men, all shoving at each other to get into a selfie. Half of them are laughing and the other half are trying to look sad. A humorous attempt at emotional blackmail gone wrong.

"We should go and put our stuff in my room," Dawn says.

"That's okay. Jared will help you." I grab the handles of the suitcases and pass them both to Jared. "Dawn, go with him so you can unlock the door."

She slides down off the barstool, flashing most of her toned thighs in the process and god, I just want to toss her over my shoulder and carry her to the nearest bed. She wouldn't know what hit her. I'd be inside her before she could utter my name.

"Kyla, can I get you a drink?"

"Sure," she says. "Dawn told me I have to try a Seventh Heaven."

"You do. Lachlan makes those the best. Lachlan?"

He nods and I rest against the bar next to Kyla. I should make some small talk before I cut to the chase, but I don't have a lot of time before Dawn returns. "She's leaving, isn't she?"

Kyla folds in her lips and shifts her balance. She doesn't need to say a word. I can see the truth of my statement in her discomfort.

"She doesn't stay still for long," she says. "If it's not traveling, it's a new job, a new man, a new hobby, a new favorite restaurant. I'm just grateful it's not a new best friend." She grimaces in the way people do when they're apologizing on someone else's behalf.

"She doesn't stay still because she's running from something."

Kyla bites on her bottom lip. "She's my best friend, and I won't betray her confidence."

"Even if it would help her?" I run my fingers through my hair, and tip my face to the ceiling, inhaling deeply before pushing out the breath and some of my frustration. "We want her to stay."

"You're trying to pin down a hummingbird." She touches my arm with a tenderness that makes me like her even more. I can see how much she cares for Dawn in the way she accepts her for all her idiosyncrasies.

"Even hummingbirds need to rest sometimes," I say. "I just want her to fly because she wants to, not because she has something pushing her. I know there's something going on. I can feel it."

Kyla shrugs. "If she wanted to bare her soul to you, she would have. I know it sounds harsh, and I don't mean it to. I really like you guys and the way you treat Dawn. She's not an easy person to treasure. She pushes and prods at every boundary. She wants to break through every chain."

"That's what we love about her." The words are out of

my mouth before I can think them through, and Kyla's head jerks back, registering the important four-letter word in the middle of my sentence.

"Love?"

It's my turn to shrug. "Of course, love. You, of all people, shouldn't be surprised with what's happening here."

"Love works in mysterious ways."

"I see myself in Dawn," I admit. "Maybe that's why I'm so sure there's something bad going on. I was diagnosed with cancer four years ago. As soon as I heard that word leave the doctor's mouth, I wanted to run. I've never been a runner. Swimming's more my sport, but suddenly, I wanted to feel my legs pumping and my muscles screaming. I wanted to feel pain in my body, so I'd know I was alive. And I couldn't sit still. I was out all the time, even though I should have been resting. With a potential end date to my life in sight, I just wanted to make the most of every day."

Kyla's mouth drops open and I focus on every little expression change because I'm hoping my confession will lead her to give away something...anything.

"The thing is, Kyla. None of that made me happy. None of that made me feel peaceful or anchored me to the people who love me. Feeling like you have ants under your skin is uncomfortable, and I see it in Dawn. I want to help her, but to do that, you have to help me, before it's too late."

"If I tell you, you have to promise me you won't tell Dawn what you know. You have to promise not to tell her I told you. I don't want her to feel betrayed. Not when she needs all the friends and support that she can get."

"I promise," I say.

"I know she'll understand one day," Kyla says, almost as though she's trying to convince herself. "Not that long ago, she pushed me out of my comfort zone because she knew what was good for me better than I knew myself. Now it's my turn to do the same."

"Exactly." I sit on the bar stool that Dawn vacated so that our eyelines are matched, hoping that it will make it easier for Kyla to share Dawn's secret.

"Her mom died of cancer when she was young. Her dad is worried that Dawn potentially carries a gene mutation that could put her at high risk of the same kind of cancer. She went for genetic tests but hasn't found out the results. Her dad made her promise that by a certain date, she'd find out the truth, one way or another, but she can't face it. She's avoiding knowing and running from her potential future by living in the present, doing anything and everything like a crazy person."

I hang my head, feeling Kyla's confession like a knife to my heart. No wonder Dawn acts the way she does. No wonder she's here in Australia, living with nine men and looking to run away before anything gets serious. She's frightened and in denial. I know both those emotions only too well. I place my hand over my abdomen where my scar marks a past I'm glad is firmly behind me.

"She can't keep running," I say eventually. "All of this...everything she's doing right now is just a mask for her fear. She needs to find out those results and take action, whatever it is, to deal with what comes next. Facing up to it is the only way she's ever going to find peace."

"Her head is so deep in the sand, she's up to her toes." Kyla touches my arm again and I place my hand over hers, feeling so affectionate toward her. She's traveled around the world to support the woman I love. That's the kind of friendship I appreciate. The kind of friendship Dawn needs in her life.

"I'm going to get her to tell me what's going on. Don't worry. I'll find a way without letting her know you ever said a word."

"And what if she tells you, but still doesn't want to find out the results?"

"We have to think positively. She'll tell me, I'll encourage her to call the doctor, and they'll tell her everything is fine. If we hope for it enough, maybe it'll become true."

"You're a good man, Logan. I'm sorry you've been through so much, but I guess your experiences are the reason you've been able to identify so much with my best friend. All our trials and tribulations can be used for good. At least, that's the way I like to see it."

"And what trials and tribulations are you using for the benefit of humanity?" I ask.

"Well, living with eight men is definitely trying," she smiles. "They're the most awesome thing that's ever happened to me, but if I have to pair another black sock, I may just obliterate half of the US with my frustration."

I'm laughing so hard that when Dawn returns with Jared, they both stare at me, surprised. Standing, I press another soft kiss to Dawn's forehead. "Forget Lachlan making your drinks. Tonight, you get to taste Logan's Seventh Heaven."

"You realize that sounded really dirty!" Dawn's grin is lit up with pure filth.

"Only to you, my smutty girl." I round the bar and begin to search for the ingredients for the cocktail.

As I mix the sweet concoction, I try to imagine doing this same thing three years from now, with Dawn happily laughing across the bar. I have to find a way to make it a reality, for all our sakes, but mostly for Dawn's.

My little hummingbird needs to rest and I'm going to do whatever is in my power to help her see that this is a safe place for her to rest her wings.

32

DAWN

"You want to go shopping now?" I glance at my watch as Kyla nods.

"I still have gifts to buy. There isn't just one man waiting for me at home. There are eight! That's eight times the shopping!"

"Can't you just buy them all the same thing?" I ask, the logistics of birthdays and Christmas in a reverse harem relationship boggling my mind.

Kyla slides her feet into her white Converse sneakers. "Gifts are about showing someone you know them, aren't they?"

"I guess, but they all like the same stuff. Band shirts and tattoo stuff."

My friend grins and shakes her head. "Wait until I come back, and you see all the different things I've found for them."

I glance again at my watch, wishing I could rewind the stupid hour hand that's telling me I have to start my shift in an hour. I'm on early set-up duty today. "I can't come with you. I don't have time."

"That's okay." Kyla's already hooking the strap of her purse over her shoulder. "I'm fine to go by myself. I know my way around now, and I have Google maps to rescue me if I get lost."

"It would have been fun, though." The thought of having to find easy conversation with the nine men who are looking at me like sand that's slipping through their fingers makes me want to scream. How did I let things get so complicated?

"We can shop together all the time when you come home." Kyla's raised eyebrows say it all. Do you even want to go home? That's the question beneath that statement. Her knowing eyes scan mine for a reaction, but I try to keep my face impassive. I don't want to go home, but I also can't stay here. I can't string these amazing men along any more than I already have. It's not fair to them or to my heart.

My attention drifts to my empty suitcase and the chair currently stacked with my clothes. I have so few possessions with me. So few items to move to another place with less complicated feelings and fewer expectations.

I'm tired of people expecting things from me. I'm worn out from being a disappointment.

As I wave Kyla off, the weird sense of uncertainty that clouded my first days in Australia returns. I arrived and didn't know anyone. I wanted to be here, but at the same time, I missed home. Now, the thought of leaving this place is what's rocking my foundations.

I press my back against the cool wood of the door, inhaling slow deep breaths to try to squash the anxiety bubbling in my belly, but before I have a chance to find equilibrium, there's a knock on the door. When I open it, I find Logan waiting for me.

"Dawn," he says softly, his serious eyes searching my face. I turn away quickly, knowing that my emotions are plastered all over my face. He follows me into the room, closing the door behind him, and I'm trapped with a man who always seems to know when I'm hiding something.

There's only one way for me to escape the conversation I know is coming. One way to distract us both from facing emotional truths.

Sex.

I need him inside me. I need the release that I know he'll be able to give me, so I step forward before he can say anything and trap his words behind a kiss.

He's surprised, but it doesn't take more than a couple of seconds before he's kissing me back. His cock stirs against my belly, and I know I've got him. Men are easy to please, easy to satisfy. At least, they are if you're the kind of person who enjoys fucking. And I do. I really do.

Logan's body is lean and warm. My hands explore the skin beneath his shirt, finding hard muscle that makes me ache between my legs.

There's no uncertainty about how this is going to go. We've done it enough already that our movements are choreographed by experience. Within a minute, I'm on my back with my legs open and his tongue working me closer to the orgasm I'm craving.

"Dawn," he murmurs against my skin when I come.

Words are dangerous.

I pull at his arm and twist beneath him to find a condom in the nightstand drawer. He climbs over me, gazing at me with watchful eyes that I know don't buy my lighthearted, happy act. I can make him believe it, though. I just have to try harder. His jean buttons are stiff, but I manage to open them with fumbling fingers and dogged determination. When I pull out his cock, it's hard and ready. Easy to slide a condom over. Easy to angle until it's resting against my entrance.

"Dawn?" he says again, this time raised enough at the end to sound like a question.

"Fuck me, Logan," I say, tugging at his hips until he's pressed inside me just an inch.

He hesitates, but I rise to kiss his lips, and run my hands down his sides, and it's enough to convince him that this is what we need to do.

Lose ourselves to each other.

Connect what's become unfastened.

Hold tight to what will drift away in the days to come.

He moves in me, pushing his arm beneath my body so he can hold me closer. I kiss him with a searing intensity that I hope will keep his attention focused on the act rather than the emotion, but even as I pretend that this is only sex, only physical, only for escape, the word liar rings out in my mind.

His body feels like home to me; familiar and protective. In his arms, I feel safe. But safety is dangerous for me. Safety makes me want to stay here and be the person these nine amazing men want me to be.

But I'm not that person. I can't be that person.

I focus on the movement of his hips against mine, the perfect rhythm our bodies make with each other. I imagine Lachlan and Thomas are with us, watching. Jared and Joshua too. Bradley and Bryce, and Cooper and Mitchell. I want them all.

I arch my back, imagining their hands and mouths teasing me while Logan fucks me, and that's all it takes for the pool of pleasure building to spill out over my whole body.

Logan doesn't interrupt his flow, even when my pussy is bearing down on his cock in pulsating waves, even when I cry out and go slack beneath him. He strokes my face, kisses my panting mouth, and finishes inside me with a cry of his own.

For seconds, the oblivion of our release is like a dome of peace over us. Logan tucks me against his body, and we breathe fast synchronized pants. I make the mistake of trailing my hands over his body, finding the scar that runs across his abdomen.

Before I can twist away and make an excuse to disengage, he takes my wandering hand and kisses it.

"When they told me I was sick, I felt like my life was over," he says softly. I know he's not trying to hurt me on purpose, but the words are like spikes beneath my feet. "I couldn't breathe properly, as if one of my lungs had suddenly disappeared. I walked through my diagnosis and the first weeks of my treatment like a zombie. I didn't want to be there to face it. I didn't want to accept that it was happening. My mom had to force me back into the hospital. I just wanted to hang out with my friends and bury my head in the sand. I wanted to make-believe it was happening to someone else."

He pauses, waiting for me to ask a question or make a comment, but there's a boulder in my throat and tears welling behind my eyes. Everything he's saying resonates with me so much. Too much. I don't want to hear more, but at the same time, it feels good to know I'm not alone in handling life's challenges badly. Logan's a level-headed man. If he struggled, then maybe I shouldn't feel so ashamed of my own inability to face up to the truth.

"But there came a point where I realized I couldn't run anymore, Dawn. A time when I had to face up to the fact that my fear was going to hurt me. I faced the very real prospect of death, fought it, and came out the other side."

He hugs me closer, running a tentative finger down my arm, sending tingles over my skin. "I've been in remission for long enough to hope that I've beaten it for good. My mom went through so much. Maybe more than I did. The worry a parent has for the safety of their child is different from dealing with cancer yourself. I had control of my choices. She had to sit by and hope that I made the right decisions."

I think about my dad and how worried he's been since Mom passed. I think about his frustration at my avoidance of finding out the truth of my own destiny. I've been selfish and I've had to live with the fact every day. But my fear has been greater than my shame for not listening to him. My fear has been greater than everything.

"If I'd had a chance to find out about my odds of getting cancer years before, I'd take it in a heartbeat because I know it's easier to fight a battle that's planned than one that takes you by surprise."

I blink tears back, still fighting against the emotion that comes whenever I think about the result that's waiting for me in a dusty filing cabinet back home.

Logan continues, still holding me close. "I lost my dad to a stroke, something he knew was a risk for him because of the lifestyle choices he made, and I was so angry when he died. So hurt that he didn't choose to live his life in a way that would have possibly avoided his death. And I was so angry with myself for feeling anything other than sadness."

His mirrored understanding of everything I've faced and everything I'm living with is too much. Tears slip from the corners of my eyes, leaving cool trails down my cheeks, and my chest hitches with a sob that I can't hold inside anymore.

Does he know? Did Kyla tell him? I don't even care anymore because, for the first time in forever, I don't feel so alone. Logan knows what it's like. He's been through so much more than me and has come out the other side fighting.

I gather my strength and tell him about my mom and the agreement I made with my dad. I tell him why YOLO has been my mantra, and why I don't ever want to settle when there's so much out there to see and experience before it's too late. And Logan holds me so tightly, like I'm a wispy dragonfly, wings fluttering, ready to move on to greener pastures.

And when I'm empty of secrets and tears, he kisses my forehead and looks into my eyes.

"I want you to imagine what it would be like to not have the uncertainty hanging over you, Dawn. Imagine picking up your phone and calling to find out the results. Imagine having a plan for what happens next. Imagine living in knowledge rather than fear. And imagine doing all of that with me by your side."

I touch his face, seeing the emotion in his expression that I don't deserve. Softness and kindness. Maybe even love.

Can I imagine those things?

Can I imagine him by my side as I take a step so far into the unknown that I may never return to the me I am right now?

There isn't another person in the world who I'd want to be with when I make that phone call. But even though Logan is my rock, I'm nothing more substantial than the seeds on the head of a dandelion, light and fluffy and ready to blow away as soon as the breeze picks up.

33

BRADLEY

When Logan knocks on our door early in the morning, I know he's got something to share beyond work. "Come in," Bryce says, stepping back to let Logan pass. "You look like you're carrying the weight of the world on your shoulders."

"Dawn told me."

"She told you?"

"The thing she's running from. The thing that made her get the tattoo."

Instinctively, I sit on the edge of my mattress, feeling sweat prickle under my arms. The way Logan's talking makes it sound bad. Really bad. I'm not the only one who's considered that she might be sick, even though she exudes health and vitality. It's a thought I've been pushing away, too terrible to dwell on.

Bryce closes the door solemnly, letting it click shut quietly. "Is this one of those things that you wish you didn't know as soon as you know?" he asks.

Logan nods. "She's waiting on results to find out if she has a high risk of developing the cancer her mom passed away from."

"What?" I ask. All I heard were the words cancer and results.

He raises his hands. "She's not sick. At least, not right now. It's genetic testing. But if it shows she is high risk, there is a whole list of things she will have to consider."

"Like what?" I ask, feeling ignorant. It's the kind of thing I should know considering what Logan's been through.

"Removal of parts of her body that can stimulate the cancer."

I grimace, and Bryce shakes his head, his fist clenching by his side. "I don't even want to ask what parts," I say. "This is fucked up."

"She doesn't want to find out the result?" Bryce asks.

"Yeah. That's pretty much it. The result is waiting for her but she's avoiding finding out. It's why her dad keeps calling. That's why she came to Australia in the first place."

"She's running from the truth," I say.

"She's running from a potential future she doesn't know how to deal with."

Bryce straightens, tipping his head to one side. "But it's only a possibility, right? She could get the all clear?"

"Exactly. Anyway, I just wanted to let you know what I found out. I've done my best to encourage her to make the phone call. She's terrified and I don't know if what I said is enough to change her mind. I don't know if it will affect her thoughts about us in any way. Maybe she'll still move on, whatever she finds out. If the result is bad, she'll have to return home if she decides to take preventative action. It's a whole fucking minefield."

Logan's jaw ticks as he considers the possibilities and

what it might mean for us all.

I don't want her to leave. I want her to stay whatever she finds out. I want to be there for her, to support her, to be a rock through hard times, and I know my friends all feel the same.

When Logan shakes his head, it's obvious just how much this is getting to him. Maybe it's raising old memories of his own experiences. They were times we all wish we could wipe from our minds. "Don't worry about telling the rest," I say. "Me and Bryce have got that covered."

He nods once, his shoulders dropping with relief.

"I don't think anyone else should talk about this with Dawn. Can you tell them? It's raw, and it won't serve any purpose. I've pointed her to the right path. She needs to make the decision to follow it."

"But we have to do something," Bryce says, his voice conveying the frustration I feel.

"All we can do is continue to show her how much we want and need her. How much we want her to stay. And how supportive we can be."

"How much we love her, you mean?" I say. It's not our usual tone of conversation, but Dawn is wrestling a huge monster right now. We have to at least be able to say the words that have defined our relationship.

"Yes," Logan says, as Bryce nods, too. "But whatever you do, don't say that word to her. She's not ready to hear it. If anything, it'll scare her. We could lose her forever."

"So what do we do?" Bryce asks.

"We do everything in our power to show her just how incredible living here with us can be," I say. "That's what you mean, isn't it, Logan?"

"Yeah." He shrugs his shoulders, as though he knows it's not really enough, but he's resigned to follow it through, anyway.

By lunchtime, everyone knows and even though we resolve to hide our worry from Dawn, there's a somber blanket of worry over us all.

When Dawn says goodbye to Kyla, who's returning to Sydney to spend some time with a distant relative, the tears that streak her face seem woven with greater emotion. Kyla's leaving Australia in seven days, and we're all fearful that Dawn will return to the US with her.

So that she doesn't return to her room to overthink, I ask Dawn to help me organize the meat in the refrigerator and write a list for the next order. It's not exactly a cheerful or sexy job, but at least it gives me a chance to spend time with her. Between us, we find a conversation that brightens Dawn's expression.

"Have you spoken to Chantelle since you got back?" I ask.

"Yeah," she says, wiping her wet hands on a cloth. "She read the article and gave me a brief synopsis of what it's going to say. She's happy that it doesn't paint her in a negative light. And Crystal seems confident that it's going to bring other women out of the woodwork. It will be published soon."

"It wouldn't surprise me. That seems to be what happens. All it takes is just one person to be strong enough and other people find the confidence to back up their stories."

"The police have been good, too, apparently. Lachlan and Cooper have been supporting her, but she's been okay. If anything, she's felt a lot better since giving a statement. Before, she was bottling it up. Now, it's in someone else's hands."

"That's good to hear. Bryce and I wanted to help, but Cooper thought it would be better to minimize the number of people she has to talk to about the situation, so as not to relive everything multiple times."

Dawn nods, grimacing at the thought. "That's definitely a good thing. There's nothing worse than having to regurgitate your pain and fear over and over. And has Barrow come to the bar again?"

"No. Not since the fire. He's been working behind the scenes, though. He sent another ridiculous offer filled with veiled threats through the post. Fucking coward."

I shove a box of prime burgers back into the freezer.

Dawn makes an angry growling noise in her throat. "He's going to get what's coming to him. I can feel it in my bones."

I rest my hand on her shoulders, needing to feel her warmth and hoping to reassure her. "If it wasn't for you, we wouldn't be feeling hopeful at all."

"Me? I didn't do anything." She shrugs, dismissing her role in helping us. "This is all you guys and Chantelle."

"What?" I squeeze her shoulder, searching her face for insincerity and finding none. "If it wasn't for you, Lachlan would probably have a permanently busted hand, and we'd all be floundering around trying to work out what to do. Your advice and contacts have helped so much. And your determination to fight. Never underestimate the contribution you've made here."

She blinks quickly a few times and I pull her against my chest, fearing she might doubt my words, or worse, she might cry.

"You guys don't need me," she says softly. "You're an amazing team. You've got this."

In the bar area, Cooper shouts something to Thomas, and a rumble of laughter spills into the surrounding air, like a cosmically timed confirmation of what she just said. We are a great team. We were before she arrived, and nothing has changed except we want her to be a part of our team and a part of our lives.

For the first time, I allow my mind to imagine Dawn leaving, and the emptiness she'll leave behind feels hollow and dark. You could go back to the US with her. It's a whisper of a thought that I wish I didn't have because I miss home, but I love this place and my friends more. If it came down to a choice between our lives here and Dawn, there would be no right path to take.

It would be an impossible choice.

So, we have to find a way to make her stay.

One of my momma's favorite sayings is 'you can catch more flies with honey than vinegar.' And maybe that's true in this case. If we make staying the sweetest option, maybe she'll choose right.

"Tonight, after closing, we're going to do something special," I say. She tips her face to mine, eyes searching back and forth.

"What?"

I press my finger to my lips and smile. "It's a secret," I say. And even though I haven't run the idea past anyone else, I begin to hatch a plan to show Dawn what life could be like if she decides to stay.

33

COOPER

Bradley's idea is simple. We come up with ways of showing Dawn how beautiful life could be with us, and hope that she decides to stay. Our Cloud 9 WhatsApp group becomes a place to brainstorm, even though we're all busy working and shouldn't be using our phones. The criteria are basic. Anything we do has to feel like it's a natural part of our lives because there's no point in making grand gestures that can't be sustained. There's no point in setting ourselves up to fail.

Bradley and Bryce start immediately by taking Dawn stargazing, setting up a blanket in the back of the ute so they can stare up at the sky.

So, we set to work, bringing each idea to life.

Mitchell, Thomas, and I take Dawn for a bottomless brunch where we eat way too much and finish two bottles of prosecco between us. Dawn laughs more that day than at any other time since she entered our lives, and for blissful hours, I think we might have cracked it. But then we get back to Cloud 9 and work a shift, and Dawn's expression becomes distracted and distant.

The next day, twenty people turn up for cocktail-making and Dawn seems to enjoy showing the cocktails she's learned and interacting with the attendees, but afterward, I catch her staring at her phone, her shoulders curled, and her bottom lip gripped between her teeth.

Logan, Lachlan, Jared, Joshua, and Bryce take Dawn kayaking and they have a blast. They even spot a turtle which was on Dawn's list of things to do in Australia, so our efforts feel promising again.

Except later, she's on the phone to Kyla, talking in whispered tones. Even Chantelle confides in me, expressing her worries about her usually buoyant friend. Dawn has lost her sparkle and there doesn't seem to be anything we can do about it.

The days are ticking past, and we're hurtling closer to Kyla's departure, no nearer to proving to Dawn that she should stay with us.

My frustration builds because all I want to do is tell her we love her. That should be enough, shouldn't it? Maybe I'm just an old-fashioned romantic, but I can't understand how someone could look at us the way Dawn looks at us or touch us the way Dawn touches us without truly feeling a love that's impossible to leave behind.

If the situation was reversed, I couldn't leave her.

Maybe we just have to face up to the fact that Dawn won't be able to see what she has here until she's dealt with the issue she's running from. We can keep trying, but it'll be like pouring water into a bucket with a hole in the bottom.

The last idea we implement is the picnic because we all want to be there, but we're worried about leaving the bar unattended. It takes some organization to pull together our friends to bar-sit, but they come through after some begging and the promise of free drinks. Craig, who introduced Dawn to us in the first place, is the first to arrive just before closing time. Then Jason, who works security, and Gary, who works at the wholesaler.

Chantelle has also been kind enough to wait up until we return. It must be a constantly intimidating thought that Barrow can show up at any minute, but she seems to be so much braver now than when we first met her, and she'll have three big strong men to protect her.

Dawn seems surprised when Bradley and Bryce emerge from the kitchen carrying wicker baskets of food. Logan has two large blankets, and Mitchell and I have the coolers. Lachlan has an industrial flashlight to light our way. Thomas has a speaker and a million playlists on his phone. The rest bring themselves. "We're stealing you away," I say, grabbing Dawn's hand and spinning her like I'm planning to take her dancing.

"Stealing me to where?"

"The beach. It's a full moon tonight," Jared says. "And a full moon calls for a full moon party."

"Really?" Dawn says, her eyes alight with surprise. "And you're all coming? What about the bar?"

"It's fine," I say, leading her outside before she has a chance to object. "Our friends are here to keep watch, and sometimes life has to come before business."

Her fingers squeeze mine and she turns to watch my eight best friends gather to make their way to the beach. It's the first time we've all been together outside of work for what feels like forever, and the buzz amongst the group is contagious.

The beach is deserted, which is exactly what I hoped for. With the light of the moon and the flashlight, we can see well enough to lay out the blankets and set up the food and drink. Dawn watches everything with her hands clasped together and her bottom lip clamped between her teeth. Not exactly the vibe I'm hoping for.

"You get to sit in the middle," I say, holding out my hand so that she can balance while she removes her shoes. When she finds her spot, she seems so little and lost.

Jared and Joshua already have their feet in the water, and Lachlan is talking about the moon. They're distracted and need to refocus on why the hell we're here before Dawn's mind drifts away and we lose our chance to make the kind of impression we planned.

"Come on guys," I say. "Let's eat." It takes a determined wave of encouragement and an expression that mothers aim at naughty toddlers to get the group onto the blankets.

"So, Dawn, have you had a beach picnic before?" Lachlan asks.

"With my family a long time ago."

Oh great. Way to go, bringing up memories of her mom.

"I didn't have one before I came here. Scotland's a little cold for nighttime paddling," he tells her.

"Scotland's a little cold for most things," Jared says, grinning to accompany his playful banter.

Bryce and Bradley pull out boxes of sandwiches that look like they came from an upmarket deli and dips, chips and chopped up vegetables. There are mini chocolate cupcakes, blueberry muffins and what looks like millionaire's shortbread, topped off by boxes of strawberries and whipped cream. For a picnic assembled at short notice, they did well.

We eat, and laugh, and Dawn seems to go along with everything, but nothing feels genuine. It's as though she knows what part we want her to play, but she can't quite bring herself to make it reality.

I know I'm quieter than usual because I can't work out a way to make this work. After turning over ideas in my mind, I'm no closer to a solution. All I come up with is trying to get her to remember the fun we had before everything felt serious and laced with troubles.

"Me and Dawn played a twenty-question game when we went to the wholesaler."

"It ended up being ten questions because we didn't have time." Dawn smiles softly at the memory.

"Did Cooper ask you lots of sex questions?" Lachlan rolls his eyes like he knows me so well. He does, but I am deeper than the puddle he's suggesting.

"Some sex questions," she says. "But I'm okay with that."

"We hit the jackpot, boys," Logan says, reaching for Dawn's hand.

"We did," I say, reaching for her other hand and lacing our fingers together. She stares at me, the intensity of the moment buzzing between us like the static of a storm.

"We know what we've got," Bradley says.

Dawn nods, and then withdraws her hands.

The harder we push for her to hear us, the more distance she seeks.

The only part of our relationship that she ever feels comfortable with is the sex. Maybe that's where we're going wrong. We should focus on the part that Dawn feels most comfortable with, and the rest will hopefully follow.

So instead of us trying to tell Dawn how we feel with words, I suggest we all go for a midnight swim.

Stripping off on a deserted beach feels strange. The cool temperature of the water makes the hairs on my legs stand to bristle but getting to see Dawn in her pretty white cotton underwear makes it all worthwhile.

I grab her hand and lead Dawn down to the sea. As soon as the water touches her toes, she freezes and gasps.

"No hesitation," I say. "No looking back. We're going

to run."

Her green eyes meet mine, wide and afraid, but I know her expression comes from more than just a fear of the ocean at night. I pulled her out of the sea once. She's not frightened of the water.

"You only live once, baby," I whisper, as Jared and Joshua fly past us, spraying water in giant arcs as they bound into the surf.

"You only live once," she whispers.

It's Dawn who takes the first step and ends up dragging me into the sea. We laugh with gasping wheezes as we plunge beneath the waves, coming up for air with salt stinging our eyes and burning the inside of our noses.

It's Dawn who presses my hand between her legs, urging aside her soaking panties so that my fingers can seek her warmth, and that's all it takes for an innocent midnight swim to turn into so much more.

It's hard to keep track of everything we do in the dark, beneath the swirling ink of the sea, with so many men and just one beautiful woman, but I keep my eyes on her face, seeking the reassurance that this is really what she wants.

Dawn cries out, over, and over, her pleasure like a living, breathing thing connecting us all. And even though I know this night will be one that none of us will ever forget, I don't know if it's enough to tip the scales to keep Dawn with us for good.

35

DAWN

Kyla messages me at four am. I'm tucked up in my bed alone, my limbs aching and my flesh tender. Just seeing her message makes my heart burst open like a ripe fruit that's fallen to the ground.

Kyla - Sydney is a riot. How's Byron? Miss me?

Tears well in my eyes, and I blink them away, turning my face into the pillow.

Dawn - Byron's good. Just tying up loose ends.

I watch the screen as Kyla types for what seems like ages. My heart begins to dread what she's going to say because even though everything is always rooted in love, sometimes what she says hurts. The more truth there is in her words, the worse I feel.

Kyla - You're still planning to leave?

I guess she deleted whatever she originally typed and replaced it with a simple question.

Dawn - It's run its course.

More tears leak from my eyes, losing themselves in the softness of my pillow and my tangled hair, because lies are toxic, but the lies we tell ourselves are the worst of all.

Instead of another message, my phone rings. Sniffing, and swiping at my face, I consider declining the call, but I know it would only make Kyla worry more.

"Hey," I answer.

"Hey yourself." The rustle of her bed covers shifting travels down the line before she clears her throat. "Look, Dawn. I convinced myself that when we said goodbye the other day, that it was likely going to be a long time until I saw you again. I was convinced you'd see what's in front of your face and believe it's worth trying to hold on to. I was desperately hoping you'd begin to find an image of a future worth trying for."

"Kyla…I…"

"No, Dawn. I don't want to hear excuses anymore. I've left this long enough without telling you how destructive your behavior is becoming. And I did it because I thought I was being a friend. But being a friend isn't just about having fun. It's about helping you through the tough times and letting you know when you're wrong. When you got that tattoo, I thought it was a phase. All the crazy things you've done recently…I just put them down to something you'd outgrow. None of it really mattered until it started hurting other people…until it started hurting you."

"They understand, Kyla. They know I'm only here temporarily. They don't really want me to stay. Everything between us is based on this being a vacation fling."

"Except it isn't, is it? That's just what you're telling yourself, and I don't get it. You've stumbled into something so awesome that everyone around you can see, but you seem intent to ignore. You're hurting yourself, honey, and I understand. And what about your dad? I get you don't want to deal with finding out the results, but this is hurting him, too." She clears her throat, and the background rustling sounds as though she's switching ears. "Please listen to me because you're not tying loose ends by leaving. You're slashing at people's hearts. People who love you."

"You've got it wrong," I say, wiping at more tears, wishing I'd just let Kyla's call go to voicemail.

"I haven't. You just don't want to hear what I'm saying. And I get it. It's easier to run than to face something massive. But you're not a coward, Dawn. You're a fighter. You always have been. So please, listen to me. It's time. It's time to deal with the past once and for all so you can plan a future that you want to live."

We're both silent for a few seconds that feel like hours because there is never space in our conversations. We've been talking nonstop since kindergarten.

"I love you," she whispers. "I can't watch you lose yourself anymore without saying something."

"I love you too," I whisper back.

"Think about what I said, and we'll talk tomorrow, okay?"

"Okay."

When we hang up, I turn my face into my pillow so that my crying is muffled, not because I'm worried that anyone else will hear, but because I don't want to listen to myself.

There are moments in our lives that feel big and unwieldy. Moments that make our hearts skitter and our palms sweaty because we're just not ready to face them.

Will I ever feel ready, or do I have to do what Logan and Kyla are urging me to do? Face into the fear. Acknowledge the truth and find a way to live in the present that doesn't involve running.

Am I strong enough?

I really don't know.

Flip a coin, Mom's voice whispers. When I was little, and I couldn't make a decision, it was her go-to solution. Flip the coin and whatever it lands on, you'll understand your true feelings. Happiness and disappointment sit on either side of the little metal disk. This is too big a decision to decide in such a flippant way, but I can either lie here awake all night, worrying about what to do, or I find a way forward, one way or the other.

I find a coin in my purse, and turn it over and over, remembering how Mom would hand me a quarter, and it would feel like a key that would open a new door. Heads, I'll call Dr. Castor. And tails? I guess I'm free to decide what that will mean.

Tossing it up feels like the strangest release, and when I slap it onto the back of my hand, my heart skips a beat. Everything rides on this little piece of metal.

A new path will open before me if I can just find the courage to lift my hand.

36

DAWN

Once upon a time, there was a girl who wanted to feel the wind in her hair and her feet pounding against the ground, who wanted to leave her cares behind in a cloud of dust and focus on the bright sun of each new day.

Once upon a time, there was a girl who found a place that felt like home and quicksand all at the same time. A place she wished she could wrap around her like a warm blanket and wriggle free from, like rope binds.

Once upon a time, there were nine men who held her hand and tried to show her that constantly moving on wasn't what made her heart sing. That friendship and love give life its meaning.

Once upon a time there was a girl who felt the power of the ocean, and the passion of nine men. A girl who heard wise words and felt tired to the marrow of her bones.

Once upon a time, there was a girl who decided she couldn't live under the shadow of fear anymore.

37

DAWN

My fingers tremble as I clasp the phone and dial the number I've long been avoiding. I take a deep breath and raise it to my ear, listening for the international dial tone. The beat of my heart accelerates at such a pace that it makes me feel woozy.

Logan, understanding the dread and fear pulsating through every cell of my body, reaches out and places a big, warm, strong hand in the middle of my back. The contact is like a weight on a helium balloon, suddenly anchoring me to the ground.

"You can do this," he says softly. "You're ready."

Am I? the little voice of doubt whispers in my mind. For all my resolve, I've been bowing to fear for so long that it's hard to shake off. Hang up, the voice whispers. There's still time.

But with Logan next to me - brave Logan who's been through so much and has come out the other side stronger and wiser - I don't give in.

"Hello, Dr. Castor's office." The receptionist sounds oddly cheerful today, but maybe it's just that her mood is not clouded like mine.

"Hi, yes. It's Dawn Mitchell for Dr. Castor. He's expecting my call."

"Ah, yes. Dawn. Hold the line and I'll put you through."

Logan is still as he stands beside me, listening to what's being said by craning a little closer to the phone. I don't mind him listening. Whatever I find out, I know I won't be able to hide my reaction. Good or bad, the news is going to make me crumble.

"Dawn. It's good to hear from you," Dr. Castor says warmly.

"I wish I could say the same thing." My voice is breathy and my throat catches on the last word.

"I know this process has been difficult for you. It's to be expected. At least, what I mean to say is that no one knows how they will react to this kind of thing until they're in your position."

"My dad has been frustrated with me," I admit. "He's the kind of man who faces things head on. He struggled with understanding my decision to avoid finding out the answer."

"Yes. I understand that. But it's your body and your life. If you find out, you won't just be able to forget if it's painful. That knowledge will always be with you. You have to be sure you want to know and accept that there may be consequences to knowing."

"I am," I say, suddenly more confident. "It's time. I've run from it for long enough."

"Well, then." Paper crackles at the other end of the line, raising my anxiety until my heart feels like it's going to burst from my chest. "Your tests were conducted over twelve months ago." There's a pause, I assume, because

268

he's reading my results in front of him. "I can confirm that you are not carrying the gene, Dawn."

When my knees go out from under me, Logan is there to catch me. I don't even have the strength to hold the phone to my ear, such is the overwhelming sense of relief at finally knowing I'm going to be okay.

All the catastrophizing I've done since Mom passed away falls away from me like ash caught by the wind. I'm so relieved that there's no space for the emotion of happiness. Not yet, anyway.

Logan takes my hand and supports the phone.

"Dawn, are you there?"

"Yes," I say, as tears leak from my eyes and drift in cool trails down my hot cheeks.

"It's good news. I'm so pleased to be able to give you the result you wanted to hear."

"I'm so pleased too." I don't tell him that there's a tiny part of me, one that doesn't make any sense at all, that feels guilty. For a long time, I've wondered if my life was going to be cut short like my mom's. In a strange kind of way, that uncertainty was a kind of connection. Now I know I haven't inherited the gene, that connection feels severed.

"Well, I guess you'll want to call your dad now. Put the man out of his misery."

"Yes."

"I know it's a lot to take in, but if you want to call me and talk some more when the news has settled, I'll be happy to make time."

"Thank you, Dr. Castor. I really appreciate that."

He says goodbye, and Logan gently takes the phone from my hand, placing it on the table. Then he adjusts me in his arms, so I'm held close to his chest and my face is nestled into his warm neck. His scent, now so familiar to me, relaxes my racing mind. I breathe him in deeply, pushing out the coiled tension that was wrapped around all my internal organs.

"This is great news," he says softly. "Really great news."

"I should have tried to find out sooner," I say, suddenly feeling stupid. There's no gun to my back anymore, nothing to push me from place to place and experience to experience. I'm free of the burden of trying to appreciate every second of life. How different would things have been if I let Dr. Castor share this news after I took the test?

Vastly different.

I wouldn't be in Australia. I wouldn't be wrapped in the strong arms of this handsome, kind, brave man. I wouldn't be craving the arms of eight other men who've shown me that life can be settled and peaceful and still beautiful enough for me to want to exist in it every day.

I wouldn't know myself the way I do. Pushed to the brink, I know I'm strong enough to bear the weight of life's troubles and come out the other side.

"You found out when you were ready. Today was the right time."

"You wouldn't have waited."

"Maybe. But there's no going back, Dawn. Only forward. What's the point of regretting what you can't change? This is the moment you have. You'll never get it back, so appreciate it for all of its joyfulness."

"You only live once," I whisper, the tattoo on my back suddenly taking a different meaning. A quieter, more mindful meaning. Living for the day doesn't mean running from tomorrow. It can mean existing in contentment.

"Exactly," he says.

"Did anyone ever tell you, you're a wise man, Logan?"

"One or two people, but I don't like to boast."

I chuckle against him, feeling the press of his lips on the top of my head, so gentle and reverential, that I have to close my eyes so I won't cry.

"What do you want to do next?" he asks, after a time.

"Call my dad," I say. "I've been avoiding him for so long, and it's not fair to make him wait another second."

"Okay. Do you want me to stay?"

I shake my head, drawing back to stare up at his serious face. "Can you tell the others? I don't think I can face it."

"Of course." He bends to kiss my forehead and then relaxes his arms so that I can step out of his embrace. "Take the night off, okay? But when we've closed up the bar, come for a nightcap. I think we need to open a bottle of champagne to celebrate."

The warmth of Logan's smile and his reassuring hand on the top of my arm are his parting gifts, and the feeling stays with me as I perch on the edge of the mattress to dial my dad's number. Logan shuts the door quietly behind him just as my dad picks up.

"Dawn?"

His voice is gravelly and uncertain, and it kills me to hear it. What I've put him through is unforgivable and the guilt will stay with me for the rest of my life. "I talked to Dr. Castor. It's good news."

"You did? It is?"

"Yes. I'm clear of the gene."

Dad clears his throat, and I try to picture him standing in our kitchen, looking out at the back yard, one hand in his pocket or holding a steaming cup of coffee. He's been standing in the same place for so many years, the rock who kept us both going when the unthinkable happened to our family. How he managed it, I'll never know.

"I'm sorry," I say, not being able to find more words to express everything that I'm feeling or to better acknowledge his pain, too.

"Don't be sorry," Dad says softly. "Be happy. That's all I've ever wanted for you."

My throat closes with a huge ball of tears that I fight back, even though there's no one to witness them. He's right. Crying is often associated with grief and sadness, but today, the tears threatening to spill are filled with nothing but joy.

"Thanks."

"So, where are you right now?"

"Byron Bay. I'm working in a bar called Cloud 9."

"Sounds interesting. And are you planning to come home anytime soon?"

I think about what my life was like before I left. An asshole boss and a job that didn't stimulate me. A man who I was just passing time with, longing for more. I'm blessed with great friendships, but everyone is moving on, determined to find their own happiness.

I don't miss the place or the person I was in it.

I like this version of me and this new life I've stumbled into so much more.

"I don't know, Dad," I say. "I love it here."

He clears his throat, a sign that he's not sure about what he's about to ask. "Have you met someone?"

"Maybe," I say. "But you know I don't talk about that stuff."

"You will one day," he says. "When it's right. When whoever it is has won your trust and truly knows you inside and out. You will when you find what I had with Mom."

The tears I've been holding back spill over my cheeks and a shuddering sob leaves my lips. I don't know if I'll ever fully get over my grief at her loss. I know Dad won't. She was a part of him, and it's hard to live with a piece of yourself missing.

"Just enjoy your life, Dawn. Not because you fear that it might not be that long, but for the sheer hell of it."

"I will, Dad. I will."

"Promise you'll call and message more often. I just need to hear from you every so often so that I know you're safe."

"You mean you're not checking my Insta?" It's said with a hint of sarcasm because he likes and comments on every photo I post.

"I don't get to hear your lovely voice over Insta, do I?"

"Point taken." I wipe my damp cheeks as I say goodbye and then slump back onto my bed, staring up at the cracked ceiling, no longer feeling like a bird in the cage. For the first time since Mom died, the door to my cage is open. Now, all I have to do is fly through.

But which direction should I go?

38

BRYCE

The night Dawn finds out she is in the clear will forever be etched into my mind. We somehow manage to work a full shift, even though all we want is to take Dawn in our arms and tell her how happy we are and encourage her to stay.

Dawn gets the night off, of course. There's no way she'd be able to concentrate after her experience.

Eventually, when the last customer leaves and Lachlan stashes the money in the safe, we head out back to the chill-out zone. We find Dawn resting in a hammock with a book propped open on her chest and her eyes closed. In the soft glow cast from the tall iron night-light, she looks like an angel.

"We should leave her to sleep," Lachlan whispers, holding his arms out to stop the rest of us from getting too close and disturbing her.

"We should wake her," Logan says more firmly. "It's what she wants."

Jared disturbs an empty beer bottle on the floor and

the sound of glass against stone is enough to disrupt Dawn's dreams. Her eyes flash open and her gaze flitters between the nine of us.

"We all heard the good news," Mitchell says, reaching out to take her hand. "How are you feeling?"

"Relieved," she says. "Sad too, but I'll get over it. It's all just been a tremendous shock, but in a good way." She pauses, inhaling a deep breath and pushing it through pursed lips. "To be honest, my emotions are all over the place."

"That's understandable," I say, pulling a magic rose from my back pocket and presenting it to her. "How can we help you?"

"Smooth, dude." Bradley rolls his eyes in a way that he only gets away with because he's my twin.

"Thank you," Dawn says softly, bringing the rose to her nose. It's made of fabric, but I scented the petals with rose oil. "And I know how you can all help me."

"I think we know too," Cooper says hopefully.

"Dude, you have sex permanently on the brain," Lachlan grumbles, which is rich coming from him.

"We all have sex permanently on the brain," Mitchell says.

"Only with me, I hope," Dawn says, frowning at us all with pretend jealousy and when we all nod, she laughs and places a hand over her heart. "Aw, you guys make me feel all warm and squishy inside."

"We will if you ever get off that bloody hammock," Jared says, sounding so British that Dawn stares at him with fascination.

"Keep talking like that, baby," she says, finally scrambling to leave the fabric confines.

All night we show her exactly how happy we are that she's okay and exactly how much we want her to stay. We tell her with our fingers, lips, tongues, and cocks, losing track of the number of times she cries out in release.

We could tell her what we want. We could share what we need.

Just her. Just Dawn Mitchell in all her flawed perfection.

But words aren't Dawn's love language. Physical touch is how she communicates.

Sex is where she loses herself and emerges again, reborn.

Two days pass. Two days of perfection where we all believe that this is it. Dawn's allowing herself to feel and believing this amazing thing between us can be real and true and long lasting.

We hope the universe will smile at us and give us the girl of our dreams.

Then Dawn tells us she wants to travel to see Kyla in Sydney, and all seems lost.

She disappears from our lives in a cloud of coach fumes, with no return date confirmed. The whole of Cloud 9 feels like it has fallen back to earth in a catastrophic tumble.

We receive a one sentence message, confirming she's arrived safely and then we don't hear from her again.

No phone calls.

No more messages.

Nothing.

All nine of us walk around like bears with migraines.

In a strange way, it feels as though Dawn was just a

figment of our collective imaginations, just a dream we shared.

Except Chantelle is still here, and when the article that Dawn's journalist friend wrote is published, all hell breaks loose.

The bar is inundated with other reporters seeking interviews, and we have to close to protect Chantelle from the onslaught.

Without work, Dawn's absence hits even harder. Jared and Joshua lose themselves in surfing. Thomas composes a melancholy melody and won't stop strumming it on his guitar. Logan, Cooper, Lachlan, and Mitchell exercise to dull the pain. And me and Bradley take long hikes up to the lighthouse and back, restless with nervous energy.

No one says what we're all thinking. What if she doesn't come back?

What if this is it?

No one contemplates what we'd do next if it is.

Then, as if she never left, Dawn appears, with Kyla and three huge, tattooed dudes, bounding into the chill-out area where me and Bradley are playing cards, throwing her arms around my neck and kissing me passionately. When she moves to do the same to my brother, I stare at her back, blinking because I half expect her to disappear again.

"Did you miss me?" she asks. In her gym leggings and slouchy yellow shirt, with her hair scraped into a messy bun, she exudes life and vitality, and once again I say a silent prayer to the universe that she's clear of the worries of the past.

"Of course we missed you," Bradley says, hauling her into his lap and beaming like a kid at Christmas. She squeals and wriggles in a half-hearted attempt to escape. Then, she remembers the people she brought with her and flushes pink.

"Bryce. Bradley. This is Carl, Noah, and Dex. Three-eighths of Kyla's boyfriends."

Carl, a big dude with blond hair tied in braids like a Viking, and eyes the color of sea ice, holds out his hand, and I stand to shake it. "Carl," he says with a serious expression and fierce grip that reminds me a lot of Lachlan.

Noah follows, smiling enough for both him and Carl. Dex is last, and then Kyla kisses me and Bradley on the cheek.

"So," I say. "How was Sydney?" But I'm not interested in the answer. Not really. I just want to know if she's back for good or if this is the proper goodbye.

"Sydney was fantastic," Dawn gushes. "We climbed Harbor Bridge and went to look around the Opera House. We rollerbladed through Centennial Park and made fools of ourselves trying to surf at Bondi Beach. We ate some seriously weird food." She counts off her fingers. "Crocodile, snake, wild boar, ostrich. Did you know you can eat snake?"

"I did," I say. "I wouldn't choose to, but I've seen it on menus."

"Crocodile was tasty. It was cooked with ginger." She wrinkles her nose as though she's not sure about whether or not she should have enjoyed the dish.

Carl grimaces. "Crocodile was weird. I think I'm happy to stick with chicken and beef."

"You can take the American out of the USA..." Dawn trails off, smiling as Carl shrugs.

Dex looks pointedly at Dawn. "We had a fun time, but Dawn couldn't shut up about you guys. We've forgiven her because she's the one who set Kyla on a path into our lives, but damn. If I hear another story about how awesome you guys are, I'm going to have to plug my ears."

When I meet Dawn's eyes, they're as light as sun dappled grass, and her expression is soft and warm. "Is it true?" I ask.

Bradley doesn't seem to need any confirmation because he plants a firm and lingering kiss on her cheek.

"It's true," she admits.

"What's true?" Mitchell asks, as he appears behind Dex, Noah, and Carl.

"Dawn's obsessed with you," Dex says, totally deadpan.

Kyla swats at his arm. "Less of the dropping statements that might make men run for the hills."

"These men aren't going anywhere, are you?" Noah asks with a knowing grin.

"We aren't," I say. "The bigger question is whether Dawn's going to stick around."

All eyes focus on the girl who's driven us crazy in the best and worst ways since she drifted into our bar looking like sin and sunshine. She turns to look at Bradley, then at Logan, Cooper, Thomas, Jared, Joshua, and Lachlan, who must have all heard voices and come to find out what the fuss is about. Finally, she looks at me.

She pulls a coin from her pocket and looks at it. "Heads, I stay. Tails I leave." The coin is flying through the air, spinning as it goes, before any of us have a chance to object. She can't seriously want to rest such a massive decision on the turn of a coin. Dawn catches it and slaps it onto the back of her hand.

"Dawn," Kyla squeals. "You can't be serious."

"Deadly." Dawn grins broadly and I don't understand how she can be so happily flippant about something that carries so much meaning and consequence to me and my friends.

She inhales deeply as though the strain is finally hitting, but there's a tug of smile on her lips. Or at least, I think there is.

She's been through so much, and we all want her to be our girl, but there's no way any of us will be happy for her to stay on a coin toss.

When she lifts her hand and peeks beneath, my heart skips a beat, then thuds in one big squeeze. My fingers grip so tightly to the edge of the chair, because it's like watching the climax of a thriller movie.

"Put them out of their misery, for the love of god," Dex says, shifting to broaden his stance and fold his inked arms over his chest. The man seems as impatient as the rest of us and it's not even his future hanging in the balance.

"It's heads," Dawn says softly.

Heads. That's it! That means she's staying!

I glance at my twin, then around at Kyla and her men, and all my buddies who gather with such a vested interest in this moment.

Then Dawn slides off Bradley's lap and sits next to me, handing the coin.

I raise my palm to look at it, curious, realizing it's not Aussie currency. There's something strange about it. Flipping it over, I see what it is and why Dawn's given it to me.

The coin has a head on both sides. She didn't decide to stay on the flip of a coin. She knew before she came back.

"I bought the coin in a magic shop in Sydney," she says softly. "I thought you'd appreciate a little magic. That's what you've all brought into my life."

I pull Dawn to me, pressing a hard kiss against her lips. "Damn you, Dawn," I whisper. "For being so infuriatingly perfect."

Then I turn to everyone. "SHE'S STAYING," I shout, the reality of this fundamental knowledge finally landing.

In a rush, Jared, Joshua, Logan, Lachlan, Thomas, Mitchell and Cooper surge forward. Dawn is passed from man to man, disappearing into fierce embraces that convey the relief and excitement they feel. Mitchell spins Dawn around, kissing her on her forehead. Lachlan presses her head against his broad chest, cradling her like a child who was in danger but is now safe.

We're watched by Carl, Noah, and Dex, whose expressions are wildly different. Carl's is serious, as though he's trying to assess if the feelings being expressed are genuine or maybe he's viewing everything with a protectiveness over Dawn. Noah is grinning, seemingly ecstatic that Dawn is getting her happy ever after moment. Dex nods as though what he sees meets his approval. Kyla has her hands clasped together, and tears glazing her eyes, genuinely moved by the turn of events.

"I can't believe you made us think you'd leave on the turn of a coin," Cooper says, as he kisses Dawn's forehead and then draws back to meet her pretty green eyes with his own. "I swear, I was considering tossing you over my shoulder and carrying you off into the sunset if that coin had shown tails. There was no way I was going to let you throw away something this good."

She reaches out to cup his cheeks and draws him closer for a soft kiss. "Thank you for sticking with me," she whispers, her eyes drifting to connect with each of ours. "I know that being with me has been a little like riding an out-of-control rollercoaster."

"That's an understatement," Mitchell says, with an accompanying broad grin.

"But I promise things will be a little more Zen from here on out."

"Zen?" I say. "Please no. If we wanted someone Zen, we never would have gotten into a relationship with you."

Everyone laughs, including Dawn, whose cheeks are pink, and eyes are bright.

"Just be your crazy, fun, passionate, inspiring self, Dawn. That's all we want. Just be you, and we'll be happy every single damn day."

I get a second hug from the girl whose rollercoaster ride I hope I never have to get off. And when my eyes meet Carl's over the top of her head, I finally see him nod his approval.

EPILOGUE

DAWN

Six Months Later

"I'm nervous," Logan admits as we wait in arrivals at Brisbane airport.

Dad's flight is running late, which has left poor Logan with more time to think about the seriousness of this visit. He's convinced that Dad is flying to Australia to assess their worthiness rather than simply wanting to spend time with his daughter.

He's probably not wrong. Dad is used to me being a do-now-think-later kind of person, but I think announcing I'm in a relationship with nine men he'd never heard about let alone met was a step too far. To be fair, I think it would be a step too far for all dads.

"Don't be," I say. "He's going to love you all, after he's sized you up and given you a grilling about your intentions." I laugh, but that's likely to be exactly what happens. "Anyway, he's like half the size of one of you. I think if anyone is likely to be nervous, it's Dad, coming face to face with so many huge and imposing young men."

"Has he met Kyla's crew?" Logan shifts on his feet and bites his lip, and I have to rest a hand on his arm to help him relax.

"No," I say. "Although I was upfront with him about her living situation as soon as I knew it was serious. I'm not a big believer in keeping secrets." Logan arches a masculine brow, his intense eye casting doubt on my statement. "Or at least, I should say I wasn't a big believer in keeping secrets until…"

I trail off and Logan nods. "I understand," he says. "You don't have to say anymore."

I'm about to apologize for the millionth time for the way I kept all my gorgeous Cloud 9 men hanging, but I know he doesn't need to hear it. Just being together for the last six months has more than wiped away those terrible memories.

"Dad," I squeal, spotting his familiar shape, thinning hair and eyes that match the color of mine exactly. I dash toward him, surprised at my instinct, and he drops the handle to his suitcase and wraps me in a fierce hug that knocks the wind from my chest.

"There's my girl," he murmurs, kissing the top of my head. Compared to my men, Dad's frame seems small and frail, but he is over fifty now and more of a runner than a weight trainer.

"Dad, this is Logan." I hold my hand out to the man who was instrumental in helping me face my greatest fear, who inspired me to reach out for my destiny and face it with courage, whatever it might hold.

"Logan." Dad holds out his hand and gives a purposefully firm handshake. "Thank you."

I blink for a second, wondering what he means. Then he claps his spare arm against Logan's and pulls him into a hug. "Thank you for helping Dawn. You achieved what I failed, and I'll always be grateful for that."

"Dad!" I rest my hand on his shoulder, feeling choked up, and when Logan is released, his eyes are glassy.

"Let's get on the road, Mr. Mitchell. You must be exhausted."

When we get to Cloud 9, I watch my dad sweep the place, taking in everything with an approving gaze. He's traditional in a lot of ways and knowing I'm going to be taken care of is important to him. "This is quite a place," he says, as he shakes hands with Lachlan.

"We're relieved it's still in our hands," Lachlan says.

Dad nods somberly. "Dawn filled me in on what's been happening. Terrible thing you've all been going through."

"We're turning a corner," Lachlan says, looking pointedly at me. "Thanks to Dawn's journalist contact and the exposure she got us, Barrow is on trial for three sexual assaults and five shady property deals. Last week, the mayor committed to investigating the planning department. That's been a major turning point."

"Public pressure can be a great motivator," Dad says, moving on to shake Mitchell's hand, then Coopers, and Thomas. They each introduce themselves and Dad apologizes in advance for how terrible he is with names.

"Maybe they should wear badges with their names," I suggest and Dad nods enthusiastically, even though I was joking.

"That would help me a lot," he says, and we all laugh.

We can't all take the night off, but Lachlan arranges cover for half of us, so I get to take Dad for dinner at our favorite restaurant with Bradley, Thomas, Mitchell, and Jared.

All the nerves that have been buzzing around in my stomach like a swarm of locusts fly away because, despite all my concerns, Dad gets on well with everyone.

He talks with Jared about the time he spent in London in the nineteen nineties, raving about Cornish pasties and sausage rolls and scones with jam and cream. He compares grilling marinades with Bradley and talks music with Thomas. He laughs with Mitchell, who always seems to find the perfect joke to tell for every new person he meets. I sit back and watch each of my men bond with my father, and the fluttering anxiety is eventually replaced with warmth.

We walk home, our bellies full, and I slide my arm into Dad's, remembering how my mom used to do the same. I'm her height now, with her hair color and her curves. Sometimes, I catch myself in a shop window or a bathroom mirror and, for a fraction of a second, I think I see her looking back at me.

Does that make it harder for Dad to be around me? I've never asked him. I've never really asked him anything about his feelings since she passed. I slow my pace, letting my men walk ahead and allowing the gap between us to lengthen. On this warm night, with more peace between Dad and I than we've had in years, I feel like I should change that.

"I miss Mom," I say softly, waiting for his response. Dad says nothing, just lifts his free hand and rests it over my arm as I continue. "I miss her every day. I miss her when I'm eating pancakes, or when I hear a song she used to listen to, or when I smell another woman wearing her perfume. I miss her when I hear something funny that I know she'd laugh at, or when I try a new cake that she'd have wanted to learn the recipe for. And it doesn't get any easier."

"I know," he says softly. "It doesn't matter how many years pass, there is always a hole in my life, the shape and size of your mom, which will never be filled. She was unique and brilliant and special, and as hard as it is, I'm happy she was so exceptional that I still miss her after all this time. She was a gift."

"She was." I smile, remembering the way Mom used to chew the end of every pen or pencil she used, and how her ears would always end up peeking through her hair.

"You're a gift too," Dad says. "You're so much like her."

"I am?" I turn to gaze at his side profile, noticing the additional creases around his eyes and the deeper set of his mouth.

He smiles and turns. "You are."

"Do you think Mom would have liked them?"

Dad slows, and then stops, turning to face me. When he places his hands on my upper arms, my heart does a little jump, anticipating he's going to say something negative. Maybe all his smiles and easy chatter were just a polite cover and now he's going to tell me how he really feels. "She would have loved them, Dawn."

I blink tears that trickle over my cheeks and he brushes them away with the pads of his thumbs. "I can see how much they love you, sweetie. I can see how they put you first. That's all a father can hope for his daughter."

"But I'm here now, and you're so far away," I say. "I wish…"

"You wish you could be closer?"

Nodding, I bite my lip. Many times I've turned over the hand that fate has dealt me, or rather, the place that my decision has brought me to. I love Australia and I love my men, but knowing I'll hardly see Dad is a bitter pill to swallow.

"Well, I'm thinking about early retirement, honey. And I don't have much tying me back home. If you want, I can spend a few months here each year."

"You'd do that?" I ask, and when he nods, I throw my arms around his neck, hugging so tightly that I shake when he starts to laugh.

"Of course, I'd do that, especially when you give me some grandbabies."

I take a step back, covering my mouth with my hand in shock. "I'm not ready for babies, yet!" I laugh.

"You've got a lot of boyfriends, honey. They're going to want at least one baby each."

Shaking my finger at him, I walk away quickly. "NO NO NO!!! I'm not having nine children. You're crazy. They won't expect that of me. I'm not a cat!"

He laughs, a booming deep chuckle that I haven't heard for years. "You better have that conversation, sweetheart."

When I put my hand out towards him, he laughs even more.

Mitchell, Jared, Bradley, and Thomas turn at the commotion, and watch with curiosity as I storm towards them, with Dad trailing behind. "He thinks you're going to want me to have nine babies and I'm freaking out."

Mitchell snorts with laughter and pulls me into a hug, patting my back like I'm a restless baby. "Well, I want at least two of my own, so it might be more. We should get started soon or you won't be able to fit them all in!"

I struggle from his arms in horror, but he runs his hand through his messy auburn-brown hair and gazes at me with the softest eyes, and I realize he's joking.

"I wouldn't mind having three. Will that be enough?" I bite the edge of my fingernail, stressing out that this should have been something we talked about months ago and even more that it could be a make-or-break issue.

"As long as you're our girl, anything will be enough," Thomas says.

Back at Cloud 9, we help until closing while Dad heads to bed for some well-needed sleep. As we're emptying the trash, Chantelle and Craig arrive, hand in hand, as they always do on a Saturday night. "Ready to lose at poker?" Craig asks with a challenging wink.

Chantelle swats his shoulder. "Be nice to Dawn. If it wasn't for her, we never would have met."

I grin, and plant two kisses on Chantelle's cheeks, happy as always to see her content, and settled with Craig. The night my boys took me on a beach picnic was the first time they met, and they've been thick as thieves ever since. The last few months, with all the coverage about Barrow and the impending trial, have been tough on Chantelle, but with Craig's love and support, she's holding her own and feeling confident about testifying in court. There might be over twenty years of age difference, but they really are a match made in heaven.

"As long as he's nice to you, that's more than enough for me," I say.

I miss my besties back home, but I'm so grateful to have found Chantelle to keep me company on my Aussie adventure!

"He's very nice to me," Chantelle says, pushing her black-framed glasses up her nose.

"Let's not drift into TMI territory," I say with a raised hand.

"Deal," Craig says.

We head to the chill-out area, pulling rattan sofas and beanbags into a circle big enough to hold us all. And we play poker and drink beer until my eyelids are drooping and my body is screaming for bed.

As Craig and my men are laughing, I take the opportunity to ask Chantelle for an update on the court hearing. As she tells me everything she's dealing with, a familiar feeling of guilt wells inside me. "I'm so sorry," I tell her, reaching out to rest my hand on her arm.

She pats my hand and shakes her head. "You know I don't want to hear you apologize anymore. If I didn't meet you, I'd still be stuck feeling powerless about what happened. I'd probably be living with my parents, depressed and miserable. You gave me a route to take back control, and you showed me I had the backbone to stand up for myself. If it wasn't for you and these guys, I wouldn't have met Craig. That night we met at that bar changed both our lives for the better."

I blink back tears and lean in to give my resilient friend a hug. She's so strong and so kind. I really am blessed to have her in my life.

Later, as I'm showing Craig and Chantelle out, hugging them both before they leave to make the short walk back to the hostel where I started my Byron Bay experience, my phone vibrates in my pocket.

When I see Allie's name on the screen, I squeal. "You better be calling to tell me you're coming over soon," I say, instead of hello. She's been promising for months that she'll take some time off work and come for a vacation down under, but so far, it's all been empty words.

"I wish," she says. "I asked my boss for time off and instead; she's given me another ridiculous assignment."

"What's it about this time?" I groan. "Fifteen ways to style your pubic hair?"

Allie laughs dryly. "That would be easy. I have to write an article on the question 'Does size really matter?'"

Snorting, I perch on the wall and cross my leg over my knee, ready to help my girl out with all the experience I've accumulated over the years. "In one word, yes! There you go. Article written, now get your butt out here."

"She's told me to write from experience," Allie says

quietly. "I think she thinks I'm a real sex-pert. She doesn't realize that my history could be written on the back of a postage stamp."

"All work and no play have made Allie an innocent girl."

She chuckles nervously and I suddenly realize that this isn't a catch-up phone call. She's looking for advice.

"Do you feel comfortable researching with other people and passing it off as your own experience?" I ask. "Because I'll be more than happy to help with information."

"I guess," Allie says. "But I don't think that's her plan. She handed me keys to a beach house and the names of ten men who are apparently going to help me answer the question."

"Ten," I gasp. "That's more than Kyla and me!"

"Well, they're just interviewees, not boyfriends," she says weakly.

"Imagine if this is fate," I say, overflowing with glee. "Imagine if you're going to be the one to top out the reverse harem ladies club."

"How about we imagine me finding a way to write a four-page spread without having to validate the size of ten strangers' cocks."

I can do that. Although my other idea sounds like more fun."

Allie groans, her misery reverberating down the line. "Did I really spend all that time in school for this?"

"You can always leave, sweetie," I remind her.

We talk some more, and I promise that I'll be available for any dick size related crises over the next few weeks.

When I finally make it back to my room, I find Cooper, Logan, and Thomas waiting for me.

"We just wanted to make sure you got to bed, okay,"

Logan says.

"Yeah," Cooper says. "We're just here for your wellbeing."

Thomas shakes his head. "Yeah, real knights in shining armor."

I punch him in the arm, and then kiss them all, teasing their lips until we're all breathless. "You don't need to pretend, guys. It's your night."

"This schedule rocks," Cooper breathes, holding my door open. We all troop through, ready to rock each other's world.

"It really does," I grin. "Just don't forget, we need to keep the volume on mute."

"Tell yourself," Thomas says, pulling my shirt over my head, not wasting another second. "If anyone's going to disturb your dad with moaning, it's going to be you."

Our laughter trails off as soon as their hands are on my body. Like a well-oiled machine, we move together, me at the center of three men intent on worshiping me.

Logan kisses my mouth, while Cooper uncovers my breasts and Thomas kneels, pressing kisses to the bottom of my spine. Tonight there are three. Tomorrow there will be nine.

You only live once used to be my mantra. I was scared and running from the future I thought was inevitable. I never imagined the future that was my destiny.

Nine men showed me that facing my fears was the key to finding my place in the world. And I'll spend the rest of my life making their lives a little slice of heaven on earth.

ABOUT THE AUTHOR

International bestselling author Stephanie Brother writes high heat love stories with a hint of the forbidden. Since 2015, she's been bringing to life handsome, flawed heroes who know how to treat their women. If you enjoy stories involving multiple lovers, including twins, triplets, stepbrothers, and their friends, you're in the right place. When it comes to books and men, Stephanie truly believes it's the more, the merrier.

She spends most of her day typing, drinking coffee, and interacting with readers.

Her books have been translated into German, French, and Spanish, and she has hit the Amazon bestseller list in seven countries.

Printed in Great Britain
by Amazon

28375297R00169